Melody
OF THE Heart

Melody
OF THE Heart

KATIE ASHLEY

ISBN-13: 9781502962676
ISBN-10: 1502962675

Dedication

To the readers who loved the men of Runaway
Train enough to keep the series going.
And to Kim Bias & Paige Silva—my two wranglers who keep me
sane, make me laugh, & keep me focused.

BRAYDEN

THE PRESENT

The wind whipped through my hair and rippled through my clothes as I drove over the Bull River Bridge that connected Tybee Island to Savannah. I couldn't help feeling seventeen again. With a Beatles CD blaring, I sang along at the top of my lungs like I didn't have a care in the world. Of course, a day at the beach always made me young again. It reminded me of summer vacations with my parents and grandparents. A smile tugged at my lips when I pondered how in the world we were able to get my two younger sisters, my parents, my grandparents, me, and all of our shit into one van. Of course, I'd faced a similar predicament today with the convertible I'd rented for the day at the beach. It had taken two or three times of repacking before I'd managed to get my three children and all of our beach gear inside.

My phone buzzed in my pocket, and I dug it out. Glancing down at the screen, I motioned to my eleven-year-old son, Jude, who sat next to me. "Cut the volume. It's your mother."

After he reached forward to turn down the music, I answered the call. "Hey, baby. What's up?"

"Where are you?" she demanded.

I could tell by her tone I was already in deep shit. "Almost back to Savannah. Why?"

"Because we're supposed to be sitting down with Giovanni Coppola right now for an interview, remember?"

"Shit!"

"Daddy!" my daughter, Melody, admonished from the back seat.

"Sorry, sweetie, but at the moment, that's the only word that will suffice."

When I glanced in the rear view mirror, my less vocal daughter, Lucy, shook her head at me in disapproval. Although their father was a rock star surrounded by men, and sometimes women with mouths like sailors, their mother taught them that swearing was wrong. I don't know what Lily was thinking when she started that up with them. It was like she was setting my bandmates and me up for failure. Besides, she'd been known to let a few juicy words slip before, especially in the heat of the moment when we were in bed.

"Time just slipped away from me, baby. I'll put the lead out and be there in ten."

"Don't you be driving crazy with my babies in that car. You're carrying precious cargo."

I smiled at her admonishment. "I won't, I promise."

"Bye," she said, tensely.

"Bye, honey." Grimacing, I hung up the phone.

"Is Mommy mad at you?" Melody questioned.

"Just a teeny bit."

"What did you forget this time?" Jude asked, with a grin.

It was common knowledge among my children that I was a little scatterbrained. Without a wife like Lily, I'm not sure if I would be able to survive. It was a personality quirk that had been a part of my life since I was sixteen years old. "This interview thing with a very important rock magazine."

"Epic fail, Dad," Jude said, shaking his head.

With a chuckle, I replied, "Ya think?"

Eyeing the speedometer, I then eased my foot down on the accelerator, slightly increasing the speed. I kept my promise to Lily to be safe, but I still wanted to get back as fast as I could. For over half of my life, Lily Marie Gregson had been keeping me on my toes. More than that, she'd been the love of my life through thick and thin, the good and the bad, for better or worse and all that jazz. She'd given me the family I'd always dreamed of with our three beautiful children. And after all these years, she could still get my blood up and running.

The five of us had left our family farm in Roswell, Georgia and had descended on Savannah yesterday. Actually, the entire Runaway Train family, sans Rhys and Allison, had flown in on our band's jet. We had come to the capitol of Southern grace and charm to see our last single bandmate tie the knot. That was also the reason I had Lily on my ass to get back for the interview. Rolling Stone had decided to do a feature on Rhys and Allison's wedding. After all, it wasn't everyday a rock star married his bandmate's little sister, who was also a rising star in the fashion industry.

But it wasn't just the soon-to-be newlyweds they wanted to focus on. They wanted to devote a large part of the spread to Lily and me. While the media often loved to focus on Jake and Abby being music's power couple, Lily and I had been singled out this time as music's lasting couple. To them, we were an enigma—high school sweethearts whose twelve-year marriage had stood the tests and trials of the rock star lifestyle. Our envied relationship was put on a pedestal for the rest of my bandmates and their significant others to aspire to. All the attention was a little overwhelming. It was one of the reasons I'd wanted to escape to the beach.

The other reason being that today was Allison's bridal luncheon. Since Lily was a bridesmaid, I had offered to take the kids to the beach to get them out of her hair. AJ and his girls had joined us as well. Poor Jake, as the brother of the bride, had been roped into staying for the luncheon and helping Abby out with their twins, who rounded out the wedding party as the ring bearer and flower girl.

With all the fun in the sun, I had let time get away from me. I cherished every damn minute we had off the road. Although I now had my own bus that enabled Lily and the kids to travel with me, I thoroughly enjoyed the time away from all that craziness. In the last few years, we had drastically scaled back our touring. Once AJ and Jake became fathers, coupled with Abby wanting to be a hands-on mother, the call of the road was no longer as alluring as living at home with our families. In the end, fame, Grammys, and money are fleeting. Your family is really all you have, all you can count on, and everything that keeps you centered in this crazy world.

I eased the convertible up to the valet stand. After Jude and I hopped out of the front, we worked to quickly extract the girls and our plethora of beach gear. I then handed off the car keys to the attendant and corralled the kids inside the hotel. After the elevator let us out at our floor, I drew in a deep breath as I neared our suite. I dug in my pockets for the key card but came up empty. "Dammit, what did I do with the key?"

"Daddy!" Melody admonished again as Jude waved the key card in front of my face.

"Sorry," I mumbled before taking the key from Jude. "Thanks." I didn't even want to begin to wonder how he had the card.

The girls pushed past me to run into the suite. As I drew in a breath, I couldn't help feeling like a pussy. I mean, I was a grown man for fuck's sake, but I was practically cowering from the impending wrath of my wife. Maybe it was because Lily was usually so easy going and laid back. She very rarely lost her temper, and she was the level-headed one who evened out my manic side.

I hustled down the short hallway. Peeking around the corner, I watched as Lily embraced our girls, planting a kiss on the tops of their dark-haired heads. They had both inherited my dark hair and eyes, but they each had the same dimple in their left cheek that their mother did. While the reporter might've thought Lily's affection was all for show, I knew better. The sight caused warmth to flood my chest.

Glancing over Lucy's head, Lily met my gaze. The beaming smile she had for our girls tightened considerably. "So glad to see you finally made it home safely." While the reporter might not have caught her veiled hostility, I heard it loud and clear. I had to do something fast to get my ass out of the doghouse.

Plastering on my most apologetic smile, I power-walked around the corner. I then threw my hand out to the reporter. "Brayden Vanderburg."

As he pumped my hand, he replied, "Giovanni Coppola."

"I'm so sorry I'm late. I'd love to blame the kids, but sadly it's all my fault."

He laughed good-naturedly. "It's okay. You guys have a lot on your plate with the wedding. I just appreciate you making time for me."

"We're just honored that an esteemed magazine like yours would want to interview us," I drawled, laying it on extra thick.

When Lily raised her brows at me, I winked. She ignored me and turned to the kids. "Okay guys, Mia is waiting on you next door. She's had an early dinner delivered from her dad's restaurant."

"Mama Sofia's!" Melody squealed while Lucy gave an enthusiastic smile.

"Good. I'm starving," Jude replied before he headed to the door with Melody and Lucy trailing behind him.

Before Lily could ask me if I had also managed to forget to feed our kids, I held up my hands. "He ate everything you packed as well as raiding the concession stand twice. I swear that kid will be eating us out of house and home when he turns thirteen."

Lily cocked her head at me. "I seem to remember you having the same appetite when you were a little older than him."

Sensing an opportune moment for interrogation, Giovanni asked, "Just how hold were you when you met?"

"Sixteen," Lily and I replied in unison.

Our shared reply brought a beaming smile to Giovanni's face. "Do you finish each other's sentences, too?"

"Sometimes," Lily replied.

"I'm usually forgetting what I want to say so I need her to finish," I joked.

Giovanni scribbled something down in his notebook. When he glanced up, he motioned to the patterned sofa. "Why don't you two sit there, and I'll have a seat here?" His hand fell on the back of one of the antique chairs.

I nodded. Easing down on the sofa beside Lily, I leaned over and gave her a quick kiss. "You smell good," I complimented.

The tight expression that had been on her face since I came in receded, and a genuine smile appeared. "You smell even better because you smell like the ocean."

I then turned my attention to Giovanni. "Once again, my deepest apologies for being late."

"It's all right."

Cocking my head at him, I asked, "Did my lovely wife give you the sad sap story as to why I'm not always with it?"

Giovanni grinned. "Yes, she did. And I have to say it was quite fascinating hearing about your head injury and how without it, you might not be where you are today."

With a chuckle, I replied, "I would have to say that's the truth because if it weren't for the short-term memory issue shit, I would have been here a lot earlier."

Waving his hand dismissively at my joke, Giovanni said, "I don't think most of our readers or your fans know you didn't grow up playing guitar or having the desire to be a rock star. That without the football related injury, you would have never taken up the guitar or written your first song."

I shifted in my seat. Talking about my injury always made the hairs stand up on the back of my arms and neck. It was one of those life-altering moments that set me on an entirely different path I could never have imagined. At sixteen, my entire universe revolved around the emerald green grass of the field and the smell of pigskin in my hands. I had my eye on a college scholarship and maybe some time in the NFL. I was that good.

But life changes in an instant—a play you had executed flawlessly a hundred times before can go so very wrong. Instead of being carted off victoriously on the shoulders of your teammates, you leave in a neck brace laid out on a stretcher. A brain injury coupled with a cracked vertebrae that narrowly missed severing your spine brings the curtains down on your dream. But then you realize the life you thought was ending was truly just beginning.

The squeeze of Lily's hand brought me out of the past and back to the present. I cleared my throat. "Yes, it is true that my life would be so very different and not for the better. But I don't mean in the sense of not having the fortune or the fame." I turned to gaze at Lily and smiled. "I might not have Lily by my side."

She brought my hand to her lips and kissed it. "When I was seventeen, I told you I'd follow you anywhere and everywhere. If your life had taken you somewhere else, I would have been there."

"Thank God," I murmured.

"So was it love at first sight for you?" Giovanni asked, leaning in expectantly.

Lily tilted her head at me before giggling. "Not exactly."

Giovanni's dark brows knit together. "Oh?"

I couldn't help the smile that stretched across my face as the familiar memory played in my mind. "I owe my marriage to my lovely wife's penchant for apple thievery."

Lily sputtered with outrage. "I was not stealing apples. We had just moved in, and I wasn't sure where our property ended and your grandparents' began."

After winking at her, I focused my gaze on Giovanni's amused one. "The first time I ever laid eyes on Lily she was wearing a blue sundress with a satin ribbon in her hair. She could have had the face of an angel, but I wouldn't have noticed because she had the hem of her dress flipped up to cradle the apples she was picking from my grandparents' tree. All I could focus on were her long, tanned legs and the brief glimpse I got at what was between them."

"Brayden Michael Vanderburg!" Lily exclaimed. Just hearing her call my full name caused warmth to enter my chest. I loved her voice, I loved her outrage, and I loved that a woman as amazing as she was actually loved me.

"I'm just answering the man's question, sweetheart," I replied. Leaning forward in my chair, I then began the story of the day that changed my life....

BRAYDEN

THE PAST

With my guitar resting on my lap, I closed my eyes and began strumming the familiar chords. The peace I often searched for through the music hummed throughout my fingers and then spread throughout my body. I focused only on the music while the rest of the world faded into the background—the heave and sigh of the porch swing, the shrieks of happy children, and the soft snores of my grandfather who slept in a rocking chair across from me. In moments like these, I was one with my instrument. It became an extension of myself—the best and purest parts.

"Speaking words of wisdom, let it be," I sang softly. Although I had been a Beatles fan all my life, the song had come to mean more to me in the last six months. Learning to let things be was the very reason I'd taken up the guitar in the first place. And like Paul, I'd had my own hour of darkness to which music pulled me out of and sent me to the light.

My foot tapped out the rhythm on the worn floorboards of my grandparents' front porch. Even from my place outside, I could hear the faint laughter and chatter of my father and his siblings. The noise barely lessened even when I worked the strings of my guitar harder. My cousins, ranging in age from three to eighteen, roamed about the large two-story, plantation-style house as well as the massive front yard.

Sunday dinners held a place of reverence in my family. I suppose they did in every old-school Southern family. I couldn't remember a time in my life when we hadn't spent every Sunday around the antique table that overflowed with home-cooked food.

My fingers hit a wrong note, and I grimaced as I remembered the one time I was absent. It had been six months ago. While a colorful array of red, orange, and yellow leaves coated the ground, I remained a prisoner in a white-walled room. Even if I had been able to leave, I doubt I would have noticed the colors. My world had faded to black the moment a doctor in a white coat had held up an X-ray and started rattling off my prognosis.

"Intense trauma to the cerebellum."

"Irreparable damage to the C1 and C2 vertebrae due to the cervical fracture."

"Inconceivable to play contact sports of any kind. Ever. Again."

And while the physical pain was bad, the emotional agony that clawed its way through me had me ringing the nurse for more medicine. I'd toddled out onto the Pee Wee football field at barely three. As a freshman, I was starting on the varsity team. The next two years, I racked up more titles and broke even more records. On that crisp, October evening, I had scouts from both Georgia Tech and Auburn watching me play. Unfortunately, they had a front row seat to the demise of my football career.

I'd spent a week in the hospital, and then three months doing physical therapy to repair some of the nerve damage I'd experienced. It was in the middle of therapy that a guitar was put in front of me. Before that day, I'd never even considered playing an instrument. But the therapist thought it might be good for me. While she'd explained that it would help rewire the parts of my brain that had become scrambled, I think she really suggested it because she thought I needed an outlet. The anger, the frustration, and the grief about what had happened to me were at a boiling point. I'd started lashing out at those around me—those who just loved me and wanted to see me get better.

But what neither one of us could have imagined was how easily learning the guitar would be for me. It was like a switch had been flipped in my brain. What had once looked like a bunch of jibberish on a sheet of music suddenly made total sense to me. The neurologist gave some name for it—acquired savant syndrome.

While savants were usually geniuses, I was nowhere near being a Paul McCartney or Jimmy Hendrix. And even though reading and playing music came a lot easier to me, it didn't hurt that all the time I'd once spent practicing football or watching it on television was now focused elsewhere. Any spare time I had, I was sure to have my guitar on my lap, just like today.

"Hey dickweed! Get your pansy ass out here and play," my cousin, Mitch, called from the front yard. I didn't even have to glance up to know that he was tossing a football up and down in his hands. Growing up, we both lived and died for football. But Mitch was the only Vanderburg still playing.

"Go fuck yourself," I shouted.

"Language, Brayden," my grandfather chided. I guess Nick and my yelling had woken him up.

"Sorry, Papa."

Mitch came to the edge of the porch. Gazing up at me, said, "Come on, man. You can at least throw it back to me."

"Leave him be, Mitchell," Papa said, as he shuffled across the floor and then into the house.

Ignoring Papa, Mitch bounded up the stairs. "Dude, you're wasting a perfectly good day sitting up here on your ass, screwing with that guitar."

"Once again, go fuck yourself," I growled. Trying to tune him out, I started playing *Let It Be* again.

"Hmm, hello, hottie."

My fingers screeched to a stop on the guitar strings as I jerked my head up. Mitch's hungry gaze was trained off the porch and far down the hillside where a grove of apple trees stood. Rising up from the swing, I peered farther into the distance. With her arm raised to one of the branches, a tall blonde was picking apples, her long hair cascaded over her shoulders. Even from where I was, I could tell she was beautiful, and it wasn't just the way her sundress molded to her body.

Mitch flashed me a wicked grin. "Let's go have some fun."

I groaned. "Can't you for once not let your dick make every decision for you?"

"And what would be the fun in that?" As he started down the porch, he glanced at me over his shoulder. "That kind of attitude is exactly why you're still a virgin."

"Douchebag," I muttered, as I put my guitar back in its case. I then followed reluctantly behind him. Since we were kids, he had been the Pied Piper, leading me from one adventure to the other. Most of the time, he got us both in trouble. He was the closest thing to a brother I had, and although he was an overbearing, egotistical jackass most of the time, I still loved the hell out of him.

We trailed down the grassy hillside. Silently, I hoped the blonde would leave before we could get to her. Mitch had a way of being a sexist pig around girls. He was a legendary ladies man at school—the love em' and leave em', manwhore type. Although I probably didn't stand a chance with her, I sure as hell didn't want Mitch tainting her.

As we neared the tree, the blonde reached up on her tiptoes to pick another apple. "Fuck me," Mitch murmured. The blonde had the hem of her dress flipped up, cradling the apples she'd picked. If she moved just another inch, I would be able to tell what color her underwear was. But even if I didn't get a peek of that, her tanned thighs were enough to cause my dick to twitch in my pants.

When I stepped forward, a branch snapped beneath my sneakers, causing the blonde to practically jump out of her skin. One of her hands holding onto her dress's hem flew to her chest, causing a few apples to tumble to the ground.

"Sorry, I didn't mean to scare you," I apologized.

As she rubbed her dress over her heart, she gave me a weak smile. "That's okay. I just wasn't expecting anyone."

Mitch cut in front of me. "You know stealing is a pretty serious offense around here," he said, a teasing lilt in his voice.

Her brows creased in confusion. "Excuse me?"

"You're stealing our apples."

She gasped as her blue eyes widened. "I'm sorry. I didn't know. I thought the trees were on our property."

"Your property? So you've just moved in next door?" I asked.

"Yeah, well, we've been here a couple of days."

"My grandfather said his new neighbor was the chief of police," I said, finding it easier than usual to make conversation with her.

She bobbed her head. "That's right."

Mitch nudged me and chuckled. "How ironic that the new chief of police's daughter is an apple thief?"

She jerked her chin up at him. "I said I was sorry. You can't fault someone for not knowing."

"Don't mind Mitch. He's just being an asshole as usual."

Her expression lightened. "Okay, I won't."

"What do you want with those apples anyway?" I asked.

"I wanted to bake a pie for my dad. Apple is his favorite, and I wanted him to have some tomorrow on his first day at work."

"Damn, you're just as sweet as you are pretty," I blurted, to which the girl giggled.

"What's your name?" Mitch asked.

"Lily."

"Nice to meet you, Lily. I'm Mitch, and that's Brayden."

I gave her a lame wave. "Hi."

"Hi," she replied, with a smile.

"Why don't I make a deal with you for the apples, Lily?" Mitch asked.

"What do you want?" she asked cautiously.

"I let you have the apples, and you let me have a taste of your pie."

Smacking him hard on the chest with my palm, I tried pushing him away from Lily. With a determined raise of my brows, I said, "We should be getting back now. We've bothered Lily long enough."

Unfortunately Mitch didn't back down, and Lily didn't get the message. "You really want me to bring you some pie?"

"Aren't you generous?" Mitch remarked, with a wolfish smile.

"Mitch," I growled in warning. I knew my cousin all too well, and if I had a breath left within me, I wasn't going to let him work his usual sleazy numbers on Lily. Even though I had just met her, I could tell she wasn't like one of his usual conquests. And I sure as hell didn't want him corrupting her. Even if I wanted to corrupt her seven different ways, I didn't want Mitch to.

Ignoring me, Mitch closed the gap between him and Lily. "Mmm, yeah, baby. I want that sweet, warm pie that's between your legs."

Lily's eyes widened in shock. "You're disgusting!" she shrieked. Throwing down the hem of her dress, the remaining apples bounced onto the ground before she turned and fled up the hillside.

"You're a fucking jerk," I muttered.

Mitch grinned. "Just wait. I'll be tapping that ass before homecoming."

Ignoring his comment, I swiped up four apples and then ran after her. It had been a long time since I had done any running. Within seconds, my body ached from the exertion and my lungs burned. When I started to feel a little lightheaded, I debated stopping. But then Lily's enraged and embarrassed face flashed before my mind, and I trudged on.

Just when I reached her, Lily abruptly stopped and threw her arm straight out, clotheslining me at the throat. I flew back, tripping on my own feet and stumbling. I got my bearings again just as the world cloaked dark around me.

Something warm and soft cradled my aching head while someone was stroking my cheek. As my eyelids fluttered, I tried desperately to bring myself around. Where was I? What had happened? At the pain throbbing through my skull, I groaned. "Shh, you're okay. I've got you."

My eyelids snapped open. When my vision finally focused, it was Lily I was gazing up at. It only took me a few seconds to do the math that if I was staring up at her I was flat on my back. It also meant that I had come off looking like a fucking pansy in front of the most beautiful girl I'd ever seen. "Oh shit," I grunted, trying to pull myself into a sitting position.

"Easy now," Lily murmured, her fingers stroking through my hair. At that moment, I realized I was a fool to try to get up when I had such an angel of mercy looking after me. Her blue eyes locked with mine. "You had me really scared there for a minute. I mean, I didn't think I had hit you that hard, and then you were passing out. I thought about going for help, but I didn't want to leave you."

"Yeah, well, what the fuck were you doing closelining me anyway?" I demanded a little too harshly.

"Y-You were chasing me…After what your friend said, I thought you were going to try and do something…," she swallowed hard as her cheeks reddened. "Nasty to me," she whispered.

"First of all, I would never, ever hurt you. Second, that guy is not a friend—he's my cousin and generally a pain in my ass."

"Oh," she murmured.

"I came after you because I wanted to give you the apples."

She gave me a sheepish grin. "I realized that a little too late."

I couldn't help smiling back at her. There was no way in hell I could be angry with her considering her delicious thighs were pillowing my head, and her fingers threading through my hair felt amazing.

"I really am sorry," she said, softly.

"It's not your fault—" When she started to protest, I shook my head. "Really it's not. Most dudes wouldn't have had that reaction to being hit by a girl."

"Is that right?" she questioned icily.

"I didn't mean it like that. You see, six months ago, I got hurt playing football." My hand automatically went to my neck. "I guess that's putting it lightly. After getting tackled, my helmet sorta malfunctioned, and I got a major brain injury along with a cervical fracture. A few more inches and I would have been paralyzed."

Lily gasped in surprise. My heart did a funny little sputter at the concern and empathy that washed over her face. "I'm so sorry."

"Yeah, I was lucky in some ways, but it means no more contact sports like football. If I got hit hard enough again, I could end up in a wheelchair."

I nearly jumped out of my skin at Lily's shriek of horror. "Oh my God, what if I hurt you that bad when I hit you? Or what if when you fell, it caused more damage?" Her blue eyes left mine to gaze below my waist. "You haven't moved your legs yet."

"Lily, I'm—"

Remorseful tears streaked down her pretty cheeks before she buried her face in my shoulder. "I'm sorry. I'm so, so sorry."

"Hey now, stop crying. I'm fine. I can move my arms and legs. Everything is fine," I reassured her.

With a sniffle, she pulled her head up and then peered down where I was shaking my legs and feet. A long exhale of relief escaped her lips. "You had me so scared."

"I'm sorry I scared you."

"It's okay," she sniffled.

I reached one of my hands up to brush away some of her tears. With my head still throbbing, there was no way to censor my thoughts. "God, you're so pretty."

Lily giggled. "Is that you or your head injury talking?"

"It's me," I replied. The moment between us seemed to be broken, so I sat up. Glancing at her over my shoulder, I said, "Guess a compliment like that doesn't mean much to you."

Her brows furrowed. "What do you mean?"

"A beautiful girl like you—I'm sure you get told that all the time."

"Maybe," she replied. As I brought my knees to my chest, Lily leaned closer to me. "A compliment like that only matters when it comes from someone you want to hear it from."

"You care that it came from me?" I questioned incredulously.

"Of course I do."

Before I could think better of it, I blurted, "Do you want to go on a date with me?" The moment the words left my lips, I cringed. Although I wasn't bad to look at, I had never been good with girls.

When they would flirt or come on to me, I was too shy to follow through. I was a sixteen-year-old virgin who had only gotten to second base with a girl and had one short-lived hand job.

Her blue eyes widened. "Seriously?"

"Um...yeah. I mean, it's only if you want to. I don't want you doing it out of pity cause you hit me and caused me to pass out."

Lily laughed. "I would never go on a pity date with you, Brayden."

"You wouldn't?"

She shook her head. "But I would love to go on a *regular* date with you."

I couldn't keep the goofy grin off my face. "Really?"

"Yep."

"That's awesome."

Cocking her head, Lily asked, "So where are you taking me on our date?"

"Hmm," I muttered. I hadn't even bothered to think that far ahead. "Well, next Friday night I'm playing at a frat house."

Lily's brows shot up in surprise. "You're in a band?"

"Not exactly. You see, I have an audition with these guys on Friday night. If everything goes well, then I'm in their band."

"Wow, that's really cool."

"So would you want to come to the party? I'd have to meet you there since I have to help with set-up and sound checks."

"I'd love to come."

"Great. The set starts at nine, and then I could take you to dinner afterwards. You know, so we could actually talk rather than having to shout over the loud-as-fuck music."

Lily grinned. "That sounds like a great plan."

A throat cleared above us. Lily and I jerked our heads up. I could only guess it was her father staring down at us. "Hi Daddy," Lily said.

"Hello," he replied. The corners of his lips twitched. "Would you like to tell me what's going on here?"

"Oh, yeah, um, I was just meeting our new neighbor." Pointing to me, she said, "This is Brayden..."

"Vanderburg," I finished for her.

"Hello Mr. Vanderburg," Lily's father replied dryly.

Turning to me, Lily said, "This is my father, Paul."

I threw my hand out. "Nice to meet you sir."

"Likewise."

Shooting to my feet, I quickly said, "Actually, it's my grandparents who are your new neighbors. I live across town."

This time Paul gave me a genuine smile. "That's good to hear."

A nervous laugh escaped my lips. Breaking Paul's intense gaze, I stooped over to pick up some of the apples I had been bringing to Lily. Lamely, I thrust them out to Paul like a peace offering. "They're from my grandparents' tree. She kinda forgot them when my cousin was being a dick." I winced at my language. "I mean, I was bringing them to her because she wanted to bake you a pie on your first day at work." When I realized my mistake of ruining Lily's surprise, I muttered, "Oh fuck."

Paul cocked his head at me. "Damn son, you sure know how to put your foot in your mouth, don't you?" I didn't realize I was fully off the hook until Paul started chuckling. Amusement danced in his blue eyes—the same ones as Lily's. "I'm sure there's a very interesting story about how the two of you ended up on the ground. Together."

"Uh, yessir, there is." I then proceeded to have the worst word vomit ever by telling Paul not only about Mitch being an asshole, but also all about my injury.

"Sounds like you've have a rough couple of months."

"Yessir."

"Since you're supposed to avoid physical injury, do you really think it's a good idea for you to start dating my daughter?"

My brows lined in confusion as I asked, "Excuse me?"

Crossing his arms over his chest, Paul shot me a hard look. "I'm merely stating the fact if you hurt my daughter, I'm going to hurt you."

"Daddy!" Lily shrieked in horror.

Paul shook his head. "You see Mr. Vanderburg, I was blessed with four daughters who are my heart and soul. There isn't anything I wouldn't do to ensure their physical and emotional safety. While I'm thankful that two of them are now happily married, I still have Lily and Kylie to worry about. Lily just turned sixteen—to me, she's still my little girl." Narrowing his eyes, Paul added, "I'm a lawman, so I can ensure the body is never found."

Lily smacked her father's arm. "Daddy, stop it right now!" She glanced from him to me with tears sparkling in her eyes. "I'm sorry, Brayden. I'll understand if you don't want to go out with me considering my father is an overprotective jerk."

"No, no, of course I still want to go out with you."

"You do?" both Paul and Lily asked.

"With all due respect, Mr. Gregson, I know I just met Lily and don't really know her, but I do know that there's really nothing you could say or do that would keep me from wanting to date your daughter."

To my utter shock, Paul gave me a beaming smile. "I'm glad to hear that." He drew Lily to him. "I think you've made a wise choice in accepting this boy. He's certainly passed my test."

My eyes widened as his comment. "Really?"

He nodded. "I'll even talk her mother into extending her curfew a little."

"Wow, thank you, sir."

"Just don't disappoint me."

"I won't. I promise."

Lily gave me a shy smile. "Thank you, Brayden."

"You're welcome."

"Why don't you come up to the house and meet the rest of the family?"

Jerking my thumb over my shoulder, I replied, "I appreciate the offer, but I really better be getting back."

"Well, at least let my oldest daughter, who is a nurse, take a look at you. I don't like the look of your pupils."

"Oh, um, okay."

Paul nodded. "You can call your parents from the house. Let them know where you are." With a wink, he added, "Maybe we can get Lily to go ahead and make us some pie."

I laughed. "I would like that a lot."

He started on up the hillside, leaving Lily and I to walk together. Feeling a slight ego boost from my encounter with her dad, I held out my hand for Lily to take. She smiled and quickly slipped hers in mine. We then started walking hand in hand up the hillside.

LILY

THE PAST

Turning left and right, I surveyed my appearance in the bathroom mirror. Even though I was only going to be in a frat house tonight, I had dressed up a little. It was Brayden's and my first official date, and I wanted to look really nice for him. After going through my entire closet, I'd decided on a pink and purple floral, baby-doll dress. The material flowed when I turned, and with its spaghetti straps and low cut back, I felt sexy. I'd spent extra time putting waves into my long, blonde hair, and I was also wearing way more makeup than I did to school.

To say I wasn't as nervous about tonight as I had been about starting my new school last week would be a lie. The last time I'd been the "new girl" had been in sixth grade when we moved from Slidell, Louisiana to Birmingham. At my high school in Birmingham, I'd been a cheerleader and found myself on the Homecoming Court. I had no idea how I would be accepted here in Roswell. My mom always said I was a natural born pleaser—someone who wanted everyone to like me. I guess that was true. But as much as I always wanted to please people, I also wanted them to be happy. My disposition often resulted in good-natured teasing from my sisters who loved to mock the people who praised me for my sunshine disposition and big heart. "Lily is just so lovely, isn't she?" they would say with a teasing lilt in their voice.

But as soon as my shaky legs took me through the front door, Brayden had swooped in to meet me and make me feel at ease. "You okay?" he asked, as we started down the hallway.

"Oh, I'm fine. Never better," I lied. When Brayden cut his eyes over at me, I wrinkled my nose. "Yeah, I'm petrified."

He smiled. "It's going to be okay, I promise. We'll stop by the counselor's office to pick up your schedule. The secretary is a friend of my mom's, so I can get her to put you in the classes with me. Then you won't have to worry about not knowing anyone or getting lost."

My brows shot up in surprise. "You would do that for me?"

"Of course I would. I've lived here all my life, so I don't know what it's like to be the new kid. I just know how much it sucked being the 'injured kid'."

"Thank you. I appreciate it so much."

"It's good for my popularity, too. Getting to be seen around with the prettiest girl in school."

My cheeks warmed a little at his compliment. "I'm glad it works for both of us then."

He laughed. "Come on, Lily. Let's show Roswell High their newest star."

Fortunately, Brayden's group of guys and girls welcomed me with open arms, and I was really enjoying school. Through his former football connections, he had even managed to score me a late tryout for the cheerleading squad. I'd secured my spot yesterday with what the coach had called a "flawless routine". While some of the girls hadn't been very welcoming, most of them became fast friends, making my transition even easier.

Although I'd barely known Brayden a week, I found myself already falling for him hard. I'd had a few boyfriends over the years, but I'd never had a relationship that lasted over a few weeks. Surprisingly enough I could see myself being with Brayden for the long haul. I'd never met a guy who was as sweet and caring as he was handsome. When I'd randomly in conversation expressed how much I loved kids and wanted to be a teacher one day, he'd even managed to get me the hookup for an afterschool program job at the school where his mother taught. Even though I would only be working two days a week, I loved every minute being with the kids.

After spritzing some perfume on my neck and wrists, I headed out of the bathroom. I found my thirteen-year-old sister, Kylie, lounging on the bed, reading my latest issue of YM magazine. "Hey

Kyles, I know we're still getting used to the house, but this is my room. Your room is across the hall."

"Har, har," she muttered. She then glanced up and took in my appearance. "Wow, where are you going tonight?"

"Nowhere special."

She rolled her eyes. "Bullshit."

"Watch your mouth. Mom and Dad will ground you in a millisecond if they hear you cussing like that."

"Don't change the subject."

Ignoring her, I went over to my jewelry box to dig out a pair of earrings that would go with my outfit.

"Come on, Lily. Give me the dirt. You know I won't tell the 'rents."

"That's because you're already too much of a troublemaker," I mused.

"And you're too much of a goody two shoes," she countered with a grin.

Throwing my hands up, I replied, "Fine. If you must know, I'm going to a frat party tonight to—"

She squealed with excitement as she bounded off the bed. "Oh my God, Lils, I'm soooo jealous!"

I shook my head at her. "When you turn sixteen, Mom and Dad better never let you out of the house."

"Whatever. So you're seeing a college guy?"

"No, it's not like that. Remember Brayden you met the other day?"

Lily's blonde brows furrowed. "I thought that guy was in high school."

"He is. But he's auditioning for a band that happens to have college-aged guys in it."

"Hmm, he must be really good."

I shrugged as I finished putting on my earrings. "I don't know. Tonight will be the first time I've heard him play."

Lily's blue eyes widened. "What if he like totally became a famous rock star? You'd be a famous rock star's girlfriend."

With a giggle, I replied, "We're not even dating, Kyles. I mean, I haven't even kissed him yet." It's not that I hadn't wanted him to the last few times we were together. Just when I thought he was going to lean in and lay one on me, he would abruptly turn away. I chalked it up to him being nervous, not that he didn't want to kiss me as much as I wanted him to.

"Damn, what if he's a shitty kisser?"

I rolled my eyes at her. "I need to wash your mouth out."

"No, you need to start talking this way to keep up with your filthy rocker boy."

"Brayden is not filthy."

"He could be if the band asks him to. Besides, I heard Daddy telling Mom how he cussed like a sailor in front of him because he was nervous."

"You don't miss anything, do you?"

She grinned. "Nope."

I glanced at the clock on my nightstand. "I gotta go."

As I started for the door, Kylie hopped up to follow me. "So does Mom and Dad know you're going to a frat party?"

My purple Sam and Libby ballet flats skidded on the hardwood floors as I came to an abrupt stop. When I turned around, Kylie smirked at me. "I'd take that as a no."

"Why do you have to be so annoying?" I growled.

"Because I'm your little sister, that's why," she replied diplomatically.

"They think I'm going to the ten o'clock movie with some of my new friends from the cheerleading squad, and that Brayden and I aren't going out until tomorrow night."

"Good lie, especially since I assume you're going into Atlanta… *alone.*"

"Are you going to say something to them?"

"Nope."

I eyed her suspiciously. "And why not?"

"Because I'm going to file it away for the next time I need a favor…or a lie from you."

"Why am I not surprised?" I muttered.

Kylie smacked me on the butt. "Go on. You don't want to be late for your rockin' Prince Charming."

I laughed in spite of myself. "Okay, okay. I'm out of here."

"Be safe. Don't forget to take the phone."

For my sixteenth birthday, my parents had gotten me of those bag cellphones. It was for emergencies only—not to be calling my friends to chat. I hated the huge thing, but Kylie had a point. "Don't wait up for me," I called over my shoulder as I headed out the door.

"Don't do anything I wouldn't do," she replied, her voice laced with amusement.

I didn't reply. Kylie's rebellious attitude already worried me for her and for my parents. My two older sisters, Natalie and Melanie, were pretty much on the same level as me. They might've had a few moments where they snuck out or lied to our parents, but for the most part, they were kind of boring. I had a feeling Kylie was going to end up giving my parents even more grey hair.

After I pounded down the stairs, I grabbed my purse and keys off the end table in the foyer. "Lily?" my father called from the living room.

Just when I thought I was in the clear to escape down the hallway and out the garage door, my father would have to call me in. "Yes, Daddy?" I asked, after I stuck my head in the living room archway.

My dark haired, dark eyed two-year-old nephew, Asher, sat on my father's lap. They were watching *Aladdin* for probably the hundredth time. My parents spent most of their Friday and Saturday nights babysitting their grandchildren so my sisters could have some alone time. No one loved and appreciated their two grandsons and granddaughter more than my parents.

"You be careful tonight. Make sure to take the phone."

"I will, Daddy."

He smiled. When I turned to start out the door, he said, "Tell Brayden I said hello."

I froze. For a few seconds, I couldn't blink, least of all breathe. Slowly, I turned back around to face my father. "But I'm not seeing Brayden tonight. I'm going out with the girls," I argued feebly.

Daddy gave me a look that clearly said I wasn't fooling anyone. "Just remember you have to be back by midnight."

"You're still letting me go?"

"Sure. Why wouldn't I?"

"Because I lied to you about where I was going."

Daddy adjusted Asher on his lap. "I like Brayden. Most of all, I trust him. He personally called me up to ask if it was all right for you to come hear his band play."

"He did?" I asked incredulously. While I thought it was terribly sweet of Brayden to do that, I wished he had let me know, so we could get our stories straight.

"Yep. So any boy who goes to that extreme to make nice with me has only the best intentions when it comes to you."

"Okay," I replied.

"So go on, and have fun."

I grinned. "Thanks, Daddy."

Just when I thought my father couldn't be any cooler, he said, "I'll be waiting up for you to do the breathalyzer, so don't even think about drinking."

"Yes, Daddy." I silently cursed having a father in law enforcement before I hurried out of the living room and down the hallway before he could say anything else. Unfortunately, my quick escape plan had issues when I ran into my mom and my four-year-old niece, McKenzie, in the kitchen.

"Lily, you look pwetty," McKenzie said.

I grinned down at her. "Thank you, sweetie."

"You gots a date?" she asked.

"Um, no, I'm going to meet some friends," I lied. I wasn't sure if my dad had made my mom aware of my real plans.

Apparently he hadn't because Mom just smiled at me. "Have fun. Maybe next time you can invite the girls over here so you won't be out so late."

As my hand reached for the doorknob, I replied, "Sure. I'll see."

"'Bye, honey. Have fun."

I exhaled a sigh of relief when I was finally out the door. I hustled over to the early 90's Honda I had inherited from my older sister, Melanie. It would be mine until I could buy my own car, and then it would go to Kylie.

Thankfully, there wasn't much traffic, so it only took me the usual thirty minutes to get downtown. When I got onto Fowler Drive, cars lined the street. Since there were a lot of frat houses on the street, I glanced down at the sheet of paper with the directions. Once I found it, I quickly parked as best I could.

Taking a few calming breaths, I then did a final check at my reflection in the rear-view mirror before I grabbed my purse. The yard was packed with people, and it took a while to get through. A glance at my watch told me I had ten minutes before Brayden was supposed to go on. When I finally got inside, it was just as packed. As I made my way through, I was offered a red solo cup by at least three different guys. I shook my head in refusal and kept weaving my way in and out of the crowd, trying desperately to reach the stage. When I got as close as I could, I craned my neck as I searched for Brayden. Four guys worked on setting up equipment like amps. As I squeezed in closer, I recognized Brayden's dark head of hair.

"Brayden!" I cried over the roar of the crowd and the music.

His head jerked up before he whirled around. A broad smile lit up his handsome face. He held up a finger before turning back to the guys. After they exchanged a few words, he came to the edge and hopped down. "I'm glad you made it. I was afraid you might've backed out."

"And miss hearing you play?" I shook my head. "Never."

He chuckled. "I'm glad to hear it."

"Yo, Vanderburg. Get your ass back up here," one of the guys called from the stage.

Brayden grimaced. "Listen, I'm sorry, but I have to go finish setting up. But I'll catch you after, okay?"

"Of course. I'm holding you your promise to buy me some dinner."

He grinned. "I'm a man of my word, I promise." He then surprised me by leaning in and kissing me on the cheek. "See you later."

"Okay," I murmured breathlessly. Just the simple touch of his lips on my skin had me enflamed. I knew in that moment I wouldn't have anything to worry about when it came to Brayden being a shitty kisser. I knew he would be able to make my toes curl.

I remained by the stage as the guys hurried around getting everything ready. From time to time, Brayden would meet my gaze, and he would wink or smile at me. I felt like I was in heaven.

"Well, hello again," a voice said behind me.

I instantly recognized it belonged to Brayden's jerk cousin, Mitch. Reluctantly, I turned around and gave him a smile. "Hi."

"I didn't think I was going to know anyone here." He flashed me a wolfish smile. "I'm glad the one person I know turned out to be so fucking pretty."

"You're such a flatterer," I responded sarcastically.

"Now don't be that way, Lily. If you and Brayden get serious, we'll practically be family."

"Shouldn't family not hit on each other?"

He laughed. "I'll keep that in mind for later on."

Before I could respond with some smart remark, a screech came over the microphone. I turned my attention away from Mitch and put it back where it belonged on Brayden. My heart stopped and then restarted at the sight of him. With his guitar strapped over his shoulder and with the stage lights coming down on him, he had been transformed. He looked every bit the rocker.

A tall, blond-headed guy with a major ego stood in front of the microphone. "Thanks for coming out to the party. We're the Benders. I'm Tom. That's Raul on bass, and Grayson on drums." His lips curled into a smirk at the pleasurable female shrieking. "So, how the fuck are you tonight?"

The crowd roared in response to the question. Tom nodded in approval. "I hope you all came to rock tonight. First up, we've got a special guest who is going to be playing and singing lead on two songs. Let us know what you think, and we may give the sad little fuck a place in the band."

My gaze went from Tom to Brayden. His face flushed at Tom's words, but he managed to wave to the crowd. When Tom motioned Brayden to the microphone, he didn't hesitate. Instead, he strode confidently up there. "Hey guys, I'm Brayden. Hope you like what I have to play and sing tonight. I thought we'd start off with some Green Day and *When I Come Around*."

The applause around me was somewhat more subdued than when Tom was up. Cupping my hands around my mouth, I screamed his name. As he adjusted his guitar and pick, he grinned at me. "Two, three, four," he said. Then he strummed the opening chords of the song. The loud amps blared the music as the drummer came in.

"I heard you crying loud all the way across town..." Brayden sang into the microphone. Like being hit by a lightning bolt, I immediately fell in love with his voice. Even though the song didn't call for it, his voice had a deep and soulful quality. I couldn't believe that until the last six months of his life he hadn't been singing, least of all playing the guitar. He had such a natural talent for both.

When it came time for the guitar solo, Brayden totally nailed it. The audience screamed their approval, which caused Brayden to grin. The song came to a close, and he took a bow. "Thank you," he said breathlessly into the microphone.

I clapped until my hands were blood red and stung from my efforts. Gripping the microphone, Brayden said, "To change things up a little bit, I wanted to do one of my favorite songs from Bush—*Glycerine*."

Brayden pinched his eyes shut and strummed the opening chords of the song. He looked so sexy when he was deep in concentration, focusing on the music and the lyrics. I thought he was handsome walking around school in jeans and a T-shirt. The muscles he'd developed from playing football were not really hidden behind his shirts, but tonight they seem larger than life. But it seemed amplified by a thousand with the glow of the lights on him, his fingers working magic over the strings of the guitar, and his heart and soul being poured out as he expressed the lyrics.

He finished his performance to another round of applause and cheering. He ducked his head, but I could see the grin that spread across his cheeks. "Thank you again. You guys have been great," he said.

Tom slid over to stand beside Brayden. "So what do you guys think? Should we give the fucker a chance?" Tom asked, to which the crowd roared their approval. I yelled until my throat burned. Tom grinned and turned to Brayden. "I guess you're in."

Brayden's face broke into a beaming smile. "Thanks. I appreciate it." He then turned to the crowd and held up his hand. "Thanks to you guys, too."

As Brayden started to leave the stage, Tom grabbed him by the arm. "Where ya going, man? We still got a show to play."

A red flush crept along Brayden's cheeks. "Oh, yeah, sure, I'll stay." He then eased to the side to let Tom take back the lead singer role. I didn't know if Brayden was prepared to play with them or not, but when they started up the next song, he fell right in.

"Wanna dance?" Mitch asked.

Since it was a fast-paced song, I didn't think it could hurt. "Sure. But if you try to molest me once, I'm going to knee you in the balls."

Mitch threw back his head and laughed. "I'll be a good boy. I promise."

True to his word, Mitch didn't try to grind on me or do anything disrespectful. After two fast songs, it changed to a slow one. We just stood there staring at each other in the middle of the dance floor. "I can still be a good boy even though the song is slow."

Reluctantly, I nodded. "Okay." Tentatively, I reached out to wrap my arms around his neck. He pulled me close against him.

"So you think you're going to like it here in Roswell?"

"Yeah, I think I am. I mean, everyone's been so nice, it's hard not to like it."

"I wouldn't know. I've lived here all my life."

"You're really not missing anything. Moving basically sucks."

"But then you get a chance to meet new and interesting people. Especially guys."

I laughed. "I guess so."

When I glanced over Mitch's shoulder, I noticed Brayden glaring at the two of us. Feeling uneasy about what I was doing, I tried to pull away. "Where are you going?"

"This isn't right. I shouldn't be dancing with you."

Mitch tugged me back to him. "You're not dating Brayden, so there's no reason why you can't dance with me."

Thankfully, the song came to an end. "Thanks everyone. Give us a ten minute break, and we'll be right back."

The loud screech of a guitar came from the stage, and when I looked up again, Brayden had torn off his guitar and stormed off the stage. He made his way through the crowd to us. But then he started past me. "Brayden, where are you going?"

"Don't talk to me right now," he growled, as he brushed past me.

I didn't even have time to ask what was wrong before he shoved Mitch hard against the wall. "Fuck you, man!" he shouted. He then stalked out of the room. Without a word to Mitch, I rushed after Brayden.

"Would you please wait!" I called after his hastily retreating form.

Brayden ignored me. He blew through the front door and stomped out onto the porch. I followed close on his heels. "Look, I'm sorry I danced with Mitch. If I had known it would bother you so much, I never, ever would have done it."

He whirled around and pinned me with a glare. "You can't possibly understand it. Mitch is never satisfied until he has exactly what I do. It's been that way since we were kids. He knew how I felt about you, but he wasn't going to be happy until he had you, too."

"But I'm not his."

"It didn't look that way in there."

My eyes widened at his accusation. "It was just a slow dance, Brayden. There's nothing going on between Mitch and me, and there never will be. In case you forgot, I came here to be with *you* tonight. You and only you."

He shook his head. "Yeah, and that was a mistake."

I gasped. "How could you think that?"

The clouds that had filled the sky for most of the day opened up and a driving rain started coming down. Drops slapped angrily against the sidewalk. Brayden glanced off the porch before turning back to me with a forlorn expression. "I'm really sorry, Lily."

When he started off the porch, I followed right behind him. The rain pelted down on me, stinging my cheeks. I grabbed Brayden's shirt. "Don't you dare walk away from me!"

Without looking back at me, Brayden said, "Trust me, it's for the best. You're too good for me—too beautiful."

"That isn't true."

"I'll always have to be fighting some guy for you."

"Stop it. You don't know me well enough to be saying that."

"No, but I know me."

I skidded to a stop. Glaring at his back, I shouted, "You know what you are? A fucking coward." My hand flew to my mouth, but it was too late to stop the harsh words or cursing. When Brayden froze, I almost apologized. But then I thought about the emotional whiplash he had put me through, and anger once again boiled within me. "You think that just because your dream of football was taken away that you'll never be who you once were. In case you missed it back there, you rocked that audition. People were riveted by your performance. But more than any of the strangers in the room, *I* was riveted. Just hearing you sing and play made me feel things and want things I never had before. But now you're telling me I can't have them simply because you're afraid I don't want you? Or that you can't bear the thought of having to vie for my attention with other guys?" I stalked over to him. "Man up, Brayden. Stand up and fight for me right now, and you'll never have to worry about me and another guy again. You'll have me."

He stared at me, unblinking and unmoving, as the rain soaked us to the bone. I knew my words were heavy handed considering we had only known each other a week. But I wanted him to know how much I wanted him—that he was *worth* wanting. "Fight for me," I murmured.

Just as I had resolved myself that the boy I was falling in love with was just an illusion, Brayden launched himself at me. His lips crashed against mine as his hands came around my waist. As his warm mouth moved against mine, he jerked my body flush against his. When I moaned at the contact, his tongue darted into my mouth. I shuddered as he ran his tongue against mine. My arms came up to encircle his neck.

In that moment, time seemed to stand still. The world around us melted away. We didn't acknowledge anyone else around us. I didn't feel the harsh rain on my skin. Instead, I felt the smooth touch of Brayden's fingers as they wound their way through the strands of my hair or up my arms.

I don't know how long we stood there kissing in the rain. When Brayden finally pulled away, I gasped in a breath. He cupped my face in his hands. "I'm sorry I acted so stupid."

"It's okay."

He shook his head. "No, it's not. I promise you I won't ever stop fighting for you."

I smiled up at him. "I'm glad to hear that. I'll fight for you, too."

He laughed. "You're a little scrappy thing to be fighting, aren't you?"

"I can be pretty tough when I need to be."

Leaning down, Brayden bestowed another kiss on my lips. This time it was chaste, but I still enjoyed each and every second of it. No one had ever kissed me like Brayden had.

When he pulled away, he brushed his thumb across my cheekbone. "Wanna get something to eat?"

I nodded. "I'm starving."

As Brayden surveyed our drenched clothes and hair, he exhaled a defeated breath. "I had planned to take you somewhere really nice tonight for our first date, but I'm thinking that's not going to work right now."

"I don't care about any of that." I swept a damp strand of hair out of his eyes. "I just care about the part where I get to eat."

He grinned. "Come on, you can ride with me, and then I'll bring you back to your car."

"Sounds good."

When we got to the car, he held open the door for me like a true gentleman. "Thank you."

"You're welcome," he replied. Glancing back at the house, he grimaced. "Give me five minutes to go tell the guys I'm cutting out."

"You won't be in trouble, will you?"

He laughed. "No, I was only playing with them until the first break."

"Oh, okay."

He shut the door and then ran back to the house. It didn't seem like he was gone a minute before he was back. He hustled around the front of the car and then slipped inside. "There's some napkins in the dash if you need to clean up."

"I don't think they're going to help."

He grimaced. "I'm sorry you got so wet."

"I didn't mind." With a grin, I added, "It was for a worthy cause."

"It was the cause of a stupid idiot.

"Hey now, that's my boyfriend you're talking about like that." When the word escaped my lips, I realized it was too late to take them back. Brayden hadn't asked me to be his girlfriend. We'd barely even had one date. "Well, um, you know."

"You want me to be your boyfriend?" he asked.

"Do you want to be my boyfriend?"

With a grin, he said, "I asked you first."

I smiled back at him. "This is all new to me. I don't have a lot of experience with guys."

"I find that hard to believe."

"It's the truth. I've dated a few guys, gone to the movies, held hands, that kind of thing."

Brayden's eyes widened. "So you're a virgin?"

I couldn't help the warmth that flooded my cheeks. Ducking my head, I questioned, "Is that a problem?"

"Of course not. Why would it be an issue?"

Shrugging, I replied, "Some guys aren't interested in a girl that won't sleep with them."

"Those guys would be douchebags," he answered, as we turned into the parking lot of an older looking restaurant. The illuminated sign with red letters read "The Varsity." While there was a place to go inside and eat, Brayden drove over to the drive-in area.

Taking my hand, Brayden said, "If we're being honest, I've never had sex either."

Now it was my turn for the wide eyes of shock. "You haven't?"

He shook his head. "Is that a problem?" he asked, repeating my question.

"No. Never."

"I'm glad to hear that."

As we sat there staring at each other, Brayden's thumb rubbed circles over the top of my hand. "Lily, would you—"

A man's loud voice bellowed outside the window. "Whadda ya have?" he questioned, with his order pad in hand.

"Shit," Brayden muttered. After he rolled down the window, he said, "Can you give us a minute?"

The man nodded before he ambled over to one of the other cars. I glanced up at the menu. "So what's good here?"

"Oh no, you're not going to do that."

"Do what?" I questioned innocently.

"Change the subject."

Glancing over at him, I said, "I was trying to give you an out. You know, in case you felt pressured."

He shook his head. "I don't ever need an out when it comes to you. Now are you going to be my girlfriend or not?"

I grinned. "I am."

"Good. I'm glad to hear it." Rubbing his hands together, Brayden said, "Now that we have that out of the way, it's time to get serious about food. We're lucky this place is close because it's legendary."

"It is?"

"Oh yeah. Best chili dogs in the whole state."

"Hamburgers?"

"They're awesome, too."

"Why don't you order a little bit of everything, and we can share."

Brayden grinned at me. "I sure do love a girl who isn't afraid to eat greasy, artery-clogging food."

When the guy came back, Brayden placed an order for what should be a carload of people. At my expression, he laughed. "Trust me, I can put all that away even if you don't eat any."

While we waited for the food to arrive, we talked about anything and everything. Conversation seemed to flow so easily between us. I felt like I could tell him anything.

After biting into a hot dog smothered in chili, I moaned in delight. "Oh my God, this is good."

"I told you so."

Chewing thoughtfully, I then asked, "So what happens now with the band?"

Brayden swallowed the large bite of cheeseburger he'd taken. After swiping his mouth with a napkin, he said, "I guess I just see where it goes. I needed to get my foot in the door with college bands since they're usually the ones who have more gigs and resources. I don't know if these guys will go anywhere, but that's not the point for me right now. I just want to play."

"I think you could go all the way."

His brows arched in surprise. "You do?"

Dabbing a French fry in some ketchup, I nodded. "You've only been playing for six months, and look how amazing you are? Think about what it might be like in a year or two years?"

"Thanks," he murmured.

"For what?"

"You're the first person who has ever really believed in me and my music. Well, besides myself."

"Don't your parents think you're good?"

Brayden took a long gulp of his drink—something called a frosted orange. "My dad still hasn't come to terms with my football death sentence. I think he somehow believes that in a year, my prognosis will magically change, and I'll be back to where I was." He glanced at me. "He just thinks the music is something I'm screwing around with while I heal."

"I'm sorry," I murmured.

"It's okay. He's not a bad guy. He's just one of those Southern men who lives and breathes for football. My mom, well, she's just so thrilled that I'm all right compared to the alternative. She wants me to be happy, so I guess once she realizes it's music that makes me happy, she'll be okay with it. As long as I still plan on going to college."

"Where do you want to go?"

"I'm hoping for Georgia Tech."

"So you can be close to the guys in the band?"

"Sort of. But it's where I wanted to go before I got hurt." After polishing off his chili dog, Brayden asked, "What about you?"

"I don't really know enough about the colleges around here yet to decide."

"I think you should go to Tech, too."

I giggled. "Is that right?"

He nodded. "Or at least Georgia State."

"Let me guess. Georgia State happens to be close to Tech?" With a wink, Brayden's hand dove in the bag for more fries. "All right then. I'll start checking on the teaching programs at Georgia State."

"Sounds like a plan to me."

A glob of ketchup remained on the side of his lip, so I leaned forward and slid it off. Not taking his eyes off mine, he flicked his tongue against my thumb before sucking off the ketchup. The suction of his mouth, along with his expression, caused a shiver to run through me. To get my mind off what he could possibly do with that mouth, my eyes went to the clock on the dash. "Shit. I don't have much longer before I have to be back."

"Okay," he said softly.

Turning back to him, I said, "I wish I could stay out all night with you."

"You do?"

At the possible implication of my words, I felt warmth rush to my cheeks. "I-I mean, I wish I could stay out talking to you. I like being with you."

"I know what you mean." After he had managed to get our trash back into the bag, he hopped out to throw it away.

"Thanks for dinner."

"You're welcome. I hope I was able to convert you to being a Varsity fan."

"Oh yeah, I think I'm sold."

"Good," he replied. We made the drive back to get my car. Thankfully, nothing crazy had happened to it while we were gone. Like a true gentleman, Brayden got out and came around to get me out. As we stood there in the dark, staring into each other's eyes, words seemed inadequate.

"I just realized how historic this night really was," he said, with a smile.

"What do you mean?"

"Well, I got in my first band and I got my first real girlfriend all on the same night."

His first girlfriend? Is he for real? He was one of the sweetest, gorgeous boys I have ever met. How had he never had a girlfriend?

I smiled back at him. "That is pretty momentous."

"It feels fucking amazing, if I was honest about it."

With a laugh, I leaned forward to bestow a kiss on his lips. He pulled me to him and kissed me back. After just a few seconds, it had become an all-consuming, all-powerful lip-lock. One I didn't think I would be able to pry myself away from. Finally, Brayden released my mouth and pushed himself away. "You better get going. I promised your dad I wouldn't mess up."

"Oh yeah, about that. As much as it was thoughtful of you to call my dad, let me know next time so I can get our stories straight, okay?"

Brayden gave me a sheepish grin. "Oops. Sorry about that."

"It's okay," I replied. On shaky legs, I slipped inside my car. Brayden waited until I cranked up and started down the street before he got into his car. I couldn't think of anything but him the entire forty minutes home.

LILY

THE PRESENT

Giovanni furiously scribbled on his notepad before looking up at us. "That was quite an interesting story about how you two first got together. Although if I had to argue that from the sound of it, it truly was love at first sight."

I laughed. "I guess you're right. At least it was for me after our first kiss."

Brayden held up his hands in defeat. "Trust me, I was pretty much a gonner from the moment I laid eyes on her."

"And you were pretty much inseparable from the day you met, correct?" Giovanni asked.

With a grin, Brayden said, "I couldn't let her out of my sight. I mean, you see how gorgeous she is. I didn't want her running off with anyone else."

I gave his thigh a playful smack. "We just got a long so well that we didn't want to spend any time apart. We had our separate interests, but luckily, we were able to support each other in those."

Giovanni nodded as he chewed thoughtfully on his pen cap. "Now Brayden, during her story, Lily touched briefly on your first band, The Benders. How long were you with them?"

Scratching his chin, Brayden became contemplative. "Let's see I was a junior in high school. And then we broke up when I was twenty."

"What happened there?"

Brayden remained silent for a moment. I knew the sordid details from being in the thick of everything with him, but it wasn't my place to talk about it.

He drew in a ragged breath. "Tom and Grayson had issues with addiction. Lots of alcohol and some drugs. It derailed the entire creative process for them, but they never wanted to include any of my songs. We weren't getting anywhere on the music scene, and then things just seemed to be spinning out of control personally with them. So I left."

Giovanni nodded. "Do you ever see or hear from them?"

"Grayson died from an overdose about a year after I left. I think after that, they just dissolved the band." After looking down at his hands, Brayden shook his head. "No, I don't hear from any of them. You know, the guilt is hard sometimes. I've heard different artists talk about how you have this guilt about making it. Kind of like survivor's guilt. Like, what was it about me that deserved to make it, but Tom and Grayson didn't?"

Tapping his pen on his pad, Giovanni smiled. "I think that shows a great depth of character. So many artists lose their hearts and souls with fame and fortune."

When I tensed at Giovanni's words, Brayden sighed dejectedly. "Trust me, I went down that road. It wasn't pretty."

"We'll come back to that one in a few minutes. I'm trying to keep to the timeline of your relationship, and I have a feeling that comes during the part when the two of you were broken up."

"Yes," I murmured. When I had first agreed to the interview, I hadn't envisioned having to relive some of the darkest times of Brayden's and my relationship. It was even harder knowing that it would be documented in a magazine for everyone to read the sordid details. I guess in the end, our breakup didn't come from anything salacious like I caught him having an orgy. To some it might not even seem like that big of a deal. But for me, it was life altering.

"Lily?" Giovanni asked.

I jumped. "Yes?"

He smiled. "From those early days together, what is the most romantic thing Brayden did for you that truly cemented your feelings for him?"

Glancing over at Brayden, I found that he was giving me a concerned look. I knew he wasn't thrilled about having to dig up the past either. I smiled reassuringly at him. "I know some people will think that this was a planned response, but the truth is the most romantic thing he ever did for me was write me a song."

"Ah," Giovanni replied, scribbling something down. "Correct me if I'm wrong, but I believe that song was the first of Runaway Train's hits."

"You are right. It was the first song of ours to ever be played on the radio. Our first Billboard hit," Brayden replied.

Giovanni smiled. "And it's all because of Lily."

Bobbing his head, Brayden said, "You got that right."

"So where did you first play it for her?"

Brayden glanced over at me with a sheepish grin. "I guess you could say it was a very acoustic performance."

LILY

THE PAST

I bolted upright in my bed out of a dead sleep. Just when I thought I had been imagining things, something scratched against my window, and it wasn't a branch caused by the wind. With my heart beating wildly in my chest, I threw back the covers, poised to run down the hall to my parents' bedroom for help. But then a hushed voice outside stopped me.

Brayden's voice.

For a minute, I thought I might just be imagining things. After our first date last Friday night, we had been pretty much inseparable for the next few days, so it made sense I would think I was hearing his voice. Not to mention the fact, that he had taken me to the preseason bonfire at the school earlier tonight.

Just when I had discredited it as my imagination working overtime, I heard, "Lily!"

Sprinting over to the window, I peered out. He stood on the lawn, his guitar slung over his back. "What in the...?" I muttered, as he beckoned me with his hand. Glancing over my shoulder, I groaned as I read the time on the digital clock. It was three in the morning.

My curfew was eleven o'clock during the week, and I was pretty sure that didn't include a lawn rendezvous in the middle of the night. After hurrying out of my bedroom, I then crept down the hall, silently willing the creaky, old floorboards not to rat me out. Once I got to the backdoor, I entered the code for the alarm before heading outside. The moment I opened the door, the gentle strings of guitar music floated back to me. I ran across the steps of the deck and peered down at Brayden where he stood strumming his guitar.

"What are you doing?" I hissed.

A beaming smile lit up his face. "I just wrote a song."

"Um, that's wonderful, but couldn't you have waited until the morning to tell me?"

"It *is* the morning."

"I meant like when I wasn't asleep."

Brayden shook his head. "After I dropped you off tonight, I couldn't go to sleep. My mind kept spinning and spinning, and then I would hear this melody in my head. And when I finally got up and started writing down the words, it wouldn't stop. It felt like I was on a roller coaster or something. Then when I finished, I just had to come over here and tell you."

Glancing over my shoulder, I nibbled anxiously on my bottom lip. "That's really cool, Brayden, but you're going to get me in trouble."

"I don't care," he replied, with a chuckle.

My mouth dropped open in shock at his attitude. "Well, I do! And you should too. If I get grounded, I won't be seeing you until after graduation."

Taking a step forward, Brayden said, "Don't you get it, Lily? I've never written anything in my entire life. Hell, I could barely string the right sentences together to write the essays for my English classes." He stared determinedly up at me. "But then you came into my life just when everything had gone to shit, and I thought I could never be happy again without football. But I'm fucking happier than I've ever been. And when you chose me, it changed everything."

"Oh Brayden," I murmured, my heartbeat accelerating wildly at his words. For a moment, I had to resist the urge to pinch myself. Could it truly be possible a handsome guy with a beautiful heart was on my lawn in the middle of the night to sing a song he wrote just for me? Surely, I would wake up in a minute and find out it had all been just a dream.

"Want me to sing it for you?"

At that point, I didn't care if my parents caught me and grounded me for the rest of my natural born life. I needed desperately to be serenaded. "Oh yes, please."

Brayden grinned. His talented fingers began working over the strings of the guitar. A melancholy melody floated up to me, one I knew came straight from Brayden's previous suffering.

Disappointments twisted and crippled me with rage.
Darkness held me bound like a prisoner in a cage.
Sadness wrecked me and brought me to my knees.
Suffering had me begging "Oh lord, help me please."
There was no reason to go on
Until there was you

Winking up at me, Brayden switched chords, and the sound of the sound changed to one more hopeful.

You drove away all the dark clouds with your smile.
You made life once again seem worthwhile.
You gave me a reason to go on.
A purpose to escape the twilight for the dawn.
Your love has the power to transcend and transform.
You're my Lily of the Valley, my savior from the storm.
Nothing really mattered in my life until there was you

When he finished strumming the last chords, I couldn't hold myself back any longer. I raced over to the deck gate. I flung it open and pounded down the stairs. The moment my bare feet hit the grass, I began to run. I couldn't wait to get to him. I had to touch him to know that he was really real. Tears blinded my eyes as I threw myself into his arms.

His guitar screeched between us. He chuckled against my ear. "I guess that means you like it.

"Oh my God, I love it!" I cried, before leaning back so I could smother his face with kisses.

"I'm glad to hear it," he murmured, in between me kissing him.

"This is the most romantic thing a guy has ever done for me," I gushed.

He grinned. "Now you're going to make it hard for me to ever top this."

I laughed. "I don't know how you could." Tilting my head at him, I asked, "Did I really do all those things like you wrote in the song?"

"You sure as hell did, babe. Every. Single. Word."

When I reached to pinch his arm, he gave me a funny look. "What was that for?"

"I wanted to make sure you were real."

"Why don't you kiss me again and see just how real I am?"

"Okay," I murmured. Just as I leaned in to bring my lips to his, the flood-lights came on all around the house. With a squeal, I jumped away from Brayden and glanced up at the deck. My dad stared down at us with his arms crossed over his chest. My mother stood behind him. While she wanted to look stern, I could see she was trying hard not to smile.

Brayden threw up one of his hands to my parents. "Good evening, Mr. and Mrs. Gregson."

My dad grunted. "All right, the shows over. Lily, get your ass up here and get in bed. Brayden, get your ass to your own home and go to bed."

"I'm sorry for waking you up, Mr. Gregson. I didn't mean to cause any problems by coming over here. Lily didn't know I was coming, so please don't punish her for my mistake," Brayden pleaded.

My dad huffed out a breath. "I'll take that into consideration."

"Thank you, sir." He started backing away from me, and then he stopped. In a flash, he was back at my side to plant a chaste kiss on my lips. "Goodnight, Lily."

"Goodnight," I called, as he started running around the side of the house. Ducking my head, I walked over to the stairs. I went up them a lot slower than I had come down them. When I got to the top, I dared to peek at my parents.

With his arms still crossed firmly over his chest, my dad's jaw clenched and unclenched. "I'm sorry, Daddy. He just wanted to sing me a song he wrote. I promise we weren't doing anything wrong."

"Excuse me that I might misinterpret the situation after seeing you two with your hands all over each other."

"Paul," my mother cautioned.

"What?" he demanded.

"They didn't have their hands all over each other. They were just hugging."

His brows shot up. "Whose side are you on, Marie?"

She smiled. "I'm not taking sides. I'm just stating facts."

He muttered something under his breath before he eyed me contemptuously. "I should ground you for this. Not only were you out past your curfew, but your boyfriend woke me up out of a dead sleep."

"I'm sorry, Daddy," I said again.

"Fine then. Get in the house."

"Yes, sir."

When I started past him, he reached out for my arm. "You could smooth things over by giving me a goodnight kiss," he said, with a wink.

I grinned and reached up to kiss the salt and pepper stubble on his cheek. "Goodnight, Daddy. Goodnight, Mama."

My mother reached in to kiss my cheek. "Goodnight, sweetheart. Your Brayden sure does have a romantic side, doesn't he?"

Before I could reply, my father groaned. "You're killing me here, Marie. Don't encourage her."

She waved her hand dismissively at him. "I seem to remember someone else being awfully romantic when he was Brayden's age."

"Hey, I'm still romantic," he argued.

"Of course you are."

As my parents bantered flirtatiously at each other, I headed back into the house. I didn't know how I was going to go to sleep. I was still so wound up. Brayden had written a song just for me. He'd come to my house in the middle of the night because he had to sing it to me. It still was unbelievable.

Until There Was You—the song that started it all for the two of us.

LILY

PRESENT DAY

"How impressive that you wrote your first song when you were just sixteen," Giovanni remarked.

Brayden nodded. "Looking back, it's not the strongest one I've written musically or lyrically, but I wouldn't change a thing about it. The song represents such a time of rebirth in my life."

With a smile, I said, "I like it just the way it is."

Brayden chuckled. "I'm sure you do since it's singing your praises."

"You got that right."

Giovanni grinned at the two of us. "So that was the most romantic thing Brayden did. I'm curious to find out what was the most romantic thing *Lily* ever did."

Tilting my head, I replied, "Hmm, I'm interested to hear his answer for this one, too."

"I'm surprised you even have to ask. I would think it would be a given."

"Being the mother of your three children?"

He laughed. "Okay, I guess you need to think a little more superficially than our kids."

"Is it sitting at home in our garage with its own custom-made covering, and no one is allowed to get too close to it?"

"Bingo!" Brayden replied, his eyes wide with amusement.

"Hmm, let me guess? It's a car," Giovanni said.

Brayden winked at me. "It isn't just a car. You can't call a '68 Challenger just a car. It was my pride and joy until Lily came along, but she managed to make it special, too."

Giovanni's brows creased in confusion. "Is that where the most romantic thing comes in?"

Brayden held up a hand. "Hang on. To understand why the Challenger is the most romantic thing, we have to give you a little backstory with the car and with us."

Feeling warmth flood my cheeks, I said, "I don't know how much I can actually say about us and your car that is appropriate."

"While you're giving him the just the basics of the story, I'll be remembering all the good details...or maybe I should say the naughty details?"

"You're impossible," I muttered.

Brayden merely grinned. "But you love me."

"Yeah, I do."

LILY

THE PAST

Friday night after the last football game of the season found me in the back seat of Brayden's car. All four windows were fogged up from the heavy breathing of our exertions. The top to my cheerleading uniform lay crumpled in the floorboard along with Brayden's shirt. The rough denim of his jeans chafed against my thighs as his hips worked against mine. The friction caused more and more moisture to grow between my legs.

It had been two months since he had serenaded me in the middle of the night. We'd been an exclusive couple ever since. Any free time I had after school and work was spent with him. If I wasn't with him, I was on the phone with him. Friday nights I usually went solo to cheer at the football games while Brayden went to Atlanta to play with his band. I'd usually join him on Saturday nights. There was nothing I loved more than to listen to him sing. Of course, I loved it the most when we were alone, and he would sing into my ear.

That's what had originally led to tonight's make-out session. Something about his voice did things to me, made me squirm with an ache between my legs. After kissing in the front seat for a few minutes, Brayden had climbed over the backseat and beckoned me to join him. While we might have moved fast with our initial attraction and becoming a couple, we hadn't gone full speed with the sex stuff. I was glad that Brayden was being patient with me and taking things slow. At the same time, the more I felt for him, the more I wanted to eventually give him my virginity.

As his hand drew down one of the straps of my bra, he jerked his lips from mine. His warm brown eyes questioned if I was okay with this next step. I bobbed my head, causing a lazy smile to drag across his lips. One of his hands delved beneath me to find the clasp of my sports bra. Grunting, his fingers worked to unhook it. After a few minutes, he blew out a breath of frustration. "Dammit, I can't do it."

I giggled. "Big bad Brayden can't get a little bra undone," I teased.

"I think they're really made to keep guys out."

"Here. Let me." Pushing him off me, I sat up. As my arms reached around my back, I caught Brayden's intense gaze. Even though we were in the dark, I couldn't help feeling a little shy. I'd never let a guy see my breasts before. I'd never really wanted to until Brayden. He had been so good not to pressure me into anything. Although he was dying to lose his virginity, he wanted me to be ready. While I wanted everything with him, I was still nervous. Once the clasp came free, I hesitated, keeping the loose fabric of the bra pressed against my chest.

Brayden's hand came to tenderly cup my cheek. "Baby, if this is too fast, we'll stop."

With a shake of my head, I slowly slid the bra down to my lap. "God, you're beautiful," he said, before the hand that had cupped my cheek came to my bare breast. As he cupped and kneaded it, his lips found mine. Once again he pushed me back down onto the leather seat. He feathered kisses down my chin and neck, which caused me to shiver.

When his lips closed over my nipple, I gasped. His head jerked up in alarm. I grinned down at him. "It's okay. It felt good."

"Let me see if I can make it even better," he replied.

This time his tongue flicked back and forth across my hardened nipple, teasing it and me. The ache between my legs began to grow. He sucked at it again before pulling away to blow air across the tip. "Mmm, very good," I murmured.

As he moved to the next breast, I opened my legs wider, letting him ease deeper between them. We both moaned when he began to rub the hardened bulge in his jeans against my center. Sensing I needed more, one of Brayden's hands slid underneath my cheerleading skirt. When his fingers grazed against the cheerleading bloomers I wore over my panties, my hips bucked against him. "Please, Brayden," I said, breathlessly.

He released my nipple with a pop. "You okay with under?"

We'd been playing the over the shirt and panties feel up the last few times we had made out. But I knew I was ready for more. I wanted him to make me come with his fingers the same way I had learned to. His hand slid beneath the elastic band of my bloomers. I sucked in a breath at the feel of his hand cupping me. As he stroked me, I arched my hips in time. Although it felt good, it still wasn't enough.

I tugged at the strands of his dark hair. As if he knew what I wanted, Brayden pushed one finger inside me. "Mmm," I murmured, closing my eyes to the sensation. After swirling one finger inside to tease and test me, Brayden slipped in another. Once again, my hips rose involuntarily.

"Oh, Lily, you feel so fucking good," Brayden groaned against my neck. He continued rubbing his erection against my thigh as he pumped his fingers furiously in and out of me. As I started to climb higher and higher, I grabbed his shoulders, my fingers molding into the flesh. Although I was embarrassed, I couldn't stop the pants and noises I was making—it felt too good. When his thumb pressed against my clit, I cried out, convulsing against his fingers. I clung even tighter to him as the waves rolled through me.

When I could breathe normally again, Brayden had removed his hand from my panties. Hazily, I watched as he slid his fingers into his mouth. "Mmm, baby, you taste good. I can't wait to put my tongue inside you."

Shivering at his words, I said, "I can't wait either. I know it'll be good. Everything you to do to me is good."

He gave me a sheepish grin. "I'm not sure I know exactly what I'm doing."

I shook my head. "I wouldn't want you any other way."

"And I want you, Lily. I want all of you."

"I know. I want you, too. Just not here in the backseat of your car. I want our first time to be special."

"So do I." His expression grew serious. "But I don't just want to fuck you. I want to make love to you."

My thumb ran across his jawline. "And I want to give you everything I have, mind, body, and soul."

His brows lined while his jaw clenched and unclenched. I knew he was trying to find the way to say something important to me. Finally, he whispered, "I…I love you."

I gasped. "What did you say?"

"I said, I love you."

"Oh Brayden," I murmured.

"And I didn't say it just because I want to have sex with you. I said it because I mean it."

Tears filled my eyes, and I couldn't help letting them overflow my cheeks. "I love you, too. And I know you would never tell me you love me just to get me in bed. You have too good a heart for that."

"My heart is all yours." He then grimaced. "Am I sounding like a dopey sap?"

I giggled. "No, you sound pretty amazing to me. But I promise whatever you say to me will go no further than here."

"What happens in the Challenger, stays in the Challenger, kinda thing?"

"Yep. That goes for you especially when you're buddies want to know if we're hitting it."

Brayden rolled his eyes. "Trust me, Mitch is on me all the time wanting to know if we've lost our V-cards."

"Ugh, he's such a jerk."

Brayden laughed. "I know." He dropped his head to nuzzle my neck. "So to answer the jerk's question, when are we going to lose our V-cards?"

I smacked his back playfully. He jerked his head up to grin at me. "I thought it was a good time to ask while we were on the subject."

"Of course you did." Brushing the hair out of his eyes, I whispered, "Soon. I promise."

"You really think you're ready?"

"Even though I probably should want to wait until I'm a little older, I always knew I wanted to have sex when I was in love. I know I love you, Brayden, so there's no reason not to."

He groaned. "God, you're killing me."

"Would you rather I said no?"

His eyes bulged as he shook his head furiously back and forth. "Oh no, I'm good. I swear."

I couldn't help laughing at him. "So where would we go?"

"Hmm, let me think." Brayden remained contemplative for a few seconds. "I think I have an idea of a place that is private. I'm not sure how romantic it is."

"I'm sure it would be better than a hotel room."

"Maybe."

"Why do you sound skeptical?"

"Well, it's just an old tree house behind my grandparents' house. My Papa built it for us grandkids. The only reason I thought of it is because it's private." He glanced sheepishly at me. "I'm not sure if it's nice enough for you."

I gave him a lingering kiss for his thoughtfulness. "Anywhere with you will be nice enough."

He quirked his brows at me. "Except in the backseat of this car?"

I laughed. "Exactly."

"Then the treehouse?"

"Yes. But when?"

"Next weekend?" At my hesitation, Brayden said, "Two weeks?" When I still didn't respond, he laughed. "Hmm, I'm thinking it's going to be never."

I nudged him playfully. "Next month is your birthday, isn't it?"

"Yeah."

"Then we'll do it on your birthday."

He grinned. "That's a helluva gift."

"I hope it will be."

"Oh, I know it will." His brows lined. "Do you think it'll be too cold in November in the tree house?"

"Won't you keep me warm?" I teased.

A gleam of desire flashed in his eyes, causing me to shiver. "Oh yeah, you don't have to worry about that one bit. I'll keep you nice and warm," he replied, his voice husky. He made me feel so loved and so desired all with one look. And given how hot I felt just from what we'd been doing and talking about, I knew he would indeed keep me warm.

Reaching between us, I felt the hardness in his jeans. "I think it's only fair I take care of you since you took care of me."

He sucked in a harsh breath before giving me an erotic smile. "I won't argue with that at all."

BRAYDEN

THE PAST

Glancing down at my watch for probably the millionth time in the last hour, I once again surveyed the time. Lily was late. Five minutes to be exact. As I paced around the inside of the tree house, I began to worry she had second thoughts and decided to back out. I sure as hell hoped she hadn't for many reasons. The first being I was never more ready to have sex in my entire life than I was with Lily. Before I met her, I thought I wanted it, but it wasn't until I was with her, kissed her, and tasted her, that I knew there was no one else in the entire world I wanted to lose my virginity to.

The second reason was the fact I had gone to a hell of a lot of trouble transforming the old tree house into something romantic. I'd dragged up a queen-sized inflatable mattress and made up the bed. I'd also lit a ton of candles. For the final romantic gesture, I'd gotten a ton of silk rose petals and scattered them across the worn floorboards. I had to admit it looked pretty amazing. It wasn't some classy hotel room, but it was a hell of a lot better than the backseat of my car.

"Brayden!" I heard Lily call from outside.

I opened up the hatch in the floorboards and peered down at her. "Hey," I said, lamely.

"I'm sorry I'm late. I didn't think my parents were ever going to go to sleep."

I smiled. "It's okay. Come on up."

She started up the ladder. When she got to the top, a cloud of her sweet perfume filled my nose. "Hmm, you smell good."

With a giggle, she replied, "Thanks." I helped pull her up the last step and into the tree house. As she fell against me, we just stood there, staring at each other. Unable to stop myself, I placed my hand over her heart. I could feel it beating fast.

"Don't be nervous," I whispered.

"Aren't you even a little bit nervous?" she countered.

Ducking my head, I replied, "Yeah, a little." The truth was as much as I wanted to have sex, I was still petrified. With both of us being virgins, neither one of us knew what we were doing. I sure as hell didn't want to ruin Lily's first time by being totally inept.

"Tell me what you're thinking," she urged. Because of the love and understanding in her eyes, I told her everything that had been running through my head. "Oh Brayden, you could never ruin my first time. The very fact that it's with you—the man I love—means more to me than anything in the world."

I laughed nervously. "You can say that now because we haven't done anything yet."

She smiled. "It doesn't matter." Dropping her gaze from mine, she then took in the tree house. "Oh my God…" she murmured.

I winced. "I'm sorry that it's not what you were thinking it would be."

Shaking her head furiously, Lily replied, "It's so amazingly beautiful. And the fact that you did it to make it better for us, well, that makes it even more special."

"You really like it?"

"Yeah, I do."

A broad smile curved on my lips. "I'm so glad to hear that."

We then stood around rather awkwardly. Neither one of us sure who was supposed to make the first move or what that first move should be. "Uh, I brought my CD player with me. Let me put on some music," I said, before I went over to the rickety table by the mattress. Thankfully, I'd remembered the batteries or we would have been out of luck. I switched on the mix CD I had made for the occasion, and U2's *All I Want Is You* came out of the speakers. I turned back to smile at Lily before I went back over to her.

"Want to dance?" I asked.

"Sure," she said, softly.

I drew her to me, wrapping my arms around her waist as her arms went around my neck. We swayed back and forth to the music for a few moments before Lily started giggling uncontrollably. "What's so funny?" I asked.

"I was just thinking how everything was so romantic except I'm here in a T-shirt and my sweatpants."

I laughed. "Well, you had to have a get-away outfit. It wasn't like you could come here naked under a trench coat."

She cocked her head at me. "Is that what you would have wanted?"

"No, I mean, it would have been cool if you had, but you look great just as you are."

She gave me a teasing smile. "I have on something underneath this—something I thought you might like."

My brows shot up so far they probably disappeared into my hairline. "You do?"

"You want to see it?"

Considering my mouth had run dry, I could only nod my head. Lily stepped back from me. Her hand hesitated at the hem of her shirt, so I reached forward to gently pull it over her head. I got an eyeful of her breasts that were pushed up by some lacy, white number. It was like what women back in the day wore. A corset or something.

Lily kicked out of her shoes and shimmied her sweatpants down her legs. When she stepped out of them, my heart shuddered to a stop and then restarted at the sight of her. White lace stockings came up her legs and stopped mid-thigh. Above them a pair of frilly, white panties met the corset. I don't how long I stood there staring at her.

"I guess you like it, huh?"

"I-It's amazing." I swallowed hard. "You're amazing."

Her cheeks flushed, and she ducked her head. "I asked my sister, Melanie, to help me with something to wear. You know, for my first time and for your birthday."

"She won't tell on you, will she?"

Lily shook her head. "No, our secret is safe."

I smiled. "Good."

"Now it's your turn," Lily said, as she stepped forward. Her fingers gripped the hem of my Georgia Tech T-shirt and then lifted it over my head. Her hands then smoothed over my chest. I closed my eyes at the feel of her touch. I sucked in a breath as her fingers went to waistband of my sweatpants. She dropped down onto her knees as she tugged them down. I wasn't wearing any underwear, so my aching hard on sprang free.

Taking me in her hand, Lily stroked me up and down before sliding me into her warm mouth. It was probably only the third or fourth time she'd given me a blow job, but fuck, she was so good at it. She seemed to pick up a new move to drive me wild, each and every time. Just as I got carried away, I gently tried to push her away. But unlike all the other times, she didn't let me go. Instead, she kept bobbing up and down my length. "Lils, if you keep that up, I'm going to come," I groaned.

She still didn't let up at my warning. I gritted my teeth and jerked my hips forward, as I came into her mouth. That was certainly a first since I had pulled out all the other times, but Lily didn't seem to mind. When I finally finished convulsing, she rose off her knees. "Why did you keep going?" I asked, my mind still hazy from the amazing blowjob.

She gave me a shy smile. "Melanie said it would be better if you...well, you know, if you came once before we started to do it. Like it would help you last longer when we were together."

Crossing my arms over my chest, I asked, "You told you sister I was a virgin, didn't you?"

"Maybe." When I huffed in exasperation, she reached out to cup my cheek. "I'm sorry if I embarrassed you. Her first time was with a guy who was a virgin, too. Well, that guy is her husband now, but that's another story. She just thought the tip would help."

Deep down, I knew it was stupid to care if Melanie knew I was a virgin. I already owed her one for getting Lily the sexy-as-hell lingerie, and I'd probably owe her more in the morning. "I'm sorry for being stupid about it."

"It's okay. You were just being a guy."

I laughed. "An over-sensitive guy about my virginity, right?"

She smiled. "Maybe."

Pulling her to me, I kissed her lips. "Now it's your turn. I think you need to come before we get started to."

"Okay," she replied.

Easing us down on the mattress, I stared into Lily's blue eyes. "You are so beautiful."

"Thank you," she whispered.

I pushed her onto her back. Then I bent my head to kiss around the frilly lace where her stocking ended on her thigh. I eased one down her leg and off her foot, and then I went to the other one. Lily kept her eyes on me the entire time.

My hands came to her top. I couldn't help saying a silent prayer of thanks that it was laced up, rather than me having to work with the clasps like on her bras. Gently, I untied the ribbon, and then tugged it through the holes. The sides came apart, revealing Lily's gorgeous tits. I couldn't keep my hands or mouth off of them for one more moment. I took one breast in my hand while I began to suck on the other. Lily's fingers came to run through my hair. Taking my time, I went back and forth between her breasts. I knew I had to get her ready to take me.

Skimming my hand down over her abdomen and between her legs, I began to stroke her over her frilly panties and then under. Panting, Lily opened her legs wider. When she did, I slipped a finger inside her already wet walls. Damn, she felt so good and so tight. If her mouth around my cock had been enough to make me come so quickly, I couldn't imagine what being inside her hot walls was going to be like. I was already hard just thinking about it. Shit. My lips came to hers, and I flicked my tongue inside her mouth the same as I did the finger inside her.

Usually she came easily when I touched her, but I knew she was nervous. So I abandoned her mouth to trail kissed down her chin, her neck, over her breasts and stomach, and then between her legs. I eased her panties down over her thighs and then down her legs.

Tenderly, I kissed up her legs and thighs until I once again reached her pussy.

My tongue lapped long strokes up and down her wet slit. With her legs trembling, Lily began to raise her hips against my mouth, her fingers gripping the sheets. When my tongue began to thrust rhythmically inside her, she came apart, calling out my name.

Wiping my mouth, I then kissed a trail back up her stomach and over breasts. "Feel okay?" I asked.

She gave me a lazy smile. "I feel amazing."

I grinned. "I'm glad I could help."

I brought my lips to hers. After kissing her passionately for a few minutes, I pulled away, surveying her expression. "Are you ready?"

"Yes. Make love to me, Brayden," she urged.

I didn't need any further persuading. Instead, I reached for the packet of condoms I had placed on the nightstand. Taking one, I tore into the foil. I didn't dare tell Lily that I had practiced putting one on, so I wouldn't look like an idiot tonight.

After slipping the condom on, I positioned myself between her legs. As I stared into her beautiful blue eyes, I couldn't believe this was actually happening. Both of our chests rose and fell with heavy breaths, and our bodies both trembled with nerves and need.

Slowly, I began to slide into her. "Are you okay?" I whispered.

"I'm fine," she murmured.

When I pushed all the way in, she sucked in a harsh breath. "Still okay?"

She nodded. "Just a little sting…a little pressure."

I furrowed my brows. "I thought it was supposed to be horrible for a girl."

With a grin, Lily replied, "Would you rather I be screaming and clawing at you to get off of me?"

"No, no, of course not. I guess, I was just afraid I was doing something wrong."

"Oh, babe, you're doing just fine. Athletic girls like me usually have easier times. Something about the stretching or something."

"Really?"

"Yes, really." She raised her head to give me a kiss while one of her hands slid down my back to my ass. She gripped my cheek, urging me on. I didn't stop to check on her anymore. Instead, I began to pump in and out of her. It was instinctual, and I simply couldn't help the need to thrust inside her. Her warmth and wetness – it was so inviting. Pinching my eyes shut from pleasure, I concentrated on the flexing of my hips. She felt so fucking good, so warm and tight around my dick. I could see now why Melanie thought I should come before. I wouldn't have lasted a second inside Lily had I not come before.

"Mmm, Brayden," Lily panted, her hands gripping my shoulders. With her words spurring me on, I thrust harder and faster. Even though I wanted it to last forever, I felt myself tightening up.

And I then with a mumbling of "Fuck yeahs!", I came. Collapsing onto Lily, I buried my face in her sweet smelling hair. We lay there panting hard, our bodies even a little sweaty in the cold. "That was amazing," Lily murmured.

"You really think so?" I asked, when I pulled my head up to look at her.

She grinned. "Oh yeah."

"I thought it was pretty amazing, too." Nuzzling my head against her neck, I added, "I can't wait until we can do it again."

Lily's laughter warmed my heart. "You're insatiable, huh?"

"Oh yeah."

"We'll have to see when I'm able to go again."

"Think you'll be too sore?"

"Maybe."

When I slid out of her, Lily winced. "Okay, maybe we need to wait until tomorrow."

"I don't mind." I kissed her cheek. "I don't want to do anything to hurt you."

"My Prince Charming and Knight-in-Shining-Armor," she mused.

"Whatever," I muttered, although I did kinda like being referred to so highly. When Lily gave a resigned sigh, I asked, "What's wrong?"

"I probably should get going."

"Can't you stay a little while longer?" Even though we weren't going to have sex again, I still wanted to be with her, to hold her in my arms.

"I guess so. I just don't want to get caught." Her brow did the cute little wrinkle she always did when she was really worried about something.

"Okay, we'll get you dressed and back. Don't want you turning into a pumpkin, Cinderella."

Lily laughed and rose up off the mattress. As she grabbed for her clothes, I couldn't help watching her a little longer in the candlelight. When she started to pull on her shirt, she glanced at me over her shoulder. "What?"

I shrugged. "Nothing. I just couldn't help looking at you."

"I would have thought you would have gotten your fill of finally seeing me fully naked," she mused, as she pulled her shirt on and started for her sweatpants.

"I could never get enough of seeing you."

With a smile, she came over to give me a kiss. "I'm going to leave the lingerie here, if that's okay?"

"It's fine. We can use it next time."

She laughed. "We'll just see about that."

After one last, lingering kiss, she started down the ladder. I followed after her and walked her to the edge of the woods. "I love you, Lily," I said.

"I love you, too," she replied.

Part of me felt completed by making love to Lily, but as she hurried down the hillside to her house, it felt as though she was taking a little piece of me with her, too.

BRAYDEN

THE PRESENT

"Babe, come on. It isn't that mortifying," I said, as I tried to coax Lily to stop hiding her face in her hands.

"I just talked about making out in the backseat of your car and how we lost our virginity. I would say that was pretty embarrassing," came her muffled reply.

Giovanni chuckled. "I'm sorry I needed some details about that first time in the tree house."

His statement caused Lily to jerk her head up. "Thankfully, they were just the bare minimum."

Wagging my eyebrows at Lily, I said, "Maybe for him, but trust me, I was reliving them in all their glory."

"You're terrible," she replied, although the corners of her lips did turn up a little.

After clearing his throat and shuffling his notes, Giovanni said, "So, to do a little recap. The original question was what was the most romantic thing Lily ever did for you. I believe you were setting up the importance of this car and how it might play into the most romantic thing?"

"Yes, that was the point of that story," I replied, with a laugh.

"A '68 Challenger was a pretty impressive car to have as a teenage boy."

"Oh hell yeah, it was. That baby was my pride and joy."

"Did your parents give it to you?"

I snorted. "No, my parents believed in you getting a job and earning the money for a car. Thankfully, my mom's dad came through for me. See, she was an only child, and I was the only grandson.

He had several old cars he had collected over the years, so when I turned sixteen, he gave it to me."

Givoanni's brows shot up. "He must've been a special man to entrust such a special car to a teenager."

"Yeah, he was. When I was just thirteen, I used to go over and wash it for him, put special oil on the leather seats. He taught me a lot about cars." I sighed. "It's sad to say, but I was glad he had passed away when I had to sell it."

"Why was that?"

"Even though in my eyes, it was for a good cause, I know it would have broken his heart."

"So why did you sell it?"

"To get the cash we needed to fund Runaway Train's first album."

Giovanni's eyes bulged in surprise. "I had no idea that you weren't with a studio the first go around."

Shaking my head, I replied, "No, the one that got us the attention we needed to get that first real record deal was from the Challenger."

Lily reached over and squeezed my thigh. "I really didn't know if he was going to make it those first few weeks after he sold it. Whenever he would have to go get in the older Honda he'd bought, there would be tears in his eyes."

I swatted her hand away with a laugh. "That's not true."

She grinned. "Yeah, it is."

Rolling my eyes, I countered, "One time. I cried one time about that car, and she wouldn't let me forget it."

Giovanni's brows lined in confusion. "So if you sold the car when you were twenty one, how does it figure into being the most romantic thing Lily ever did?"

"Well, that's because my wife is really good at surprises."

BRAYDEN

THE PAST

"Are we there yet?" I asked for probably the hundredth time in the last ten minutes.

Lily groaned. "Would you stop? Jeez, I never realized you were so impatient."

I turned toward the sound of her voice. I couldn't see anything since she had insisted on blindfolding me. Today was our first wedding anniversary. I'd managed to get a night off the road to fly back home, so we could celebrate. While I couldn't wait to get my hands on her, Lily had other plans when she picked me up at the airport.

I'd missed her more than just physically. She had only been able to come out two weekends this month to be with me. Whenever she wasn't with me, I felt lost. But between her job and the pregnancy, she was worn thin. Regardless of how much I wanted her with me, I wouldn't allow her to do anything to jeopardize her health or our baby's.

When the car started slowing down, I sat up straighter in the seat. "Is this it?"

Lily giggled. "I bet you used to drive your parents crazy."

"No comment."

The car came to a stop, and I held my breath until Lily put it in park. "Okay, I'll come around to get you." When she opened her door, I was tempted to jerk off the blindfold. As if she anticipated me, she said, "No peeking, or you don't get your gift."

"Fine, fine," I grumbled.

Tapping my foot, I waited for her to come around the car. She opened my door and undid my seatbelt. Taking me by the hand, she led me out of the car. We took a few steps and then she let go of my hand. "Are you ready?"

"Yes, dammit, I've been ready the last thirty minutes."

She laughed and then pulled off the blindfold. I was momentarily disappointed to see that we were just in our driveway. But then when I saw what was in front of me, I dropped onto my knees, which earned me another laugh from Lily. "Oh. My. God."

It was a black, 68' Challenger just like I'd gotten when I was sixteen. Just like the one I'd sold to fund our first record deal. Staggering back to my feet, I said, "I can't believe you found another one."

Lily slid her arm around my waist. "I didn't find another one. I found the *one*." When I stared at her in shock, she said, "That's your old Challenger, babe."

I was speechless. She had literally stunned me speechless. "But how?"

"I ran the VIN number through some collectors, tracked it down, then explained to them the story behind the car." With a teasing grin, she winked at me. "I might have used my feminine wiles a little bit to sway them to sell it."

"Please tell me you didn't show them your boobs?"

She smacked my arm. "Honestly, Brayden. I merely tossed my hair, gave them lots of smiles, and then maybe I turned the waterworks on about my dad and the baby."

I threw back my head and laughed. "You're terrible."

"It got you the car, didn't it?"

"Yeah, it did." I pulled her to me, wrapping my arms around her. "Baby, this is the most amazing gift I think I could ever receive." Feeling her tiny bump brush against me, I quickly corrected myself. "The most amazing gift until our baby is born."

"Good save, Vanderburg," she murmured, her lips hovering over mine.

"Glad you thought so." I kissed her deeply, plunging my tongue into her mouth. When I finished we were both breathless.

She smiled up at me. "Wanna take the car for a spin?"

"Fuck yeah. But considering I'm hard as a rock, I think I would rather take you for a spin."

Lily pulled away from me. Swaying her hips, she walked over to the car and opened the backseat door. "Wanna fuck me in here like old times?"

Glancing around, I tried to gage if any of the neighbors were home to see us. When I thought the coast was clear, I hurried to her side.

Not taking her eyes off of mine, Lily lay back on the seat, opening her legs invitingly. "You want to know why this car is special to me?" she asked.

Licking my lips, I asked, "Because I love it so much?"

She tsked at me. "No silly." She then whipped her shirt over her head. "Because I had my first orgasm with a guy in this backseat."

I grinned. "I was happy to oblige you with that one."

As she slid off her jeans, she said, "I almost lost my virginity in here."

"Yeah, not the most romantic place to lose it."

Cocking her brows at me, said, "Lose the pants, Vanderburg."

"Yes, ma'am." Not caring about the neighbors, I unzipped my jeans and tugged them down.

"Going commando, are we?"

With a laugh, I replied, "I ran out of clean underwear."

Lily giggled. "Heaven forbid you have to do some laundry."

"You got that right."

The leather seat warmed my bare ass as I sat down. Once I closed the door, I covered Lily's body with my own. She brought her hands up to grip my shoulders. "You want to know the number one reason why I love this car?"

"Mmm," I muttered, as my hands came to her breasts.

"Because it was the place where you first said you loved me."

My fingers stilled their movements. "I remember that," I replied.

"In that moment, I didn't think I could love you more, but I had no idea." She cupped my face in her hands. "My love for you grows each and every day."

"As does mine." I brought my lips to hers for a tender kiss. When I pulled away, my heart did a funny flip-flop in my chest like the first time I ever saw her or kissed her or made love to her. We were coming full circle from the horny teenagers who had romped in the backseat to a married couple with a baby on the way.

And as the car rocked back and forth with our exertions, we made new memories in the Challenger with all new orgasms.

LILY

THE PRESENT

After shifting in his chair, Giovanni gave me a wry smile. I couldn't help bracing myself for his next question. The twinkle in his dark eyes told me he was about to pose a question that he really wanted to get some dirt on—something potentially salacious. I couldn't imagine where he planned on going since he'd already gotten the dirt on Brayden's and my first time, not to mention our R rated Challenger shenanigans. "This question shifts forward just a bit, but I think it will help tie everything together from your high school days to the days of Runaway Train."

"Okay," I said.

"Everyone is under the impression that the women of Runaway Train get along very well together." He cocked a brow at me. "Is that the truth or a very carefully constructed PR façade?"

"No, we really do all get along and like each other. We're so very lucky that we've become best friends, especially since we're all so very different. Abby, Mia, and now Allison feel more like my sisters, than just my friends or bandmates wives. Over the years, I've really leaned on them, and they have me. I can't even imagine how awful it would be if we hated one another."

When Brayden snickered, I cut my eyes over to him. "What?" I demanded.

He held up his hands in surrender. "Nothing. I was just thinking myself how thankful I am that you girls all get along because there's nothing scarier than one pissed off female, least of all four."

Giovanni and I both laughed at his response. Brayden then winked at me before looking at Giovanni. "It really is the truth that the girls get along well. Any bitchy attitude is usually given to their men, not each other."

"That is true. Although I would add that the men usually deserve it," I replied, with a smile.

Brayden laughed. "I would agree with that, too."

After smoothing my fingers over my skirt, I sighed. "In the end, it isn't easy being a rock star's wife. The somewhat nomadic life on the road with all the endless touring, the overeager female fans… it's an emotional landmine. I really don't think I could have survived if I hadn't surrounded myself with supportive women like the girls.

"But you didn't always have them to fall back on. You two were together before Runaway Train, or what would become Runaway Train, formed."

"Yes, that's true. Two of the guys in Brayden's first band had girlfriends, but we were all so busy with school and jobs that we really didn't get to be together that much except at shows. The Benders didn't do any touring either."

"I can only imagine it was hard being the only female with the four very different men of Runaway Train," Giovanni remarked.

I nodded. "*Very* hard.

"Now that brings me to the question I really wanted to ask. What was it like the first time you met Brayden's bandmates?"

"Oh God," Brayden groaned, burying his head in his hands at the same time a flush entered my cheeks.

Giovanni's eyes flashed like he had hit the jackpot. "Hmm, so it wasn't all fun and games in the beginning?"

As the different memories of meeting Jake and AJ flickered through my mind, I gave an embarrassed laugh. "I guess you could say that although they were hours apart, my first introductions to the men who would become my brothers were quite interesting."

LILY

THE PAST

The summer I turned twenty one was the first birthday I had to spend away from Brayden since we had become a couple. I had been accepted into a summer internship program that I received college credits for. It was a camp for troubled teens up in the North Georgia Mountains. I would only have every other weekend off, and I didn't know how Brayden and I would get through our first real separation. The day I had to leave him, I cried the entire hour trip to the camp, and I didn't stop until the next day.

I wouldn't have been able to survive if we hadn't been able to talk to each other every day on the phone. I shared stories about how far some of the campers were coming in their ability to trust or control their anger while Brayden told me more about his new band that had formed a few months beforehand. Two of the guys, Jake and AJ, were childhood friends who had formed a band in high school. Their bassist was Jake's cousin. They hadn't gotten as far on the music scene as the Benders had, but Brayden said they had way more talent. They just needed some polishing, and he hoped with his experience they could start to go places.

It was good hearing the excitement about music in Brayden's voice again. After the breakup of the Benders, he had been adrift. I had begun to worry what would happen to him if he didn't find another outlet for his music. With work and school, I hadn't had the chance to meet them yet, but it sounded like they were all a perfect musical fit.

The weekend before my birthday, I drove home so I could spend some time with my parents, but most of all, with Brayden. After we had a home-cooked birthday dinner at my parents, we left on the pretense of Brayden showing me his new apartment. The truth was we wanted to be alone. Before this separation, we had never gone longer than a few days without having sex. Now it was two weeks each time, and we were both feeling the pain enough to want to rip each other's clothes off.

Since I had left for the summer, he had moved into a loft with his new bandmates. I was really interested in seeing the place since Brayden had been hounding me for a year to move in with him. We'd both stayed in campus housing our first two years, and after that, I moved back home to save money. Most of the time, I'd end up staying at Brayden's apartment anyway.

When we drove up to the building, I began to wonder if it was a building with lofts or an abandoned warehouse. "Is this place safe?" I questioned, after I got out of the car.

Brayden chuckled. "This block was once one of the most up and coming neighborhoods in the city."

"Once?"

With a grin, Brayden replied, "Yeah, this know-it-all developer bought it and then went bankrupt. The new contractor who bought it got it for a steal. You should see the way they remodeled our floor."

"You have an entire floor?"

"Yeah, it's pretty amazing. Four bedrooms and two baths."

My brows shot up. "That's like a house. How in the world do four college guys afford it?"

"One of my roommates, Jake, his dad owns the contracting company that bought the building. His dad has this giant guilt trip when it comes to Jake, so he offered it to Jake for the same amount of rent he was paying at his old place. It's worked out well because Mr. Charismatic, Jake, has been able to rope more college kids into moving in. A win-win situation for them both."

"He's the lead singer, right?"

"Yep, Mr. Jake Ego-Trip Slater," Brayden mused, with a grin.

Wrinkling my nose, I replied, "I'm not looking forward to meeting this guy. Tom was enough of an ego-trip for me."

"Just wait, babe. I think Jake is even worse."

"Ugh, that sounds horrible."

"He grows on you once you get to know him. Deep down, he really is a nice guy. He's a helluva singer and songwriter, too. With him as our front man, we're really going to start going places. I can feel it."

"I hope so, baby. No one deserves it more."

With a growl, Brayden jerked me to him. "Enough talking. I think it's past time we got to fucking."

I smacked his chest playfully. "You're terrible. Besides, I want you to make love to me."

Cocking his brows at me, Brayden countered, "I haven't been inside your for two weeks. I won't last long enough to make love to you. Maybe tomorrow, but not tonight."

I merely giggled at his response. My laughter was silenced by him slamming his lips against my own. All other thoughts faded away as I focused on the feel of his mouth on mine, his tongue against mine. Just when I thought we might go at it on the hood of his car, Brayden pulled away. "Let's get upstairs," he demanded.

By the time we reached Brayden's floor, I was out of breath. While the three flights of stairs had been a bit of an exertion, it was more about the fact that we hadn't been able to keep our hands off each other. At each landing, we paused to let our mouths crash together, our tongues tangle in a passionate dance. When we finally got to his apartment door, I was in his arms, my legs wrapped around his waist. He grunted as he shifted me to the side, so he could dig his key out.

"Hurry," I moaned, as I kissed a trail across his jawline to his ear.

"Trying," he muttered.

Instead of putting the key in, he shoved my back against the door. His free hand delved under my top to grab my breast. "Hmm, yes," I murmured, as my nipple began to harden under his touch. He began to rub his jean-clad erection against me. It was getting to be too much.

Gripping the back of his T-shirt, I started tugging it off him. Once I had it in my hands, I dropped it to the floor beside us. He followed my lead by stripping off my shirt. He then buried his head in my cleavage, licking the tops of my breasts before moving to put his mouth over my bra covered nipples.

"I want you inside me, Brayden," I panted.

His hand with the key in it left my waist to unlock the door. When it opened, we fell through, nearly collapsing to the floor. I giggled at our sex-crazed antics as Brayden tossed the key onto the table next to the door. As we started across the room, his fingers dug into my buttocks, kneading my flesh. "I can't wait until I'm buried so fucking deep inside you that you come so hard you scream."

I opened my mouth to say how much I wanted him to do just that when a guy's voice interrupted me. "Just try to keep it down, will ya? I'm watching a movie."

At the stranger's voice, I squealed and gripped Brayden's shoulders tighter. "Dude, what the fuck are you doing here?" Brayden demanded.

"Uh, last time I checked, I lived here."

"You said you were going home this weekend to stay with your parents."

"I said I *might* go home."

Brayden grunted in frustration. "You said you would because you knew Lily was coming this weekend."

"Oh yeah, I kinda forgot about that."

"Sorry, baby," Brayden said, before he gently eased me onto my feet. Considering I was in my bra and jeans, I pivoted around to hide behind Brayden.

"You told me she was a hell of a looker, but you didn't mention that she was so shy. Of course, she didn't sound shy when you guys were out in the hallway."

"Oh God," I moaned, as mortification filled me.

I heard the guy rise off the couch and start over to us. When I shrank farther behind Brayden, he said, "Come on, mi amor, a bra is like a bikini top. Nothing to be ashamed of."

Slowly, I peeked around Brayden's shoulder. A tall, dark-haired, dark-eyed guy stood grinning at me, his arms crossed over his broad, bare chest. The only article of clothing he had on was a pair of boxer shorts that hung low on his hips. If I hadn't been totally in love with Brayden, I would have probably fallen to the floor in a pool of lust for this guy. He was that good-looking. But the thing I liked most about him was his warm smile and the mischievous glint in his eyes.

"Lily, this is my roommate, AJ," Brayden introduced.

Throwing out his hand, AJ said, "That's Alejandro Joaquin Resendiz actually. And I'm not just his roommate. I'm the drummer in his new band."

With a resigned sigh, I stepped around Brayden to shake his hand. "It's nice to meet you."

He winked. "Nice meeting you in the flesh. I feel like I already know you because Bray talks about you all the fucking time." Smacking Brayden's chest playfully, AJ said, "He's such a sap."

While Brayden's cheeks reddened, I couldn't help smiling. "I'm glad to hear that he talks about me and isn't having wild and crazy orgies while I'm gone."

AJ snorted. "This guy? Never. Jake and I have been calling him the Old Man."

"Because he's the oldest?"

"Because he acts like an old married man."

"You're full of shit, AJ," Brayden muttered.

The thought of him talking about me to his bandmates and having eyes only for me made my heart swell. Overcome with emotion, I leapt at Brayden, smothering him with kisses. "What dare you doing?" he asked, with a confused grin.

"Showing you how thankful I am that you're such a good boyfriend."

"I have some other ideas of how you could show me."

I giggled. "Is that right?"

"Oh yeah."

AJ groaned. "Would you please take it to the bedroom?"

"I'm sorry. It's just I haven't seen him in two weeks," I replied.

"Yeah, yeah, go fuck each other's brains out. I'll make sure to turn the TV up," AJ replied, before walking back over to the couch.

"There's some earplugs in one of the kitchen drawers," Brayden said.

"Tempting. Very tempting."

Brayden swept me into his arms and started for the bedroom. "Goodnight, AJ."

"Goodnight, Lovely Lily."

I grinned as Brayden kicked the door shut behind us. "Aw, he called me Lovely Lily like Paul McCartney's Lovely Linda."

"Makes sense to me," Brayden replied, with a smile.

The time apart made Brayden and me insatiable for each other. We kept at each other for most of the night until finally falling asleep just before dawn. With my naked body sprawled across Brayden's, I wasn't expecting the door to fly to open just a few hours after we had managed to go to sleep.

"Brayden!" AJ cried.

A scream erupted from my lips at the sight of AJ in the doorway. He quickly spun around to where he faced the door. My reaction freaked out a dead-to-the-world, Brayden. He shot straight up in bed, sending me tumbling to the floor.

"Ow!" I cried, as my butt slammed onto the hardwood.

"Oh fuck, I'm sorry, babe. Are you okay?" Brayden questioned, leaning over the side of the bed.

"I think I broke my butt," I replied, with a smile.

"I'll kiss it and make it better," Brayden offered. He then got out of bed and helped me up.

As he rubbed my aching backside, Brayden demanded, "What the hell are you doing in here AJ?"

With his head down, AJ said, "I knocked a million times. I guess you guys didn't hear me."

"Barging in here at—" Brayden glanced over his shoulder to look at the clock, "at fucking eight am? You better have a damn good reason."

"I do." When he started to turn around, I dove under the covers. As soon as I was decent, he turned the rest of the way around. "Jake called me just a few minutes ago. Apparently this guy down at Eastman's called him in a panic. The house band he had to perform on Friday and Saturday nights broke up, and he's desperate for an act. He wants us to play tonight."

Brayden's mouth gaped open. "You're serious?"

"I'm dead fucking serious."

"A gig? A real, paying gig?"

AJ grinned. "Hell fucking yeah!"

Brayden frowned. "But we just started together a few months ago. Are we really ready?"

I smacked his bare ass to try to knock some sense into him. "You were born ready, babe."

He glanced down at me and smiled. "You really think so?"

"Oh, I know so."

He then threw his arms up in the air. "Holy shit, we have a gig!" AJ and I laughed at him. "Now what happens?"

"We have rehearsals at noon, and then our set starts at seven. Jake and Teague are on their way home from the mountains right now."

My ears perked up at the mention of his other two bandmates. Originally, I wasn't going to get to meet them since they had gone home for the weekend, but apparently now, I would get to see all of the Runaway Train guys.

"Shit, we need to decide what we're going to play," Brayden murmured, running his hands through his hair.

"Well, first, you need to put on some fucking clothes. I'm tired of staring at your junk," AJ mused with a smile.

Brayden threw a pillow at him. "Fine, I'll get dressed."

"Then we'll start putting together a song set. Jake and Teague can agree or veto when they get here."

"Sounds good."

Shifting in the bed, I said, "While you guys are doing that, I'll get us something to eat."

"There's stuff in the kitchen to cook," AJ said.

My brows shot up in surprise. "Really? It's not growing fur on it in the back of the refrigerator, is it?"

He laughed. "No, mi amor, my mom takes good care of her boy. She brings groceries by once a week."

Brayden nodded. "She really does."

"So I could make pancakes, eggs, and bacon—Brayden's favorite breakfast?"

"Hell yeah, you could," AJ replied, with a grin.

"Then it's a deal. You guys work on the song set, and I'll cook."

AJ brought his hand to his heart and gave me a revered look. "She wants to cook for us, and she makes the most amazing sex noises I've ever heard. You really have to marry this girl, Brayden."

Now it was my turn to throw a pillow at AJ. "You said you would turn the TV up!" I shrieked at him.

"It was too hot not to listen to," he argued, with a chuckle and waggle of his eyebrows.

"If you don't get out of here right now, I won't give you any pancakes," I challenged.

Without another word to me, AJ hustled out of the door. "Oh my God," I moaned, as I collapsed back in the bed.

"He just being his big goof self, Lils," Brayden said.

"I've known him less than twenty-four hours, and he's heard me having sex and seen me naked."

"He only saw your ass."

Cocking my brows, I countered, "*Just* my ass?"

Brayden grinned at me. "It could've been worse. He could've seen your fabulous tits or your—"

I held up my hand to stop him. "I get it."

"Come on. Let's get dressed before he has the nerve to come back in here."

"Um, that's a great idea, but I seem to remember in our excitement to get in here last night that we didn't bring in my suitcase."

Running his hands over his stubbly face, Brayden snorted with laughter. "Fuck, I forgot about that." He went over to his dresser and took out a T-shirt and a pair of boxer shorts. "Think these will work until I can grab a quick shower and go downstairs?"

"I think so." Climbing out of bed, I went in search of my panties and bra in the collection of clothes we had strewn across the floor last night. After putting them on, I slipped into Brayden clothes and then went out of the bedroom.

AJ wasn't in sight at the moment, so I went to the kitchen to get started on breakfast. AJ hadn't been lying about his mom keeping the kitchen stocked. I'm sure the other guys contributed some as well, but I was able to put on quite a feast by the time Brayden emerged from the shower.

He sat down at the table at the same time as AJ came out of his bedroom, freshly showered and dressed. "Damn, that smells good," he remarked, as he slid into a chair across from Brayden. After I'd given them their plates, I brought mine over to sit beside Brayden.

When he bit into my pancakes, he rolled his eyes in exaggerated bliss. "Man, you sure can cook."

I couldn't help laughing. "It's just pancake mix, AJ. Not brain surgery."

Brayden shook his head. "She's just being modest. Lily really can cook."

"Then we need to bring her along when we go out on the road."

My brows shot up in surprise. "You're going out on the road?"

Holding up a hand, Brayden replied, "AJ is getting ahead of himself as usual. We want to be able to go out on the road to try to hit some music festivals. But it probably won't be until next summer anyway."

"If it's the summer, then I really could come with you."

Brayden winked at me. "Of course, you'll be coming with us. You and me are a package deal."

My heart did its usual tap dance whenever Brayden made me feel so loved, especially in front of his friends. "How would you guys get around?"

AJ took a swig of his orange juice before replying. "My uncle owns an RV dealership in Guadalajara." At what must have been my blank look, AJ said, "In Mexico."

"Oh. I see."

"He can get us a killer deal on an older model."

Brayden snorted. "Older model as in a hunk of junk."

AJ tossed his napkin at him. "Hey asshole, we can't afford much better than a hunk of junk."

"True," Brayden replied.

When his cellphone started ringing in the bedroom, AJ ran to grab it. He came back out a few minutes later. "That was Jake. He said they would just meet us at Eastman's at noon, rather than coming by here."

Brayden nodded. "Guess we better get busy working on that set list." When he started to rise out of his chair, he winced. "I'm sorry, babe."

"What are you apologizing for?"

"It's your birthday weekend. I know we had planned on spending today with just each other and doing all your favorite things in the city."

I smiled. "It's okay, Brayden. You just got a once in a lifetime opportunity. I think I can entertain myself the rest of the day."

AJ sighed. "Once again, you gotta marry her. Like if you don't, I think I will."

As I laughed at AJ's comment, Brayden merely grunted. While the boys started working on their set list, I cleaned the kitchen up. Then I decided to do laundry. Thankfully, the boys had a washer and dryer in with one of the bathrooms. So, I did my clothes and then Brayden's. In between bouts of folding clothes, I got dressed in jeans and T-shirt and did my hair and makeup.

I had had just about enough domestic bliss when Brayden came looking for me. "Hey, we're about to head down to Eastman's for rehearsals. Want to come with us?"

"Are you sure I wouldn't be in the way?"

Brayden shook his head. "I want you with me, baby."

My heart did a little skip at his words. "Okay then, I'll come."

Eastman's was a small bar close to the Georgia Tech and Georgia State campuses. Apparently, it catered to a younger, college age crowd, especially on the weekends. One wall was made up of Georgia Tech black and gold paraphernalia while the other was blue and grey for Georgia State.

The inside was empty except for two waitresses refilling salt and pepper shakers. "We don't open until three," one of them said.

Brayden cleared his throat. "We're here to rehearse."

The waitresses glanced between each other. "You're the new house band?" the other waitress asked.

"Yeah, we're Runaway Train. Well, we're waiting on our other two guys to get here."

As their gazes devoured Brayden and AJ, I moved a little closer to Brayden. At that moment, a middle-aged man came out of the side door. His face lit up at the sight of us. "So fucking glad you guys could help me out."

"It's our pleasure," Brayden replied, with a smile. Turning to me, he said, "Sean, this is my girlfriend, Lily."

He gave me a warm smile. "Hey, I'm Sean Underwood, owner of Eastman's." He shook my hand. "Nice to see you guys again."

"Again?" I questioned before I could stop myself.

Sean smiled. "These guys auditioned to be my house band probably about two or three weeks ago. But I was really stupid and went with another band."

"Yeah, but we were meant to be the one and only in the end, right?" AJ said, with a smile.

"Exactly," Sean replied. He then motioned for us to follow him to the stage. I noticed the waitresses continued to undress Brayden and AJ with their eyes. Brayden must have noticed my discomfort because he wrapped his arm around my waist and drew me to him.

"So everything is here that you need. Take your time setting up. I'll need you back here by six, even though the set doesn't start until seven."

Brayden and AJ nodded in agreement. "Sounds good. We'll just start setting up while we wait for the others."

At the sight of all the chairs on the tables and nowhere to sit, I started to feel out of place. Sean motioned for me to follow him. I shrugged at Brayden and then started behind Sean down the hall next to the stage.

At the first room on the right, he opened the door. Inside was a cramped but cozy dressing room. "In case you want to take a load off while they get set up."

"Thank you. I appreciate it."

"I'll tell Brayden to come get you when he's ready." He smiled and then left me. I walked around the room, taking in the somewhat lacking décor. It was pretty cool thinking that this was where Brayden and the guys would get ready tonight. Their very own dressing room.

"Well hello there," a voice said behind me.

Whirling around, I widened my eyes at the sight of the guy in the doorway. He was taller than Brayden and bigger built. An inviting smile lit up his handsome face while his deep blue eyes, that had an impish twinkle in them, seemed at odds with his dark hair.

"What are you doing in here?"

"Oh, um, I'm sorry. I thought this is where I was supposed to wait."

"Who told you that?"

"The owner. I mean, Sean. He said this is where I should wait for the band."

The guy chuckled. "Damn, we haven't even played yet, and we already have groupies," he mused.

My brows furrowed in confusion. "Wait, what are you talking about?"

Closing the gap between us, the guy stood directly in front of me. At the intense look blazing in his baby blues, I had to look away. The next thing I knew his hands had slithered around my waist, jerking me against his hard body. He stared down at me with eyes hooded with desire. "Damn, you're so beautiful," he murmured, his alcohol-laced breath burning against my cheek.

"Let me go!" I protested, my hands pushing against his sculpted chest.

As he dipped his head to kiss me, I tucked my neck to my chest, so he only ended up kissing my forehead. He grunted in frustration. When I dared to peek up at him, he gave me a pleading look. "Please, beautiful, open up to me. You're just what I need."

The sound of a voice behind us caused us both to freeze. "What the hell is going on here?" Brayden demanded.

The guy smirked at Brayden over his shoulder. "Man, your girl really has been gone too long if you don't know what this is."

In a flash, Brayden was beside us. Planting both of his hands on the guy's chest, Brayden shoved the guy hard, sending him spiraling backwards. "Dude, what the fuck?" the guy demanded, as he flopped down onto the couch.

Jerking me to him, Brayden's chest heaved up and down. "What are you doing groping my girl, Jake?"

Jake's blue eyes widened in shock as his head slowly shook back and forth. "*You're* Lily?" he asked incredulously.

"Yes," I squeaked.

"Fuck!" He jerked his hand through his dark hair. "I'm sorry." He glanced from me to Brayden. "I really am sorry, man. I had no idea she was Lily. If I had, I would have never, ever come on to her." With a grimace, he added, "She reminded me of Stephanie."

Brayden's arm remained tight around my waist. I wanted to tell him I couldn't breathe well, but I didn't want to set him off. The last time I'd seem him this furious was the night we became official—the night I'd demanded he fight for me when it came to Mitch. Now it seemed he didn't have any problem fighting Jake for me. "You better not *ever* let it happen again," Brayden finally growled.

"I swear I won't." Extending his hand, Jake said, "You have my word."

Brayden eyed it momentarily before he reached out and shook it. Jake then offered me his hand. "Lily, please accept my apology."

I glanced between him and Brayden. "Okay."

With a teasing smile, Jake said, "I guess I should have believed Bray when he told me how hot his girlfriend was. Then I would have known it was you right off the bat."

My face flushed with his compliments. "Now I know what you meant when you mentioned groupies."

Another growl came from Brayden. "You thought Lily was a groupie?"

"Shit, here we go again," Jake muttered.

I tugged on Brayden's shirt. "Babe, it was all a misinterpretation. Let it go, okay?"

Brayden narrowed his eyes at Jake. "Have you been drinking?"

Jake shrugged. "Maybe a little."

"Dude, it's only fucking noon."

"Yeah, well, I needed a little something for my nerves." Jake shook his head. "Hell, you act like I'm fucking plastered. I can still walk a straight line."

"Can you do the nose test?" I teased.

With a wink, Jake stretched out his arms. Then he brought his right finger to the tip of his nose and then his left. "You look too much like a little goody-two-shoes to know about DUI nose testing."

"My dad is the chief of police in Roswell."

"Ah, I see." He grinned. "Guess I really better watch my step with you considering you have two very protective men connected to you."

"That's right."

AJ stuck his head in the door. "Okay, guys, let's go."

The butterflies I had in my stomach for Brayden and the guys turned over to boulders. I couldn't imagine what they were feeling.

I mean, it wasn't their actual performance, but it was just one step closer.

Brayden kept his arm wrapped around me as we started out the door. It was a tight squeeze, but we made it. Glancing up at him, I smiled. "Think you're being a little overprotective?"

He grunted. "I just want to make sure Teague doesn't get the wrong idea."

"You know, you're kinda cute when you're being a caveman."

"Is that right?" he asked, with a grin.

"Mmm, hmm. It gets me kinda hot." I ran my hand up his chest. "You think that maybe you and I could christen that dressing room for my birthday?"

A gleam of lust burned in his eyes. "Oh yeah, I think I can arrange that."

"I'm glad to hear it."

He gave me a kiss on the lips before he broke away. AJ had already sat behind the drum kit near the auburn-haired guy with the bass guitar had to be Teague by process of elimination. Jake and Brayden took their guitars and then went on stage.

I eased down on one of the bar stools and prepared to hear my very first Runaway Train performance.

LILY

THE PAST

I don't think I moved from my spot for a full hour. I was that mesmerized by the guys making music. It didn't hurt a lot of the songs that they were playing were written by Brayden about our relationship. Of course, it was really strange hearing Jake sing lead on *Until There Was You*. Hearing Brayden's words of love come out of someone else's mouth was going to take some time to get used to, especially with it coming from Jake.

The guys bantered back and forth about which songs they should play, and then they finally came up with a list of ten of their own, along with a few covers by Eric Clapton, the Rolling Stones, and Tom Petty. Once they finished rehearsing, they were starving, so we made a quick stop at The Varsity, which apparently was a favorite of theirs too.

"So Lily, besides Brayden, who do you think is the hottest member of Runaway Train?" AJ asked, after we'd made a decent dent in the massive pile of food.

I couldn't help laughing at his question. "I don't look at other guys."

AJ rolled his eyes. "I don't believe you."

Throwing up my hands, I said, "I think you're all very good-looking, okay?"

"Did you hear that, Bray? Your girlfriend is hot for us?" AJ teased.

"You are impossible," I replied.

"Got any single friends you wanna hook us up with?" Teague asked.

"I have a few who are single. But it depends on what kind of guys you are."

Jake cocked his brows at me. "I would think it was pretty evident."

Wrinkling my nose, I replied, "Manwhores?"

The guys laughed at my summation. Jake took a swig of Coke and then winked at me. "I just got out of a relationship a few months back—"

Teague snorted. "What he means is he got his heart broken when his girlfriend refused to take sloppy seconds of his time anymore."

Jake smacked the back of Teague's hand. "Shut the fuck up, man."

With a shrug, Teague replied, "It's the truth."

"Whatever," Jake grumbled. "Anyway, I'm on the rebound, so I'm not looking for anything long term. These two jokers might be up for a relationship if the right girl came along."

Playing with my straw, I asked, "Why didn't you make time for your girlfriend?"

Jake glowered at me across the table. I could tell I had hit a sensitive nerve for him. "It wasn't that I didn't make time for her." At Teague's "bullshit" turned into a cough, Jake once again smacked him.

"We'd dated for two years. We were both busy with school, and then AJ, Teague, and I were trying to work on getting the band to another level, but not having any luck, which led to a lot of stress. Then last semester, I had the chance to play and sing backup with a band we met at the Moonshine Festival up in Dawsonville. So I dropped out of school and went on the road with them. Nothing much came of it career wise other than it showed me that Runaway Train really needed to get on the road and start playing festivals, fairs, and shows. As far as my personal life, it really strained things between me and Stephanie." He sighed. "In the end, she wanted a bigger commitment. The last thing I want right now is to be engaged or God forbid, married. So she broke up with me."

"Wow," Brayden murmured.

"What?" Jake asked.

"I think that is the most open and honest I've heard you be with anyone in the last few months."

With a wry grin, Jake replied, "It's because of Lily. She brings out the gentleman in me."

I laughed. "Was that you being a gentleman earlier today when you tried to kiss me?"

AJ and Teague's eyes widened at my statement. "Holy shit, where was I when this was going on?" AJ demanded.

"You were setting up," I replied.

Glancing between Jake and Brayden, Teague asked, "Wait a minute, Jake tried to kiss Lily, and Brayden didn't shed his blood?"

I waved my hand dismissively. "No, no, it was just a misunderstanding."

Jake chuckled. "It might've been a misunderstanding, but he still shoved the hell out of me."

Brayden narrowed his eyes at Jake. "You had your hands on my girl."

"I know. And I said I was sorry. I was sorry then, and I'm sorry now."

The tense expression on Brayden's face receded slightly. Dropping my hand down beneath the table, I reached out for his hand. When I squeezed it, he gave me a warm smile.

Jake broke our moment by rising out of his chair. "Well, we better get going. We need to get ready for tonight."

"What are we going to wear?" AJ asked.

Brayden frowned. "Good question."

Jake's gaze fell on me. "Why don't we get Lily to help us?"

A nervous giggle escaped my lips. "You want me to be your unofficial stylist?"

Bobbing his head, Jake replied, "Sure, why not?"

"I'm not sure I'm really qualified to do that."

Brayden kissed my cheek. "You've always picked out my clothes."

AJ grinned. "Then it's all settled. Lily is our new stylist." Scratching his chin, AJ then asked, "Do you do hair?"

In that moment, I wondered what I had gotten myself into. At the same time, I couldn't help being grateful that the men of Runaway Train were openly embracing me. I just hoped it would last.

I spent the rest of the afternoon back at Brayden's loft, going through the guys' closets. When it came down to it, they were almost as bad as a girl trying to decide what to wear on a first date. After we'd settled their outfits, I finally had a moment to slip into the shower myself. I'd brought a swanky red and black dress to wear in case Brayden and I went out to dinner somewhere nice for my birthday. Instead, I was going to be wearing it to Eastman's. I didn't care if I was a little overdressed. Tonight was about celebrating.

Just as I was putting the finishing touches on my makeup, AJ knocked on the door. "Come on, Lils, some of the rest of us need to get ready."

I laughed. "Last time I checked there was another bathroom in this place."

"Yeah, your boyfriend's been in there the last twenty minutes working on his hair."

"Whatever," I mumbled. When I opened the door for him, his eyes bulged at the sight of my dress.

"Damn, girl, you're looking hot as hell tonight!"

"Why, thank you."

As he squeezed by me to get to the counter, AJ mused, "Man, Brayden is one lucky man."

"You're such a flatterer, AJ," I replied, as I headed out into the living room.

Brayden came out of the bathroom a few moments later. "Mmm, don't you look handsome," I said, as I wrapped my arms around his neck.

He grinned. "Thank you. I must say that you are looking sexy as hell. I'm not sure I'll be able to concentrate on anything tonight but you."

"Oh, I'm sure you'll muddle through somehow." I gave him a light kiss, so he wouldn't end up wearing my lipstick. "Tonight after all the girls have screamed your name and mentally undressed you a thousand times, you just remember that you're only going home with me."

Throwing back his head, Brayden laughed. "I don't think that will be a problem."

"I'm sure it's going to be a problem. You should have seen the way the waitresses were sizing you up today."

"Really?"

"Mmm, hmm." I fixed the collar of his button down shirt. "With you guys taking this gig, things are going to change for you. You're going to have women falling all over you."

"That might be interesting to see, but it's sure as hell not something I will be acting on." When I didn't immediately reply, his fingers reached out to grip my chin, tipping my head to meet his eyes. "You do know that, Lils? There won't ever be anyone for me but you."

Feeling overly emotional, I shrugged. "I'm sure for a guy it would be tempting to see what sex was like with someone else."

Brayden shook his head emphatically. "I wouldn't do anything to jeopardize what we have, and that includes cheating." Leaning his forehead against mine, Brayden said, "You're it for me, Lily. I couldn't imagine even kissing another woman."

"I'm glad to hear that."

With a tentative smile, Brayden said, "I guess our roles are changing."

"What do you mean?"

"Remember how in high school I was always afraid you would find some other guy? I couldn't imagine such a beautiful, popular, and sweet girl like you would want me."

"Yes, I remember you being stupid about that," I replied.

Brayden laughed. "Well, it's kinda reversed. Now you're the one worrying about me."

"I guess that's true."

"So there's nothing really to worry about. Right?"

"Right." Then I brought my mouth to his for a long, lingering kiss where I didn't care about lipstick.

"Jesus, do you guys ever stop?" AJ questioned behind us.

When we pulled away, Brayden replied, "Two weeks, man. We've not seen each other for two weeks."

Shaking his head, AJ said, "I think that's just an excuse. You'd probably be all over each other no matter when you saw her last."

I giggled. "You might be right."

"Come on, let's go," Jake said, as he motioned to us from the loft's doorway. While Jake, AJ, and Teague all piled in a car together, Brayden and I went in his. We made the short drive over to Eastman's and then parked.

I don't know if Brayden was nervous or not. I could barely contain both my excitement and anxiousness. When we got inside, Sean met us. "You guys go on and get set up," he said. Brayden gave me a final kiss. "Wish me luck."

"Luck times infinity," I replied.

He grinned and then followed the guys through the bar to the stage. Just when I wondered where I might sit in the packed house, Sean took my hand. "I reserved a place for you."

"Really?" I asked, as I followed him through the crowd.

"Yes, right here," Sean said, motioning to a small, two-person table almost up on the stage.

"You're so sweet. Thank you."

He winked. "I figured I would go a long way with the band if I was good to their girlfriends."

I laughed. "That's a really good plan."

After I took my seat, I didn't have to wait long for the guys to take the stage. A roar went up over the crowd. I knew some of the people in the audience knew the guys from school. "Hey everybody, how you doin' tonight?" Jake bellowed into the microphone. A few whistles went up around me when he flashed them his most come hither smile. "We're Runaway Train, and we're the new house band. Are you ready to rock tonight?"

A resounding yell of approval came from the crowd. "Then let's get started!"

With my seat close to the stage, I could see and hear everything almost too well. My ears rang from the noise, but I kept right on singing along and clapping my hands as the guys went through their set. Jake was a natural at working the crowd. Where Brayden was too shy, Jake knew exactly what to say and do. Even behind the drum set, AJ threw a few jokes out.

After finishing up a cover of The Rolling Stones *Start Me Up*, which Jake received a pair of panties thrown in his face as his reward, Jake's amused expression grew serious.

"So, we're going to excuse one of our members for a moment." I furrowed my brows in confusion as I watched Brayden put his guitar up. I couldn't imagine what he was doing. Pointing to Brayden, Jake said, "You see this guy here?" At the whistles and applause, Jake continued on. "He's not only one hell of a guitar player, but he wrote most of the songs we just sang. But besides his talent, ladies and gentleman, he is the biggest romantic sap in the world. He's been with the same woman since he was sixteen years old."

A chorus of "Aw's" rang around the room. "Speaking of that same lady who has shackled our good man, she's sitting right here." The spotlight beamed over to me, and I fought the urge to dive under the table with mortification. "Don't be embarrassed, Lily. Stand up so the good people can see what a stone-cold-fox you are."

I don't know why I listened to Jake's command, but I slowly rose out of my seat. Before I could sit back down, I saw Brayden cutting through the crowd with a dozen red roses in his arms. "It just happens to be Lily's birthday next week, but she's not going to be able to spend it with Brayden. So, we'd like to let them have a dance right now to celebrate Lily turning twenty one."

Brayden sat the roses down on the table, and then offered me his hand. When I took it, he pulled me against him and then bestowed a kiss on my lips. "Happy early Birthday, baby."

"Thank you," I said, as I tried to fight the tears that stung my eyes from his romantic gesture.

As Brayden led me to the dance floor, Jake said, "So here's one of Brayden's favorites that adequately expresses his love for Lily." He started playing the opening of Eric Clapton's *Wonderful Tonight*.

Instead of laying my head on Brayden's chest, I kept my gaze locked on his as we swayed to the music of the love song.

"I have your presents at home for you to unwrap later," Brayden said, with a smile.

"You didn't have to get me anything," I protested.

Brayden laughed. "Yeah, right. If you went home empty-handed on your birthday weekend, I'd be cut off from sex until my birthday."

I giggled. "Okay, so maybe I expect you to get me a little something."

His amused expression grew serious. "I wanted to get you something really big this year, but the time isn't right."

"A puppy?" I asked hopefully.

He shook his head. "No, it's not a dog."

"Then what was it?"

"I can't tell you, or it won't be a surprise."

"It's not fair to tease me like that," I protested.

"Fine then. I wanted to get you a ring."

I swallowed hard. Oh wow, an engagement ring. Even though I knew I wanted to marry Brayden, it seemed like a big step since we were still so young. At the same time, I wanted to belong to him in all ways, and being called a fiancée meant a lot more than just girlfriend. "You know, you don't have to get me a ring to ask me to marry you."

He scowled at me. "What kind of asshole would I be if I did that?"

"One who didn't care about material things?"

"It's not happening."

"Fine then. I'll just wait."

"It's more than just the ring, Lily. Not only do I want you to have a symbol of our commitment to wear, but I want to go to your father and ask for your hand in marriage. I don't want to do that until I've made a little something of myself to where I can show him I can take care of you."

His earnest tone and sweet words brought tears to my eyes. "You really mean that, don't you?"

"I sure do."

Squeezing my arms tighter around his neck, I pulled him down to where I could kiss him. After a few breathless moments of making out, I eased back. Smiling at him, I said, "I love you, Brayden Vanderburg. I want nothing more than to be your wife. Although

I'd be happy living with you in just a box on the street, I'll respect the fact that you want to prove yourself to me and my dad."

"It means so much to me that you're willing to wait."

"I'll wait forever for you, Brayden."

"I promise it won't be that long. I want us married and having kids before we're twenty five."

My eyes bulged. "Twenty five? That's only four years. Please tell me you just want us to get started having kids at twenty five."

He grinned. "Maybe. I just know I want a houseful. I don't care if they're boys or girls. I just want them to be as good looking as you and have your sweetness and beautiful blue eyes."

"I hope they're as talented as their father. And have his warm, caring heart, along with his looks."

"We're going to make beautiful babies."

"Someday."

He ducked his head to kiss me. "Someday."

LILY

THE PAST

ONE YEAR LATER

"That'll be a hundred and twenty dollars," the cashier at the Shop and Go said.

Brayden reached into his wallet and handed the woman a credit card. It was known among the five of us as "The Runaway Train" card. It paid for gas in the bus and groceries and food. At the end of the month, the guys just divided the bill equally among each other. It had been a necessity when we started out on the road two weeks ago.

When I eyed all the shopping bags, I whistled for the others. "Little help here, guys!"

AJ and Jake quickly shoved the magazines they were reading back into the rack and then scrambled to grab some of the grocery bags. "Where's New Guy?" I teasingly asked. Poor Rhys, the new bassist, was constantly being called New Guy, rather than his name. I think it was some sort of initiation shit the guys were doing, and I had picked up on it.

Jake grimaced. "He got a call from the 'rents. Didn't sound pretty."

"Oh," I murmured. I didn't know much about the newest member of Runaway Train. Rhys had joined the band just two months ago. Teague, Jake's cousin and the bassist, had decided that he didn't want to embark on the summer tour with the guys. He felt like he really needed to focus on school. After he quit, the guys worried about finding another bass player who would mesh with them all.

Then they remembered a guy who had been coming to some of the Runaway Train shows at Eastman's. His name was Rhys McGowan, and he was two and half years younger than the other guys. He'd graduated high school at sixteen and was already working on his pre-law degree at Emory in Atlanta. Besides being a genius, he had mad skills at playing the bass guitar, which he had taken up only after he'd mastered the cello.

Because of my crazy school schedule, as well as preparing to be gone for the summer with Brayden, I didn't get to meet Rhys until I stepped on the bus two weeks ago. So far I liked him a lot, maybe even more than Teague when it came down to it.

As we started out to the parking lot, I cocked my head at Brayden. "What's his favorite meal?"

"Whose favorite meal?"

"Rhys's."

"How the hell should I know?"

Rolling my eyes at him, I countered, "Maybe because he lives with you and is your bandmate."

Brayden snorted. "We're guys, Lils. We don't talk about what our favorite foods and shit are."

"Impossible," I muttered.

Shifting the bags in his arms, Brayden cuffed the back of my neck playfully. When I cut my eyes over to him, he was grinning at me. "What?"

"I was just thinking how sweet you are to want to make things better for Rhys by making his favorite meal."

"The way to a man's heart is through his stomach, you know."

"I agree with that. Although I would also argue, that it's through his dick, too."

"You're such an ass," I replied, but I couldn't help laughing.

"Yeah, but you love me."

I grinned. "Yeah, I do."

We strolled up to the bus that would be our home for the summer. The guys had bought it from AJ's uncle a few weeks back. They'd each taken turns learning how to drive it. It wasn't a total hunk of junk. The inside furnishings were dated, and it had some mileage. But it also had enough storage beneath for the guys' equipment, and it would get them back and forth across the country to the festivals and venues they would be playing at.

In exchange for food and boarding on the bus, I would pull my own weight as cook, stylist, and merchandise pusher. At each of the festivals, I would sit at a table selling Runaway Train's debut CD and some of their shirts. Brayden thought it was ridiculous I felt the need to earn my keep since I was his girlfriend, but I didn't want the guys to come to resent me.

I started up the steps, but then I turned back when I realized Brayden wasn't behind me. It only took me a minute to see what he was staring at. It was a Challenger, just like the one he had sold four months ago. If he hadn't sold the Challenger, we probably wouldn't be on the road. Brayden financed Runaway Train's first album with the car, along with hiring a promoter to get them into shows.

The longing expression on his face broke my heart. "Babe," I murmured softly.

His gaze snapped from the car over to me. "Sorry. I'm coming."

When he tried to ease past me on the stairs, I stopped him. "It's okay to be sad about the car. It was your pride and joy."

He glowered at me. "I know I can be sad. It's just I look like a major pussy mooning over a lost car."

"Don't sell yourself short. It was more than just a car. We had a lot of happy memories in the Challenger."

"And happy endings," Brayden replied, with a smile.

I rolled my eyes. "You had to go there, didn't you?"

"It's the truth."

"Yeah, yeah, get on up the stairs before some of this starts to ruin in the heat."

Brayden and I found AJ and Jake putting away the groceries. Rhys was slumped into one of the captain's chairs, his expression dark. "So Rhys, what's your favorite food?"

He gave me an odd look. "Fried chicken. Why?"

"How would you like some fried chicken for dinner?"

"You know how to fry chicken?" Rhys asked, his eyes lighting up.

"I sure do."

With a shrug, Rhys replied, "Okay."

I started for the door. "I'll be right back. Don't take off without me."

"Where are you going?" Brayden called after me.

"Just the store." I raced across the parking lot and back into the Shop and Go. Grabbing a basket, I hurried to the meat section to grab the chicken I would need. I assumed there wasn't enough flour or cornmeal on the bus, so I picked that up as well. Some buttermilk went into the basket, so I could top the meal off with cornbread. I just hoped there was an iron skillet in the bus somewhere, or I was screwed.

I had a twenty of my own in my pocket that I paid for the food with. Then I hightailed it back to the bus. The guys had finished putting away the groceries by then and were staring expectantly at me. "Sorry," I said, breathlessly.

"What's in the bag?" Brayden asked.

"What I need to fry chicken."

When I met Rhys's gaze, his dark eyes bulged. Then a tentative smile curved on his lips. "Just for me?"

I returned his smile. "Yeah, just for you."

"Thanks, Lily."

"You're welcome."

Brayden clapped his hands together. "Well, all right then. We better get out of here." He went over to the driver's seat and cranked up.

"Who wants to help me?"

Jake snorted. "Men don't cook."

AJ smacked his arm. "That's so not true. I love to cook."

With a roll of his eyes, Jake replied, "I'm sorry. I should have said 'real men'."

When they started shoving each other, I took a spatula and smacked them both to get them to stop. "How kinky of you, Lils," Jake mused.

"You can roll the chicken," I commanded. When he started to argue, I held the spatula up again. He flashed me a wicked grin. "That's not really a deterrent since I like it when a beautiful woman hits me."

"You're impossible."

"Fine, fine, I'll help."

"I'll get the pan and oil heated," AJ said, as he reached into one of the cabinets.

"What do you want me to do?" Rhys asked.

I shook my head. "Nothing. This is a meal in your honor, so just sit back and relax."

After mixing the flour and corn meal together, I had Jake start rolling the chicken. When he rubbed in some pepper on the chicken, I raised my brows in surprise. He winked. "I might've helped my mom do this a couple of times."

"I see."

It was actually kinda nice having the guys help me cook. With all the teasing banter, I had a smile on my face the entire time. After opening a can of green beans and making some instant creamed potatoes, we had a Southern meal in the middle of nowhere West Virginia.

"This chicken is fucking fabulous," Rhys said, after taking a bite. His eyes rolled back in his head in exaggerated bliss.

"Thank you."

"Seriously, it's almost as good as our cook's, and she was known for being one of the best cooks in Savannah."

"High praise indeed," I replied with a smile.

While the guys continued chowing down, I took a plate over to Brayden. Sitting down next to him, I started feeding him bites as he drove. "You're so good to your man for doing this," Brayden said, after swallowing a bite of cream potatoes.

"It's my pleasure, baby," I replied.

Jake groaned. "You two with the lovey dovey shit are going to make me lose my dinner."

"Bite me," Brayden shot back.

"I wouldn't mind if Lily did," Jake teased. That earned him both a quick glower, as well as a growl, from Brayden. "Keep your eyes on the road, dickhead," Jake said.

"I'll be happy to. Just keep yours off my girl."

"All right, boys, that's enough," I warned.

"He reminds me too much of Mitch sometimes," Brayden muttered under his breath.

I smiled at him. "Once again, you are so misguided."

He cut his eyes over to me. "Am I?"

"Just like with Mitch, there will never be anything between me and Jake."

"Give me a kiss to prove your sincerity."

With a giggle, I leaned over and gave him a quick kiss. When I pulled back, Brayden winked at me. "Love you."

"Love you, too." As I forked him more chicken, I said, "At the next stop, we'll get one of the guys to take over the wheel. Then we can have some alone time."

"I like that idea very, very much."

BRAYDEN

THE PAST

"Brayden, are you coming?" Lily impatiently whined from the front of the bus.

As I slipped the ring box into my jeans pocket, I called, "In just a minute."

I couldn't help grinning when I heard her stomp her foot in disappointment. We'd pulled into the RV area of the Great Southeastern Fair somewhere in Mississippi about an hour ago. We had a show from eight until ten. While we played, Lily would be manning the merchandise, which was mainly our CD's and T-shirts.

Of course, I hadn't expected Lily to be dying to go to the fair. I hadn't seen her this excited in a long time and all for a half-assed version of what we could get back home on a much bigger scale at Six Flags in Atlanta.

She appeared in the doorway of the bathroom. "We only have three hours before you have to go on."

Cocking my brows at her, I said, "Wow, only three hours? We may not get to ride everything twice."

She poked her lips out in a pout that made her incredibly sexy. I had to fight the urge to throw her over my shoulder and head to the bedroom. I knew she would kill me if I even tried.

"Okay, okay, just let me put on my tattoo cream and pull my hair back."

Lily's blue eyes widened with pleasure when I unbuttoned my shirt. A week ago we had pulled into a tattoo parlor. Jake wanted some more ink, and considering I only had two tattoos, I thought it would be a good idea to get some as well. The one I really wanted was to go over my heart, and it was Lily's name. The guy had made it look really bad ass with these flames and the word *Lily* in the middle of them.

"There I am," she said softly, as I began to rub the cream over her name.

"Always on my heart."

She leaned in and gave me a kiss. "I love that you wanted to get my name on your body."

"Maybe we can work up to getting mine on yours."

She wrinkled her nose. "Your name is a lot longer than mine."

"So?"

"It'll hurt more. That's not fair."

I couldn't help laughing. "Am I not worth a little pain?" I countered.

"Mmm, hmm, and I consider that taken care of when I have our babies."

"I guess you're right."

"Here. I'll do your hair for you." Lily wedged herself between the mirror and me. She ran her fingers through the strands of my hair as she swept it out of my face. "I can't believe how long it's getting."

"Don't you like it?"

She smiled. "Mmm, I love it."

I grinned at her. "I'm glad to hear that." In the last month on the road, my hair had grown past its usual length on my shoulders.

"There," she said.

Glancing past her, I surveyed her work in the mirror. "What the hell is that?" I asked, pointing to the bob at the back of my head.

"It makes you look edgy."

"It makes me look like a samurai warrior or something."

Crossing her arms over her rack, Lily countered, "Well, last time I checked, samurai's were pretty bad ass."

"Hmm, Lily Marie said a bad word," I teased.

"You're impossible," she muttered before she shoved away from me.

I pulled her back to me and started tickling her. She dissolved into giggles. "Stop it, Bray!" she shrieked.

"Do you promise to lighten up?"

Jerking her chin up, she countered, "And do you?"

I grinned at her. "Yeah, I do."

She returned my smile. "Good. Now can we please go?"

"Lead away."

With a squeal, she took my arm and dragged me down the aisle. Jake and the others were milling around outside. "You guys going in too?" I asked.

Jake shrugged. "Might as well. Nothing else to do until show time."

AJ grinned. "Oh, I'm going in. I'm going to have a fucking blast."

"Me too," Lily answered.

"Race you to the ticket stand?" AJ asked.

"Deal," Lily said, and then they took off, kicking up a cloud of dust behind them.

Jake, Rhys, and I followed them at a much slower pace. By the time we caught up to them, they'd bought a ridiculous amount of tickets and were impatiently bouncing on the balls of their feet as they waited for us.

We did the bumper cars, the Tilt a Whirl, and the hokey Tunnel of Love. Lily even managed to drag me on the Merry Go Round. That's when we eventually split up from the guys. Then we hit the food stands trying fried Oreos and fried pickles. I didn't make it through half of my corndog before I was feeling way too full. Lily on the other hand had a never ending stomach when it came to fair food. I couldn't help laughing at her dainty self as she packed away the goodies.

As we walked around the other side of the fair, I nursed my growing indigestion. I knew it wasn't just the fair food. It was the ring box in my pocket and what I had in mind to do with it when the time was right.

"Let's do the Ferris Wheel," I suggested.

Lily's eyes lit up. "Okay."

As we got in line, she started trying to devour what was left of her cotton candy. "Babe, I'll get you some more if they won't let you take it on with you."

When she glanced up at me with her mouth and cheeks covered pink, I busted out laughing. "What? Do I have something on my face?" she questioned, with a smile.

"Hmm, just a bit."

"Well, get it off. There's wet wipes in my purse."

"You're always so prepared." I then opened the giant bag at her side and got out the wipes. Bringing one to her face, I slowly started to work off the pink film. "You are a dirty girl," I teased.

She giggled. "Only you would say something like that in line for the Ferris Wheel. Don't think you're going to get all happy-hands on me like Mark Wahlburg in the movie *Fear*."

Whispering in her ear, I asked, "You mean you wouldn't want to have an orgasm high up in the air?"

As I pulled back, she licked her lips. "Maybe. I'm all about new experiences."

"Mmm, I like it when you're naughty," I said, as I nuzzled my face in her neck.

"Next," the man taking tickets bellowed. Lily tossed her remaining cotton candy in the trash while I deposited the wipes I'd used to clean her up. I passed him our tickets, and then we climbed into a bucket seat.

The ring box continued to burn a hole in my pocket. I knew it was now or never. As our seat climbed to the top, I shifted and reached for the box. When I did, I ended up poking Lily in the side with my elbow. She gave me a weird look. "What are you so fidgety?"

"Just needed to get something."

As she surveyed the view of the fairgrounds from our position, I finally got the box out. When we reached the top, the wheel stopped to allow other people on. "Isn't it beautiful, Bray?" Lily asked, as she gazed at all the twinkling lights.

"Yeah, it is." I cleared my throat several times, trying to build up my nerve. Taking Lily's hand, I said, "I need to say something."

Her brows lined. "Okay."

"I want you to know that each and every day with you is like this view. I can't imagine my world without you in it. You're the greatest blessing that has ever happened to me. You're my soul mate, my other half, the very best of me. More in the anything in the world, I want you to marry me."

Lily's eyes bulged while her hand flew to her mouth. "You... me..." She shook her head. "What about going to my father and asking his permission?"

I smiled. "I went to him before we left this summer. We have his blessing and his support."

The wheel shifted us forward again, and we started to descend back to the ground. As she continued to remain speechless, I cracked open the ring box. "This was my Nana's first engagement ring. My Papa gave it to her right before he left to fight in WWII. Years later when he had made something of himself, he bought her a big, fancy diamond, but she never stopped wearing this one. Not until the day she died."

Tears streamed down Lily's cheeks. "It's beautiful—the story, the ring, all of it."

I slipped the ring on her left hand. "Just like my Papa, I'm going to get you a big, fancy diamond one day. You have my word."

Lily smiled. "You should know me well enough by now to know that expensive rings don't matter to me. Like I told you before, I would live with you in a box if I had to."

I laughed. "One day, baby, when we have a mansion and lots of cars, I'll remind you of what you just said."

"It still won't change the way I feel about you."

"I feel the same way." Twisting in the seat, I cupped her face with my hands. "I can't wait to make you my wife." I then brought my lips to hers for a lingering kiss. We continued the desperate, love-fueled kisses as the wheel made several more sweeps. When we finally got off, the guys were waiting on us.

"Did you guys enjoy the ride?" AJ asked, flashing us a wicked grin.

"Yes, it was very nice," Lily replied.

"I got several good pics of you guys making out," AJ said.

Lily gave me a dreamy smile as she answered AJ. "Good. I want to see them."

"You do?" he asked

She nodded. "Then we can have the moment we got engaged forever immortalized."

"Wait, you guys are engaged?" Jake demanded.

Holding out her hand, Lily showed them the ring. "I mean, he didn't get down on one knee when he asked me, but it was still romantic."

"*Still* romantic? I was trying to be creative with my proposal," I protested.

Jake shook his head. "I can't believe you guys are engaged. You're just twenty-two."

Lily frowned at Jake's words and harsh tone. "What does it matter how old we are as long as we're in love?"

"Whatever. It's your funeral, not mine," Jake replied.

"I thought you would be happy for us," Lily countered softly.

Crossing his arms over his chest, Jake said, "Why would you want to get married?"

"Because we're in love," Lily answered.

"And how do you even know if the love you have is real? You guys were sixteen years old when you fell—" he made air quotes with his fingers, "in love."

I crossed the space between us to stand toe to toe with Jake. "That's enough. Look, you don't have to be happy for us, but you don't need to stand there being an asshole by questioning our love and choices on one of the happiest days of our life."

He eyed me contemptuously for a moment before he relented. "Fine. I'm sorry. Okay?"

"Fine," I muttered.

Taking Lily the arm, AJ said, "Come on. Let's go buy you a celebratory funnel cake for your engagement."

Silently I thanked AJ for lightening the mood. Lily's genuine smile warmed my heart. "Okay. If you're treating, I won't say no."

As she and AJ walked off to one of the stands, I started behind them with Rhys at my side. When I turned around, Jake was gone. "Asshole," I muttered under my breath. I couldn't imagine why Jake had reacted the way he had. Yeah, his parents divorced after his dad had an affair, but I couldn't imagine that tainting him against all people getting married. The last time I checked he was crazy about Lily and enjoyed having her around.

Determined not to let Jake put a damper on my happiness, I strode up to Lily who was munching on one of the funnel cakes. "Want some?" she asked, holding out a bite for me.

Ignoring her, I pulled her into my arms and crashed my lips against hers. I moaned at both the contact and how sweet she tasted. My tongue ran along her lips, licking off the powdered sugar. When I finally pulled away, she was breathless. "You're delicious," I mused, licking my lips.

She giggled. "You sure you don't want some cake, or do you want to taste me some more?"

"I might take a little of both." I drew her to me and whispered in her ear. "Let's go back to the bus for a little while."

Jerking back from me, her eyes widened. "You want to leave the fair?"

"Yes, so I can make love to my fiancée."

"You don't play fair," she pouted.

"You want a compromise?"

"What do you mean?"

Turning to the guys, I said, "Excuse us fellas."

I took Lily by the arm and started leading her to the edge of the fairgrounds. "Where are you taking me?"

"Somewhere private."

She didn't protest anymore. We dipped into the heavy thicket of trees just beyond some of the campers. When I thought we were far enough away from prying eyes, I pulled her to me. "I want you so bad, Lily."

"Then I guess you're going to have to take me. Right here in the woods."

I grinned. "I had just the same thought."

Pushing her back against one of the trees, my fingers went to the button on her shorts. I jerked them down her thighs, along with her panties. As our lips stayed locked, I worked to free my hard on from my shorts. Grabbing Lily by the waist, I hoisted her up and then impaled her on me. Gripping my shoulders hard, Lily cried out. "I'm sorry, baby. I should have gotten you ready."

She shook her head. "Mmm, I'm good. It hurts so good."

Her words and noises of pleasure drove my hard thrusts as I pumped in and out of her. I was afraid that even through her shirt, she was going to get splinters from being banged back against the tree. After I dipped my head, jerked down her shirt, and took her nipple in my mouth, she came, which caused me to as well.

We stood there, chests heaving and panting, from our exertions. "Our first time as an engaged couple," I mused.

Lily giggled. "It's so romantic being fucked up against the tree just a few feet away from a bunch of strangers."

Cocking my brows at her, I countered, "You just came harder than you have in weeks."

"That's true." After nipping my bottom lip with her teeth, she said, "I guess we'll just have to have sex in public more often."

"I wouldn't exactly call this public, but I'm all for it if you are."

With a grin, Lily said, "Can you put me down? I'm not sure my legs will work though."

I eased her back from the tree and then sat her on her feet. After taking care of some cleanup with the wipes from her bag, I pulled her shorts and panties back up. Then I worked on getting myself presentable.

"Ready?"

She wrinkled her nose. "Yeah, I need to find a halfway decent bathroom to clean up in."

We started out of the woods together. After a bathroom pit stop, we were back in business. As we walked through the crowd, I couldn't help glancing over at Lily from time to time and smiling. When she finally caught on, she asked, "What?"

"Are you really disappointed that I didn't get down on my knee when I proposed?"

She shrugged. "Maybe a little."

"It means that much to you?"

"It's just conventional for the guy to get down on one knee."

When I stopped walking, Lily turned around. "What's wrong?"

With a smile, I sank down onto one knee. "Lily Marie Gregson, will you make me the happiest man alive by consenting to be my future wife?"

Lily's eyes widened. "Yes. Yes of course I do."

As I rose back up, people around us started clapping. Lily blushed at the attention. "Are you satisfied now?" I asked.

She laughed as she threw her arms around my neck. "Yes, Brayden. I'm very, very happy."

LILY

THE PAST

To everything there is a season, a purpose under heaven—Ecclesiastes 3:1

Those words would mean a lot to me during the difficult periods of my life. It helped me remember during the times when I thought I could not go on, that it was just a season, and the hopelessness would pass. It was also a reminder to enjoy the moment because happiness is sometimes fleeting.

The summer Brayden and I became engaged was one of the happiest times of my life. I loved being out on the road with the guys, and I was sad to see it end. In the autumn, the guys hard work touring paid off. A promoter who saw them at a show in Anaheim sent their CD to a record executive. Within two weeks, the guys were offered a very lucrative record deal. Their first two singles topped the Billboard charts.

With the back-to-back success of *Until There Was You* and *Twisted Reality*, Runaway Train's world literally went off the rails. Suddenly, they were everywhere. When I turned on the radio on the way home from class, I would always catch one of their songs. I squealed every single time, especially when Brayden came in to harmonize with Jake. They were sent out on a US tour almost immediately. Gone was the rickety old bus that had so many memories for Brayden and me. Now they traveled in style on the label's half-a-million dollar home on wheels. They had handlers now—people you had to get through just to talk to them. It was overwhelming to me, so I couldn't imagine how the guys were handling it.

And when the season changed to winter, everything in my life changed.

Nothing ever comes without a price, and the bounty to be paid for Runaway Train's success was the slow demise of Brayden's and my relationship. I'd never thought I would have to worry about him changing. He had always been so grounded and so humble. He didn't have an ounce of ego in him like Jake and AJ. He never cared about wealth—he just wanted to be able to make a living from playing music.

But something happened when he signed on the label's dotted line. It was like he sold his soul. With me doing my student teaching and working part-time at night, I was so busy I didn't notice things at first. The fact that my calls and texts went unanswered and unreturned, or he was always putting me off when I asked for their schedule so I could come spend the weekend with him. When I actually did talk to him, he sounded distant and not like the Brayden who used to talk to me for hours on end. Sometimes he slurred his words and said off-the-wall things. I began to worry that he was drinking too much, which was something that had never been an issue with Brayden before.

But then we finally reached the end of the road on Valentine's weekend.

"Hey, baby, what are you doing?" Brayden's voice boomed into my ear.

"Just pulling in the drive."

"You go to the mailbox yet?"

I laughed. "Since when do you care about me getting the mail?"

"Just check it, Lils."

"Okay, okay," I muttered, as I walked over to the mailbox.

"Did you get it?" Brayden questioned, as I flipped through the envelopes.

Cradling the phone on my shoulder, I asked, "Get what exactly?"

"The ticket."

My breath hitched. "You sent me a ticket?"

"Yeah, to come out here for Valentine's Day weekend."

His thoughtfulness caused my heartbeat to shudder and restart. At the bottom of the pile was a long envelope addressed to me. I couldn't help squealing.

"I guess that means you got it," he said, amusement vibrating in his voice.

I tore open the envelope and eyed the plane ticket. "Oh my God, Bray, thank you so, so much!"

"Well, we haven't spent a Valentine's Day apart since we've been together. I figured we didn't need to start now. You won't have a problem getting off that Friday, will you?"

"No, it should be fine." Pressing the envelope against my chest, I sighed, "I can't wait to see you."

"I feel the same way."

"Don't plan anything for us to do while I'm there. I just want to spend the entire time with you, preferably in bed."

Brayden laughed. "As much as I would like to oblige you on that one, I have to attend a party at my label on Saturday night. Wanna be my date?"

I tried hiding my disappointment that I was going to have to share Brayden. "Sure. I'd love to."

"Great. Listen, I'll have a driver waiting for you at the airport."

I laughed. "Seriously? Why don't you come and get me?"

"Because I have shit to do, Lils. I can't just drop everything to pick you up."

His words and his tone stung me. When I could finally speak, I said, "Yeah, sorry. I wasn't thinking."

"So I'll see you in two weeks?"

"Of course."

"'Bye, Lils."

"'Bye, Brayden. I love you."

But he didn't hear me. He had already hung up.

LILY

THE PAST

I sat in the first class seat Brayden had purchased for me, twirling my engagement ring around my finger. I hadn't heard from him since our last phone call two weeks ago. Well, he had sent a text this morning asking if I was still coming. I didn't know if that was more for him or more about the fact he needed to let the driver know.

The entire flight to L.A I did nothing but think. I broke apart our relationship into pieces and tried to examine each one to find the flaw. As hard as I tried, I still kept coming up empty. I didn't know how everything had gone wrong so fast. Part of me worried I was being irrational and overreacting. Relationships weren't always passion, heat, and devotion twenty-four seven. They went through ups and downs. While Brayden and I hadn't experienced many ups and downs yet, we were both under a lot of strain in our professional lives. Throw in a separation and that had to cause a little strain in even the strongest of relationships.

When the plane landed at LAX, I grabbed my carry-on and headed to the pickup area. Glancing around the drivers with signs, I tried to find the one with my name on it.

"Lily!"

I blinked in shock. Running towards me was Brayden with a dozen roses in his hand. When he got to me, he jerked me into his embrace. "Hey baby!"

The surprise of seeing him rendered me speechless. After what seemed like an eternity, I said, "I didn't expect to see you here."

"Yeah, I pulled some strings to get away."

His words caused me to smile so hard I thought my cheeks would break. It was like having the old Brayden back. I threw my arms around his neck and brought my lips to his. But the moment we kissed, all my hopes faded. It felt stilted, awkward, and forced. I kept kissing him desperately, searching to find that spark we once had. But no matter how hard I tried, it wasn't there. While I wanted to blame it on the separation, deep down I knew something fundamentally was wrong, and it scared me to death.

When he pulled away, I had to fight the tears that threatened to overflow my cheeks. "Hey, what's wrong?" he asked.

"They're happy tears because I'm just so glad to see you," I lied.

He laughed. "You always were so cheesy and dorky."

Before I could stop myself, I countered, "If I remember correctly, we both used to be cheesy and dorky."

"Glad I got rid of it," he replied. He took my bag from me. "Come on. Let's get you to the house."

With a heart that was slowly breaking in two, I followed in step behind him. "Wait until you see this place, Lils. It's fucking off the charts," Brayden said, as the driver held open the chauffeured driven Lincoln Town Car.

"I didn't know you had bought a house," I said, cautiously.

"It's the label's. They have different artists there while they're recording their albums. You wouldn't believe some of the other bands who have stayed there from time to time."

"That's nice."

Brayden snorted. "Just nice? It's on the water in Venice Beach for fuck's sake. I'd say that was a hell of lot better than nice."

Once again, I felt a piece of my heart fall away. The old Brayden wouldn't have been impressed with a house on the beach. He loved the mountains and the backwoods where he had grown up. It's the one thing that had originally endeared him to Jake because he and Jake shared the same passion.

Brayden didn't say much else to me during the drive. He fielded some calls on his phone while I stared out the window. I'd never been to Los Angeles, least of all California before, so I should have been more excited about seeing everything. But I just couldn't get rid of the nagging feeling in the pit of my stomach.

When we arrived at the house, I couldn't help feeling even more overwhelmed. It was a mansion more than it was a house. It had a sleek, modern design, and almost wall-to-wall windows to take in the views. "It's something, isn't it?" Brayden asked.

"It sure is."

He took my hand and led me up the walk and into the house. I had assumed even with the other guys at the house that Brayden and I would have some private time to talk and reconnect. The moment we entered the house, we were surrounded by people. Scanning the room, I searched for a familiar face, but I didn't see one. "My room is at the end of the hall. I know you've had a long flight, so why don't you go take a shower and rest?" Brayden suggested.

"Um, okay." I thought he might show me to his room himself, but he started talking to a tall, dark-haired guy with tortoise shell glasses. Taking a deep breath, I rolled my suitcase behind me as I went down the hall. The door on the right swung open, revealing Jake in some swim trunks. His eyes narrowed slightly at the sight of me. "Hey, Jake!" I said, a little over-enthusiastically. Since Brayden's and my engagement, things had become tense between Jake and me, but in spite of all that, I couldn't help but feel glad to see him.

"What are you doing here?" he demanded, as he crossed his arms over his chest.

I shrank a little at his tone. "Brayden invited me for Valentine's Day weekend."

"How sweet of him," he said, sarcastically.

"I thought so."

"Yeah, well, have fun."

"Thanks."

He stalked off down the hall, leaving me wondering yet again what his deal was. We had always gotten along so well, even when I was out on tour with them. I couldn't imagine what had soured his view of me unless it was he felt I was trying to saddle Brayden down with marriage.

When I got inside Brayden's room, I once again felt the sinking feeling in my stomach along with a tightening in my chest. Nothing in the room looked like him. While the furniture most likely had come with the house, there were no touches of Brayden. Even in his roost on the old bus, he had kept little mementos around to remind him of me, of home, and his family. None of those were here.

Considering how sanitized of personality the room was, I was surprised there was even a picture of us on the nightstand. Abandoning my suitcase, I went to pick it up. It was a double-sided frame. One picture was from the night we got engaged when AJ had taken a pic of us when we were kissing on top of the Ferris wheel. The other one was of us Homecoming night when I had been crowned queen. Brayden wasn't a part of the court, but he had met me as I came off the field. With roses in my arms and my glittering tiara on my head, I'd run into his open arms. The yearbook photographer had captured the moment when I pulled back and stared into Brayden's eyes. We both had such expressions of love on our faces.

I swept my hand over my heart, trying to ease the ache burning in my chest. I felt like I was in a deranged fairy tale where our once happily ever after had turned so very sour. Willing myself not to cry, I grabbed a fresh outfit out of my suitcase and then trudged into the bathroom. I hoped the shower might make me feel better, but it didn't. After I finished, I wrapped myself in one of the silky robes hanging on the back of the door. With my hair wet, I went out onto the porch that ran the length of the house.

After staring out at the ocean for what felt like an eternity, Brayden's strong arms came around my waist. "Mmm, you smell nice," he murmured, in my ear.

"Thank you."

"Sorry I had to take care of some shit."

"It's okay."

His hand trailed up my stomach to cup my breast. "I've missed you so fucking much, Lily."

"I've missed you, too."

As he pinched my hardened nipple, his teeth grazed along my neck. "Wanna go inside?"

I nodded and then let him lead me back into the bedroom. For the next three hours, we tumbled through the sheets, rolled around on the floor, and splashed water around in the Jacuzzi tub. The more I was with him physically, the more I began to slowly feel a more emotional connection to him.

My heart and mind felt even more at ease when he refused the invitation from AJ to accompany him and the guys to a club opening. Instead, we stayed at the house, eating Chinese take-out and watching goofball comedies. It felt just like old times.

Just before midnight, he took me for a walk along the beach. Hand in hand we walked along the cool sand, letting the waves lap against our ankles. Then we stripped down and made love on the beach by a secluded dune. On the way back to the house, he stopped to kiss me in the moonlight. "I love you," he said.

"I love you, too."

And in that moment, everything was right and perfect between us.

LILY

THE PAST

I yawned. "Good morning."

Brayden laughed. "Try afternoon, sleepyhead."

After I shot up in bed, I glanced at the clock on the nightstand. It was twelve-thirty. "Oh no," I moaned.

"What's the matter?"

Untangling myself from the sheets, I replied, "You shouldn't have let me sleep so long."

"Why? I figured you needed the rest."

"I don't have that much time with you, so I don't want to waste a minute."

"Sounds like you've been missing me pretty badly," he mused.

"Of course, I have." I brought my hand to his face and rubbed my thumb along his jaw. "I love you so, so much. I hate to have to spend any time away from you."

"I love you, too." Jerking the sheet away from my breasts, he grinned. "Now why don't you show me just how much you've missed me?"

"I can do that," I replied

"I'm glad to hear it." He then pushed me onto my back on the mattress.

After I showed Brayden how much I'd loved him to the tune of two orgasms for him and three for me, I slipped into the shower. Any other apprehensions I had about his feelings for me faded away when he brought me a tray of bagels, croissants, and fruit to the bedroom. Bundled in a robe, I chowed down on the feast before me.

"I have a surprise for you," he said.

"You do?" I questioned through a mouth of jelly-filled croissant.

"Remember how I said there was a party for my label tonight?"

The bite of croissant I swallowed lodged in my throat. "Yeah, I remember."

"Well, I gave our assistant your size and asked her to find you a dress for tonight."

"Really?"

"Yeah, I didn't want you to have to worry about getting a dress before you left. But more than anything, I wanted a dress you would feel comfortable in out here. I know how you feel about fitting in."

And with those words, the happy little bubble of my day burst. "You mean you were worried about me not fitting in," I countered softly.

He scowled at me. "That's not it at all, Lils. I just wanted to get you something nice. What's wrong with that?"

"Nothing." I then forced a smile to my face. "I haven't had a new party dress in a long time."

He grinned and went over to the closet. He took out a garment bag and then unzipped it. "What do you think?"

It was a nightmare—both the dress itself and the world I found myself in. It was short, and I knew from the material it would be skin tight on me. With the cutouts on the halter top, it would be showing a lot of cleavage too. While I'm sure it cost a fortune and had a famous designer's name attached to it, it wasn't me, and Brayden should've known that.

"That's some dress," I finally managed to say.

"I know, right? Fuck, Lils, you're going to look so hot in this tonight."

"You want me to look like that in front of your bandmates and the guests coming?"

He gave me a weird look. "Of course I do. Why would you ask?"

"It just seemed like it was going to show a lot of skin."

"That's the idea, babe. You've got a rockin' body, so you might as well show it off. Make me proud."

"Thanks," I murmured.

He glanced at the clock. "We've got a few hours before we have to get ready. What do you want to do?"

"We could recreate last night with the movies."

His brows furrowed. "You've never been to LA before, and you want to stay holed up here on a gorgeous day?"

I shrugged. "I just want to spend time with you."

"I think we can do that and see some of the sites." He jerked his chin at the bathroom. "Go get dressed, and we'll go for a ride."

"Okay," I agreed, although I would have much rather just stayed in with him.

After throwing on some shorts and a T-shirt, I pulled my hair back into a ponytail and went to meet Brayden. He ushered me into the garage where a sleek, black Aston Martin convertible sat. "Oh my God, is this yours?"

"No, it's the label's. But it's ours to drive as long as we're staying at the house."

"That's amazing."

"Wait until you feel how it rides."

I slid onto the seat and buckled up. Brayden revved the engine, and then backed us out of the garage. Once we got on the main road, I knew exactly what he was talking about with the car's ride. He drove me around some of the other parts of Venice Beach. Then we went to Hollywood. We strolled along the Walk of Fame and checked out the footprints at Grauman's Chinese Theater.

While I had initially wanted to stay in, I had so much fun being out with Brayden. It felt like the past when we were exploring Atlanta together during our first year of college. Of course, the one thing that was different this time was Brayden being recognized by people. He got stopped three times for his autograph.

On the drive back to Venice Beach, we were both quiet. Brayden finally turned to me and smiled. "What are you thinking about?"

"Just about how much things have changed in the last few months."

"For the better right?"

I shifted in my seat. "It's much better for the band," I replied.

Brayden frowned. "What are you not saying?"

Folding my hands in my lap, I sighed. "You don't think things have been different between us?"

"I guess so. I mean, we're both very busy right now."

"I know that. It's just..."

"Just what?"

"You're different."

He snorted. "Yeah, I guess I am. That's what happens when a nobody becomes somebody."

I couldn't help cringing at his words. "You were never a nobody, Brayden."

"In the industry I was. Now that's all changed."

"But it shouldn't change you," I protested.

Gripping the steering wheel a little tighter, Brayden said, "You can't expect me to be the same person I was, Lily. People change as they mature and then when life puts them on a different path. I sacrificed a hell of lot to get where I am. Now that I'm here, I want to enjoy it. If that means partying or drinking harder than I used to, then I'm going to do it."

"I see," I murmured.

Brayden took his eyes off the road to momentarily pin me with a stare. "What are you getting at exactly? That I'm not the man you fell in love with or some bullshit?"

"No, that's not it at all. You know I love you. It's just hard for me since you've changed."

"Sounds like it's time you did a little changing."

"So I can fit in better with you now?"

"Yeah."

Hurt pierced my chest at his callousness. "Sure. I can try."

"Glad to hear it." To signal that the conversation was done, he reached over and turned on the radio. We didn't talk the rest of the drive. When we pulled up at the house, I eased out of the car and headed inside. "We got about an hour before the car comes to pick us up. So get cracking on making yourself presentable," Brayden said, with a grin.

"We couldn't have me looking *unpresentable*, could we? That would be too mortifying," I replied, before I stalked off to the bedroom.

I locked myself in the bathroom. I took another shower before I did my hair and makeup. When it was time to slide on the dress, I had to fight the urge to rip it to shreds. I hated the damn thing and everything it represented. But instead, I put it on. Standing in front of the mirror, I saw I had achieved just what Brayden wanted. I had transformed myself into an acceptable date for a desirable rock star like him to be seen with.

A knock came at the door. "Lils?" Brayden asked.

I unlocked the door for him, and he stepped inside. His eyes bulged at the sight of me. "Damn, you look amazing. Just like I thought you would."

"Thank you," I mumbled.

"Are you going to be mad at me all night?" he questioned softly.

Turning back to him, I shook my head. "I'm not mad at you. I'm hurt."

"Just because I said you needed to be presentable?"

"It's not just that one statement. It's the way you've made me feel since I got here. That I'm not good enough to be with you."

"Jesus, Lils, that not what I meant at all." He drew me to him. "I'm sorry if I made you feel that way. You know I love you, and you're the only woman I want to be with."

I hoped, rather than believed, him to be sincere. "I love you, too."

"Good. Now let's go have some fun."

When I got into the limo at the house, I was never so glad to see AJ and Rhys in all my life. I slid across the seat to hug them both.

Neither one of them had a date with them. I wondered what had happened to AJ's last girlfriend who I met once or twice. I didn't ask where Jake was. After our initial run-in at the house, I hadn't seen much of him.

Being with AJ and Rhys felt like old times, and it helped to ease the tension still hanging in the air between Brayden and me. When we got to the venue, I gasped and tried to hold my excitement in.

Brayden turned to give me an amused smile. "Why are you so fidgety all the sudden?"

"Um, hello, we're at a party at the Chateau Marmont. This is huge!"

He gave an apathetic shrug. "I'm at these kind of places all the time now."

"Yeah, well, I'm not," I replied, as we got out of the car. On the way inside, I had to bite my tongue from squealing at some of the celebrities that walked past me.

When we got in the elevator, Brayden laughed. "You're freaking out inside, aren't you?"

I nodded. "Do you know that my students, especially the musical ones, would literally fall over in a heap at some of the singers and musicians I just saw? They might even piss their pants."

"I don't have to worry about you doing that, do I?"

I laughed. "No, but that doesn't mean I'm not nervous." Grabbing his arm, I said, "Promise you won't leave me?"

"I won't."

"Not even to go to the bathroom?"

Brayden's brows rose. "You want to go with me to piss?"

"Maybe. Or at least wait outside the door."

"Jesus, Lils," he muttered.

The elevator dinged open, and we stepped out onto the main floor. Wall to wall people packed the room. I shifted uneasily in my heels before gripping Brayden's arm a little tighter. He led me through the crowd, occasionally stopping to talk to people. Most had no idea who I was, least of all that he had a fiancée. "We've got some good PR people hiding that one, don't we?" he joked.

A middle-aged woman nodded. "Yes, they've got to keep the image that you're all young, single, and available. The image is just as important as the music."

I gave her a fake smile. I didn't see what harm it would do for people to know Brayden and I were engaged. Didn't happy couples sell records as much as single guys? I knew it would be a losing game to push the issue around these people.

We continued working our way through the crowd. I had to fight myself from yawning at some of the boring conversations. I'd already spoken to at least fifty people before one finally said, "And what is it you do?" a balding man with a large gut asked.

"I'm almost finished with my teaching practicum. I should have a class of my own next year."

"A teacher? What a noble profession."

"Thank you."

He winked at Brayden. "Since it doesn't pay shit, you better keep your hooks in this one, eh?"

"Yes, I suppose I should," I replied coolly. Brayden quickly steered us away from the man. "Great people," I muttered.

"He's an ass."

"Yeah, he is, but I'm sure most of the people here would share his sentiments about my lowly tax bracket."

Brayden ignored my comment. Instead, his attention seemed focused on the tall guy with glasses who I had seen at the house the day before. "Hey, Marcus, I didn't get a chance to introduce you to my fianceé yesterday."

Marcus sized me up. "So this is the future little woman?"

"I'm Lily," I said, extending my hand.

"Nice to meet you. I've heard only good things about you."

"I hope so."

"Are you having a good time?"

"Oh sure," I answered quickly.

Marcus laughed. "No need to lie. These parties can be so fucking boring."

"If you say so."

"Speaking of boring," Marcus said before he leaned over and whispered something in Brayden's ear. At Brayden's nod, Marcus smiled. "Lovely meeting you Lily."

"The same to you."

As Marcus started walking off, Brayden said, "The label has some people they want us to meet."

"But you promised you wouldn't leave me," I protested.

Brayden's aggravation was apparent. "Dammit, Lily, it's only for a few minutes. Give me a break."

His tone and his words stung me, but I managed to plaster a smile on my face. "I'm sorry. You're right. Go do your thing."

Without another word to me, he strode off with Marcus. I took a few deep breaths, trying not to panic in the overwhelming situation. *Come on, Lily. You were Homecoming Queen for God's sake. You know how to win people over. Go forth and win these assholes over.*

Trying to be proactive, I started to walk around the room, lingering by groups of people and trying to join in on their conversations. While I gave them my best smile, most only offered me a frosty hello before they turned back to their own friends and acquaintances.

I took a flute of champagne from one of the waiters. Sipping it slow, I willed myself not to cry. This was Brayden's world now, and because I was with him, it was mine as well. I just had to get used to it. But I couldn't help wishing for the past—the days when the band was just starting out and Brayden and I were of one mind and body.

I don't know how much time passed. It seemed like an eternity. I'd downed two flutes of champagne. After a trip to the ladies room, I ran into Rhys in the hallway. "Hey!" I cried, enthusiastically.

He grinned. "Hey, yourself."

"Sorry. It's just good to see a familiar face among all these people."

"I know what you mean." After glancing around, he made a face. "I thought I'd escaped all the pretentious bullshit when I left home. Unfortunately, I'm right back in hell tonight."

"I'm glad I'm not the only one who isn't comfortable with all this."

"If you ask me, this is the worst part of the business—boot licking and ass kissing."

I giggled. "You're right. I was just thinking how I missed the early days, especially last summer when we were all together on the bus."

"Yeah, those were some good times." He smiled at me. "I'll never forget how sweet you were to me. I was in a really bad place with my parents disowning me because of the band. You really came through for me."

"Stop, you're going to make me cry," I said, as I felt my eyes moistening.

"It's the truth."

"I feel the same way about you." Glancing around, I asked, "You guys done with your meeting?"

Rhys brows furrowed. "What meeting?"

"Marcus came and got Brayden because the label had some people they wanted you to meet."

Shifting uncomfortably on his feet, Rhys said, "Uh, I haven't met with any of the label guys tonight."

My stomach plummeted to my knees, and although I hated myself for it, tears stung my eyes. "I see."

Rhys hand came to touch my shoulder. "I'm sorry, Lily."

I held up my hand. "You don't need to apologize. It isn't your fault."

He sighed. "Look, I know it doesn't make it any easier, but we've all noticed a change in Bray over the last few months. And it's not a good one."

"Thanks," I replied, in a whisper.

"He'll come to his senses soon."

"You sure about that?"

"This world," he motioned around him, "is hard for the others to acclimate to. I grew up with money and excess, so it doesn't have the shiny appeal to me like it does for the others. AJ would be the same guy if he was living in a mansion or in a box on the street. He's just that kind of guy. As for Jake and Brayden…" He shook his head.

"The greatest prize comes from corrupting the incorruptible. He's been a target of theirs from the beginning."

"The label's?"

"Their minions, yeah."

The thought of Runaway Train's handlers manipulating Brayden made me sick. "I just thought that Brayden was too strong to let all this get to him."

"You hear their line of bullshit day in and day out, and anyone can fall for it, especially when the brand of propaganda comes in the form of houses, clothes, and cars. Money talks more than anything in the world."

"I guess you're right."

"Just give him some time. He'll come around."

"I hope so, Rhys. Because if he doesn't..." I bit down on my lip to keep from crying.

"The worst thing in the world that could happen to him would be to lose you."

I barreled forward and threw my arms around Rhys's neck. "Thank you for being so good to me."

He chuckled. "You don't need to thank me for that."

I pulled away and kissed his cheek. "Yes, there is. Just like you thanked me earlier for being good to you last summer. You have such a good heart, Rhys. In spite of what you grew up with, you are a decent, caring person."

Rhys's jaw clenched like he was fighting his emotions. "Thank you, Lily. That means a lot coming from you."

"I'm going to go find Brayden. I think it's time I left for the night. Let him do his thing."

"Good luck."

"Thanks, I'll probably need it."

After I made my way back to the main room, I started searching through the crowd for Brayden. When I didn't see him, I started down another hallway. Just as I came around the corner, AJ stepped into my path. "Hey, Lils, what's up?" he asked, a plastered smile on his face.

"I was trying to find Brayden, so I could tell him I was leaving."

"No, you can't do that." When I cocked my brows at him, he said, "I mean, you can't leave yet. Why don't you stay and dance with me?"

I knew then that Brayden was in the next room, and he was doing something that would be hurtful to me. I shook my head. "AJ, get out of my way."

"Please, Lils, you don't want to see him like this."

Closing my eyes, I willed myself to wake up from the nightmare I found myself in. "Is he with another woman?"

"No, God, no. It's just he's…really fucked up."

"He's not even been gone an hour."

"I'm sorry. But he is."

Even though I knew it wasn't the best time to confront Brayden, I side-stepped AJ and hurried around the corner. Overstuffed sofas filled the room along with the pungent aroma of pot. With his tie undone and suit disheveled, Brayden lounged on a couch with two other men—I think they were label executives. On the table in front of them were probably dozens of empty shot glasses along with a white powdery substance with a razor blade.

At my gasp of horror, Brayden jerked his head up to meet my gaze. "What are you doing in here?"

I crossed my arms over my chest. "I think I could ask you the same thing."

"I'm unwinding. Having a good time. Something your uptight ass doesn't know how to do."

"By drinking and smoking pot? I mean, please tell me you're not in here snorting up."

Brayden shot off the couch and grabbed me by the shoulders. "Keep your fucking voice down!"

I shoved him away. "Don't you dare put your hands on me!"

Glancing behind him, Brayden said, "AJ, get her out of here."

"I think it's you that needs to leave, man."

Brayden's brows shot up. "You're taking her side now? Whatever happened to bros before hos?"

AJ closed the gap between them in one long stride. Grabbing Brayden by the neck, he shoved him past the couch and up against the wall. "AJ!" I cried.

Ignoring me, he practically snarled at Brayden. "You need to shut your fucking mouth before you say or do anything else you're going to regret in the morning."

"Get off me."

"I will when you apologize to Lily."

Brayden glanced at me over AJ's shoulder. He looked like a stranger. No, he looked at me like *I* was a stranger. Tears stung my eyes at the final revelation that the man I had once loved, the man I wanted to marry, was gone.

"Sorry," he finally muttered.

"I'm sorry, too," I whispered. I was sorry for what had been lost between us in the last few months. I was sorry for the countless promises he'd broken. I was sorry that the future we had once dreamed of together would never come to fruition. I was sorry that no matter how hard he had once tried to stay grounded, Brayden was now just another casualty of fame and fortune.

Turning around, I fled the room. I desperately wanted to leave the ugliness I had seen behind, but I knew it would come with me. In a way, I needed it to. If it didn't, I would be tempted not to do what I had to do.

When I got to the elevator, AJ appeared at my side. "I'll take you home."

"Thank you, but that's not necessary. Stay here and have some fun. Find a girl to take home."

He gave me a sad smile. "Right now, none of that matters to me. You're the only girl I want to take home."

His words caused the dam of my emotions to break, and I began to sob. He wrapped his arm around me, and I drew myself against his chest. He led us on to the elevator. "I'm sorry, Lils. I'm so fucking sorry," he murmured against my ear.

"I just don't understand."

"I know. I don't either. All I do know is I'd like to throttle his ass for treating you the way he has."

"I can't stay with him. Not when he's like this."

AJ grimaced. "I know that. I wouldn't expect for you to. You deserve so much better."

I brushed the tears from my eyes. "I only deserve the old Brayden."

Taking my hand, AJ led me off the elevator. The limo that had brought us to the party was waiting outside. At AJ's wave, the driver hustled out to come open the door for us. Once we were inside, I buried my head in my hands and wept.

AJ wrapped me in his strong arms. When I had finally had my fill, I pulled away. "Will you do something for me?"

"Anything, mi amor."

"Will you take me to the airport in a little while?"

"Don't you think you should wait to talk to Brayden?"

"There's nothing left to say."

"I still think you need to talk to him. I'll call Rhys and have him bring Brayden home."

Feeling defeated, I murmured, "Fine."

When we got to the house, I went straight for Brayden's bedroom. The moment I closed the door behind me, I stripped myself out of the horrible dress. I threw on a pair of shorts and a T-shirt. Then I escaped out onto the deck. Leaning forward on the railing, I listened to the waves crashing against the shore. "Fight for me again, Brayden. Please," I whispered, as I thought back to our first date.

At the sound of the door opening, I whirled around. My heart sank at the sight of just AJ standing there. "He wouldn't come home, would he?"

AJ shook his head sadly. "He said he would talk to you in the morning."

Glancing back out at the water, I expected myself to break down, to become hysterical and sink down onto my knees. But the tears didn't come. It seemed I had shed all the tears I could at the moment for Brayden. "Will you take me to the airport now?"

"Yeah, I will."

With a nod, I turned and started down the deck to him. "I just need a few minutes to pack."

"Take all the time you need." AJ then slipped out of room, leaving me alone to do what I had to do. It didn't take me long to throw my clothes and makeup into my suitcase. I didn't even bother trying to neatly pack. I just wanted out of there and the faster the better.

I grabbed my purse and suitcase and started to the door. When I looked down at my left hand, I paused. Without a second thought, I slipped off my engagement ring. There was no reason to take it with me, and it had belonged to Brayden's grandmother anyway. Putting down my things, I went over to the nightstand and put it down by the picture frame. It belonged with the happy couple in the pictures, not what we had become.

When I started down the hall, AJ met me halfway and took my things. I knew I would miss his sense of humor, his dancing, and his larger than life personality. But what I would miss most of all was his kind and caring heart.

I was leaving California, but what happened to me in the few short days I was here would haunt me for a long, long time.

BRAYDEN

THE PRESENT

As Lily painfully recounted the demise of our relationship, I fought the urge to throw up. It seemed like she was talking about a stranger. I guess in a way, whoever that asshole was that I had become, was a stranger to me. Even after seeking out a therapist years ago, I still couldn't quite grasp why I had changed. While the therapist gave me some psychobabble spin of why the sudden fortuitous changes in my life affected my psyche, it still didn't seem to set in to me how I could have become such a superficial son of a bitch.

When the story progressed to the agonizing end that night at Chateau Marmont, I rose off the couch and started pacing the room.

"Brayden?" Giovanni inquired.

"Yeah?"

"Do you need to take a break?"

Raking my hand through my hair, I replied, "I think I need a drink." I stalked over to the mini-bar and threw it open. After grabbing three small bottles of Jack, I reached for a glass. Emptying them one by one, I then took a large gulp. When I caught Giovanni's eye, I gave a mirthless laugh. "For the record, I only allow myself to have one glass of hard liquor at a time. I might throw back three or four beers, but it's only one glass of liquor. It was this shit," I held up my glass of Jack, "that partly contributed to me being such an unimaginable bastard to Lily."

"So during your early days of Runaway Train success, you abused alcohol."

"Oh yeah. Big time."

"And after you and Lily got back together, did you try to curb your drinking?"

"Yes. That's when I first instated the hard liquor clause. I realized what it had cost me."

Giovanni frowned. "There's no record of you ever being in rehab."

"That's because I wasn't. I did it cold fucking turkey. I was that dedicated not to ever screwing up with Lily again."

"I didn't realize talking about the past would affect you so much," Lily said, softly.

Turning around to face her, I shook my head. "It doesn't just affect me. It tears me apart, shreds me. Not only because I treated you that way, but because I don't even have a fucking good reason for why I started acting the way that I did."

Giovanni cleared his throat. "If I might interject here, I think Lily touched on many reasons why your behavior towards her changed."

I rolled my eyes. "Trust me, I've already had a therapist explain that it was the alcohol, the separation, the manipulative bastards who worked for the label, blah, blah, blah." I took another gulp of Jack. "It's all bullshit. I should have been stronger. I mean, I didn't just lose myself. I lost the most important thing in the world to me—the very reason to get out of bed and make the music that I did."

Lily rose off the couch and came over to me. "It was just a bump in the road."

"Don't sugarcoat it, babe."

"Okay, it was more like a dark, cavernous crater in the road. But in the end, we got through it."

"Only because you were willing to forgive me."

Giovanni came over to us. "Why don't we move we forward, shall we?"

"That would be a good idea," Lily replied. She offered me her hand and then led me over to the couch.

Once we were seated, Giovanni started in on the next question. "After Lily left you in California, did you try to reach out to her, mend fences?"

With an anguished moan, I closed my eyes. "I called her the next morning like I said I would. She was back home in Georgia then. It wasn't a good call."

"You didn't question her as to why she left or ask her to come back?"

When I dared to open my eyes to look at Lily, tears pooled in her eyes. "I can't do this," I muttered. "I can't dredge this shit up again and hurt my wife."

"Brayden, it's okay. I'm okay," Lily protested.

"No, you're not. I've made you cry. *Again.* I swore I would never let that happen."

She reached out to cup my cheek. "You aren't that man anymore. I'm only crying again because I hate to see you in such pain."

"And to relive it," I countered.

"Yes, you're right."

Pinning Giovanni with a harsh look, I said, "I answer this and then we move on. No more dwelling about what happened in California. Okay?" He nodded. "When I called her, I wasn't looking to apologize. I wanted to hear she was sorry for leaving me…for not appreciating the new life I had or that we could have."

"And what did you say to that, Lily?" Giovanni asked.

"We're dwelling," I practically growled.

"I need to know," Giovanni replied, softly.

Lily sighed. "I told him when he found the man that I loved with all my heart and soul, his old self, to give me a call. Until then, I didn't want to see or hear from him. And he honored that."

As I exhaled a ragged breath, Giovanni asked, "So you were broken up for a year?"

With a shrug, I replied, "Yeah, give or take."

"It was eleven months, two weeks, and five days," Lily replied. When Giovanni and I both looked at her, a sad smile appeared on her face. "There are some things you don't ever forget."

Easing back in his chair, Giovanni adjusted his tie. "Look, I don't want you guys to think I'm some kind of masochist freak for having you dredge up these painful memories. I just have to paint the full story, and that has to include part of your past."

I sighed. "I don't suppose you can help it. I mean, you've got to get your story, right?"

"Yes, I do. But at the same time, I want you to know that I won't be exaggerating these hard times to sell the story. I want to juxtapose them against the people you are now—the people it made you. In the end, these hard times are what made your love so strong."

"I suppose you're right," I replied.

Giovanni nodded. "Now what happened at the end of those eleven months to finally reunite you?"

At Lily's sharp intake of breath, I reached over and took her hand in mine. The bastard I had been during the band's early success, our break-up, yeah, those were hard, but nothing compared to what had actually brought us back together.

"It was the loss of someone who meant the world to me," I said. When I cut my gaze over to Lily, tears shone in her eyes. I couldn't help thinking of the old cliché time heals all wounds. And while it sometimes lessens the pain, time can never take away the anguish of losing someone who was your entire world.

BRAYDEN

THE PAST

"Man, I'm so fucking tired," AJ groaned, as he banged his head against the gold-plated elevator wall.

"I hear ya. I just want to sleep for days," I replied, flexing my aching fingers.

Jake snorted. "Yeah, well, I just want to fuck for days."

I rolled my eyes at his response. "Give your dick a rest for one night," I mumbled.

"I never sleep as well as I do after a fuck-fest."

Rhys laughed. "I doubt I could even get it up right now I'm so tired."

With a grin, AJ replied, "I think I could get it up, but she'd have to do all the work."

The elevator dinged, and we made our way to our suite. We'd spent the last five nights on the bus with back to back shows. Tonight we actually got to sleep in a real bed before gearing up for the next hard leg of the tour, which included three nights in Vegas.

When we got inside the posh room, I whistled. "Looks like the label really came through."

"As hard as they're working us, they sure as hell better have," Jake mused before he collapsed on one of the plush couches.

"Who wants room service?" Rhys asked, as he plucked the menu off the table.

"Me. I want a steak, rare, with some potatoes and gravy. Maybe some mac and cheese or rice, too," I said, my stomach growling with longing.

Rhys nodded, and then I went in search of a shower. All of our luggage had been brought up earlier, so after I found my bag, I dug out some fresh boxers and a T-shirt. With the water on the hottest setting, I slipped inside the shower. Nothing felt as good as washing the sweat and grime off after a show. While the bus had a decent bathroom, it sure as hell didn't compare to this.

Of course, the moment the hot water hit my back, I let out a hiss of pain and cursed under my breath. After last night's show, I entertained a brunette knockout on the bus before we left. Her acrylic nails had scoured my back as we fucked. When it was over, she'd left me her number, which I tossed in the trashcan after she left. None of the women I slept with sparked an emotional connection in me. They were just a means to get off. Of course in the end, I would always end up comparing them to the one woman I couldn't seem to forget.

"Fuck," I muttered, as I banged my head against the shower tile.

When I got out, I caught my reflection in the mirror. Just like always, my hand swept over my heart to the ink with Lily's name. The familiar ache twisted and tightened in my chest at the thought of her and what we had once had. I'd made two appointments to have the damn thing covered with something else, but I never could bring myself to go.

As I stroked the lettering, I wondered what she was up to back home. I wondered how her teaching job was going. I knew she was probably busting her ass because she always was such a perfectionist. I wondered if she was dating someone. While I wanted her to be happy, I sure as hell didn't like the thoughts of her with another man. I knew that AJ and Rhys kept in touch with her through emails and texts. I was too stubborn an ass to ever ask them how she was.

My phone buzzed on the counter, and I grabbed it. I couldn't help grinning when I saw it was Mitch. "Hey douchebag, how the hell are you? I was just thinking about shit from home, and then you call me." At the silence on the other end, I said, "Mitch? Are you there?"

"I'm here."

"What's going on?"

"Look man, I don't know how to tell you this, but I figured you'd want to know."

Just the tone of his voice caused fear to reign down on me. "What's wrong?" I demanded.

"Paul Gregson was murdered last night."

The image of Lily's smiling father burned through my mind so hard I staggered back. "W-What?"

Mitch exhaled a long breath. "There was a shooting at the courthouse. Some death penalty case for a gang member where the dude's friends started shooting up the place when the sentence was read. Judge Goodwin is in critical condition, along with the new prosecutor, ten people were wounded, and Paul…"

"Jesus," I muttered, as I fell back against the bathroom counter.

"He was a fucking hero. He jumped on one of the gunmen and took him down, saving who knows how many lives, but he was shot in the chest and stomach. He never made it outside the room."

While my heart ached for Paul, my thoughts immediately went to Lily. Razor-sharp pain pricked its way through my chest. "How is she?" I asked, knowing Mitch would know exactly who I was talking about.

"Not good, man."

I couldn't even begin to imagine how she was handling this. Lily and her father had such a special bond. While she loved her mother intensely, there had never been a stronger Daddy's Girl than Lily. To lose him period would have shattered her, but to have to lose him so violently and when she was so young, it was life altering.

After a long pause on the line, Mitch cleared his throat. "She's not seeing anyone right now—she hasn't gotten serious about anyone since you two broke up. She's gone out with a few guys—half the coaches at the high school where she's teaching get permanent wood when she's around, but she's not biting."

I knew why he was telling me this now. Lily was all alone without the two most important men in her life. I had to go to her. I had to be with her during this horrible time. Regardless of what had happened between us, I owed it to her and to Paul.

"When's the funeral?"

"Friday at two."

"Okay, I'll be there."

"I'm glad to hear that."

"Well, Paul was always so good to me. I should go and pay my respects."

"This isn't about Paul and you know it."

"What the fuck are you talking about?"

"You still love her, Bray. You're no fucking good without her, and you know it."

"Look, I appreciate you calling to tell me about Paul, but when it comes to me and Lily, there's nothing to discuss."

"Oh really?"

"Yeah, really," I snapped.

"Then answer me this. When was the last time you were able to write a song?"

Motherfucker. I gripped the phone tighter in my hand. He'd gone straight for my jugular on that one. "We're not working on the album now."

"That has nothing to do with it, and you and I both know it. Admit it, Bray. You need her. You love her."

With a mirthless laugh, I said, "Since when does a manwhore advocate monogamy and relationships?"

"Since I finally fell in love three months ago."

The wind left my body, and I staggered back for the second time that evening. "You're shitting me?"

"No, I'm not."

"Why didn't you tell me?"

"Because Lily wasn't the only one who saw you change."

"Ouch man, that hurts."

"I'm sorry, but it's the truth. Talking to you tonight is the first time you've sounded like your old self in a hell of a long time."

While I could have argued with Mitch, I knew it was the truth, too. Losing Lily over who I had become should have been enough to make me turn my life around, but for some reason, I hadn't. But maybe it wasn't too late. "For what it's worth, I am sorry."

"I know you are. Just like I knew deep down you'd come to your senses one day and realize what a fucking asshole you'd become."

"That's a little ironic coming from you, don't you think?"

Mitch laughed. "Yeah, but I've always been an asshole. It suits me. But you're not cut out for it."

I chuckled. "Listen, I need to get off the phone here so I can get our PA to make the flight arrangements for me."

"Okay."

"Will you let me buy you a beer when I get back in town? I need to hear all about this girl who has reformed you."

"Yeah, I'd like that."

"Good. I'll see you tomorrow."

"Bye, cuz."

"Bye, Mitch."

I hung up the phone and quickly threw on my clothes. When I got back out to the suite, room service had arrived, and the guys were chowing down. At that moment, I no longer had an appetite. All I could think of was getting back to Lily as quickly as I could.

When AJ saw me, he motioned to my plate. "Get your grub, dude."

I shook my head. "I need to call Gretchen and get a flight out of here tonight."

Jake's fork clattered onto his plate. "Where are you going?"

"Back home to Roswell."

With his brows lined in worry, Jake asked, "Are your parents okay?"

"Yeah, they're fine. It's Lily actually. Her dad was murdered last night—well, he was shot while taking down a shooter at the courthouse."

"Damn, that's horrible," Rhys remarked.

"Poor Lils. She and her dad were so close," AJ said.

Pushing his plate aside, Jake asked, "You expect to leave during the middle of a major tour for some ex-piece of ass's father?"

I narrowed my eyes at him. "Lily is more than just an ex-piece of ass, and you know that. Besides the fact she was once my fiancée, her dad was a helluva guy who meant a lot to me."

He shrugged. "So send some flowers or a card. Or if you're really feeling generous, give them a check."

Closing the gap between us, I snarled, "You are one heartless motherfucker, did you know that?"

"I'm just being honest. Do you think the label is actually going to allow you to leave for some ex-girlfriend's father?"

"I frankly don't give a fuck what they think. There are more important things in life."

With a snort, Jake said, "I can't believe you're going to jeopardize your career over that bitch. Hasn't she caused you enough trouble already? She fucked up your mojo to where you can't write a song to save your life, not to mention trying to tie you down."

I grabbed him by the shirt. "Don't you say one more fucking word about Lily!"

"Or what?"

AJ rose out of his chair and came over to us. "Okay, that's enough."

Jake sneered up at me. "Fine. Go home to your precious Lily. She must have one more gold-plated pussy if she can get you to throw your career away."

As rage ricocheted through me, I didn't take a second to think. I just reacted. My fist connected with Jake's jaw hard enough to flip him over in his chair. I barreled over the chair and started pummeling his stomach. I got in three or four good punches when I was lifted up under my arms by Rhys and AJ. "Dude, knock it off!" AJ shouted.

With my chest rising and falling in harsh pants, I tried to catch my breath. "I'll stop kicking his ass when he says he's sorry. Lily's never been anything but good and nice to him, and he's a fucking asshole for talking about her that way!" I shouted back.

Wiping the blood from his mouth, Jake glared up at me. "Just get out of here."

I shook my head at him. "Why can't you say you're sorry? Is that too much to fucking ask?"

"You don't want to hear what I have to say," he bellowed.

"Yeah, I do. Because if you don't make things right between us, I'm not sure there's a point for me coming back."

Both AJ and Rhys inhaled sharply. "You can't mean that, Bray," AJ said.

"I sure as hell do. I can't make music with someone who is as heartless and unfeeling as Jake."

"Fine," Jake growled, pulling himself to his feet. "You want the truth about why I can't stand your precious Lily?"

His tone caused me to lunge forward, and if AJ and Rhys hadn't been holding me back, I would've attacked him again.

"She chose you," Jake said.

I could only stare at him as I tried processing his words. "What do you mean?"

"I'm only admitting this because I don't want you to leave the band. We need you too much."

"Get to the point," I snapped.

"Somewhere along the way, I kinda started to like her."

My mouth gaped open in both surprise and horror. "Like her? Like more than your friend's fiancée?"

"At first, I thought it was because she reminded me so much of Stephanie, but then the more I got to know her, the more I started to like her. She was so good to us—cooking for us and caring about what was going on in our lives. After being surrounded by groupies, she was so fucking real. I thought I could make her want me."

"So you could fuck her and dump her?" I snarled.

"No, so I could have what the two of you had. Something real."

"And then when she didn't show anything to you but friendly love, you sorta turned on her. Or at least used me to turn on her."

Jake nodded. "You guys getting engaged was kinda what did it for me. I saw then she was never going to like anyone—love anyone else—but you. When you started to change, it was easy to manipulate you into treating her worse and worse."

"But why would you do that?"

"So she would leave, and I wouldn't have to see her anymore."

"Jesus, Jake," AJ muttered by my side.

Jake sighed. "I know you want it, but you fucking deserve it too. I'm sorry, Brayden. I'm really fucking sorry. I'm sorry for all the horrible shit I said about Lily. I'm sorry her dad got murdered. She's too good to have something so horrible happen to her. But most of all, I'm sorry I treated her the way that I did there at the end."

I cocked my brows at him. "You really mean that? You're not just saying it to make sure I'll stay in the band."

He snorted. "Man, I must be some unimaginable bastard if you had to question that."

With a shrug, I replied, "I'm sorry, but with your track record, that's the way I feel about it."

"Yeah, it's the truth. Every fucking word. If she was standing here before me, I'd say the exact same thing to her." When I still hadn't budged, Jake said, "I'll even call her and apologize myself."

I knew then he was really sincere. Jake didn't get emotional for anyone, least of all a woman, unless he absolutely had to. "Okay, I'll stay."

He nodded. "Besides the band, are we good?"

"I don't know, man. I need some time to process all this."

Sadness flickered in Jake's eyes. "I understand. And hey, don't worry about the shows. We'll work something out."

"Wasn't worried, but thanks." Without another word, I turned and went in the bedroom to call Gretchen, so I could get the hell out of there.

I arrived in Atlanta around noon. Instead of a driver waiting to meet me, it was my mom and dad. They even parked and came inside the airport, so they could hug and kiss me. Even though

I was twenty three and far too old to be fawned over, I let myself truly enjoy it. For one, I'd missed them, and the other reason was I thought of how Lily would never get to put her arms around her father again.

My mom chattered non-stop on the drive home, asking me questions about the guys and the tour as well as filling me in on how my sisters were. When I was with Lily, she always ensured that I skyped or texted my sisters once a week. They never knew that I needed prompting. Well, I guess they did now since I rarely, if ever, messaged or called them. "Have you seen Lily?" I asked.

When she glanced over at my father, I knew the reason why she had been talking so much. They had hoped to avoid the subject of Paul's death and my ex-fiancée as long as possible.

"They haven't started having visitation yet, but I think people have been going over to their house."

"I want to go the minute we get home."

"Can't you wait and have lunch with us?" Mom asked, her fingers working nervously with the locket around her neck.

I rolled my eyes. "You're doing it again."

"Doing what?"

"Trying to keep me from Lily. You never liked the idea of us."

My dad met my gaze in the rearview mirror. "We just didn't want you to ruin your life by getting too serious too soon. You were too young to be thinking about marriage. Honestly, Bray, you have your whole life ahead of you. Why would you want to shackle yourself down?"

"Why don't you say what you really mean?"

Dad's brows rose. "Excuse me?"

"You don't want me to settle down young because that's what happened to the two of you. Of course, that's really my fault, isn't it? I mean, I was the reason you got married."

"Brayden!" my mother cried, her hand flying to her throat. I almost felt bad when I saw the tears in her eyes.

My dad, on the other hand, clenched his jaw. "Just because you're famous now, I won't allow you to speak to us this way."

"I'm an adult now, Dad. I can say whatever the hell I want to. I'm not that eighteen-year-old kid you threatened to cut off any financial support if I dared to propose to Lily."

Releasing one hand off the steering wheel, my dad pinched the bridge of his nose. I knew he was trying to calm down and weigh his words carefully. After all, they enjoyed the money I sent them from time to time too much to risk pissing me off. "Maybe we made some mistakes in the past. But what we did was out of love," he replied. My mother nodded in agreement.

"If that's true, then I don't want any argument about giving me the car or when I'm coming back. I'm sorry, but I didn't come home to be with you. I came to be with Lily. And if I can, I'm going to get her back. I'm going to buy her a big fucking diamond this time around, and finally make her my wife."

While I'm sure I floored my parents, I was just as surprised by the words that left my lips. Was that what this trip was really about? Getting Lily back? Could just twenty-four hours completely change the person you were the day before? I guess the better question was could I have so easily changed back to my old self in just the span of a day?

My dad cleared his throat. "Okay, son."

I cocked my brows at him. "That's all you have to say?"

"We just want you to be happy, honey," Mom replied.

"I really hope you mean that."

Mom reached back to pat my leg. "We do." After I gave her a small smile, she turned back in her seat. "Oh, I almost forgot to tell you about what happened with your Uncle Sam." She then began rattling on again like nothing had happened at all. Leaning back against the seat, I closed my eyes and willed the car to get us home faster.

BRAYDEN

THE PAST

As I turned onto the familiar road, an agonizing ache tightened in my chest. If I had closed my eyes, I could have found the way there by heart. The two greatest loves of my life had called this road home—my grandparents and Lily. And I had lost them all.

Before I reached the familiar driveway, my foot eased up on the accelerator, and I found myself pulling over. Rolling down the window, I stuck my head out and took a long look at what once had been my beacon in the storm.

More than anything in the world, I wanted to see my Nana shuffling along the front porch, outfitted in one of her house dresses with a green water pitcher in her hand. As she hummed a gospel tune, she would give nourishment to the plants she loved. With a chaw of tobacco in his mouth, Granddad would be sprawled out in a rocker, watching Nana's every move with lazy, hooded eyes, which were drifting between being alert or slipping into a nap. Of course, the moment he heard Nana squeal, "Brayden Michael, get yourself on up here and give me some sugar!" he'd be out of the rocking chair in a flash.

Tears welled in my eyes as I surveyed the empty porch. Only the ghosts of happy memories resided there now. If I stopped by the personal care home, Granddad wouldn't know me. After Nana's sudden death from a stroke two years ago, he had lost his mind. Once the light of his world had been extinguished, he gave up the will to live and retreated into his own shadowy existence where he didn't have to live without his love.

Even though I was only twenty four, I realized more than ever that you could never truly go back home—at least not literally. Sometimes home had to simply reside in your heart.

Easing down on the accelerator, I passed my grandparents' house and headed on to Lily's. Cars lined both sides of the road, and I had to park on the curb a few houses down. I drew in a deep breath to try to prepare me for what I was about to face. I had to worry not only about the suffocating panic that always filled me around death and grief, but also, the fact that I might be met with open hostility by Lily and her family.

I started up the hillside. Even though the funeral wasn't until tomorrow, people still were all outfitted in black. While conversation filled the air, it was silently muted and reverent. I made my way across the yard and pounded up the porch steps.

Craning my neck, I searched the crowd for Lily. As I walked down the length of the porch, my skin burned from the stares of people I'd once known. When I dared to meet some of their expectant gazes, I simply bobbed my head and gave a tight smile. At the moment, I didn't give a fuck if they were thinking I was some sellout for leaving town and not looking back. All that mattered at the moment was finding Lily.

"Brayden?" a voice questioned behind me. I whirled around to see Lily's younger sister, Kylie, staring at me with wide eyes.

"Yeah, it's me," I replied lamely.

"I didn't expect to see you. I mean, with the way things were left with you and Lily, I didn't think you'd have any reason to come..." She shook her head. "Shit, that came out all wrong."

"It's okay." As I cleared my throat, I desperately tried to find the right words. "I had to come if just for Paul. He was..." My voice choked off with emotion. "Paul was a good man. I loved him very much."

Tears shimmered in Kylie's blue eyes—eyes that were so much like her sister's. She reached out for me, and I wrapped my arms around her. "Thank you," she murmured into my ear. After I pulled away, she gave me a sad smile. "He loved you, too. I don't think he ever gave up hope that you would patch things up with Lily."

Kylie's words caused the ache in my chest to grow. The memory of going to him and asking his permission to marry Lily flickered through my mind. The emotions were so strong that I staggered back from the pain. To try and get a hold of my emotions, I asked, "How's Lily?"

Kylie grimaced. "Not well. She hasn't slept or eaten since we got the news. She's refused to see or talk to anyone."

The enormity of Lily's grief didn't surprise me. "Where is she?"

"Holed up on the back porch in Daddy's favorite rocking chair."

"I need to talk to her."

"Good luck with that," Kylie replied. She then motioned me with her hand. After we got into the house, we started weaving our way through the maze of mourners. I spoke to a few familiar faces. When we got to the kitchen, Kylie led the way over to the door that led to the back porch. Kylie took a key from her pocket and unlocked the door.

"Hey, sis, there's someone here to see you," Kylie said.

Lily's body shuddered. "Not now. I don't want to see anyone," her voice, hoarse from crying, croaked.

Glancing at me over her shoulder, Kylie gave me a look like she had tried. When she started to push me back into the house, I shook my head. I'd come too far not to see her.

"Lily," I said softly.

Her gaze jerked from staring out at the yard to mine. Her hand flew to her mouth. The range of emotions that went through her face ran from agony, to hurt, to anger, to elation.

Scrambling out of the chair, she then raced down the length of the porch to meet me. She threw her arms around my neck, burying her face in my shoulder. Her body shook so fiercely with her sobs that my body trembled as well. I wrapped my arms tight around her, cocooning her against me.

"I'm sorry, baby. I'm so, so sorry," I whispered into her ear. I said the words for so many reasons. For the loss of her father just as much for the asshole I was to let her go. As she continued to weep, I couldn't stop feeling so helpless. I didn't know what to say or do.

I just knew I needed to do something to ease her suffering. "Lils, I want you to know if there was anything in the world I could do right now to take your pain away, I would."

"I know," she murmured against my chest.

I rubbed small circles across her back, anything I could think of to give her some comfort. Her crying slowly started to ease. Then she slowly lifted her head to stare into my eyes. "I can't believe you're really here."

"I had to come. Your dad was always so good to me. I considered him a good friend who was taken too fucking soon."

"It would have meant a lot to him. You know, that you came so far just for him."

I shook my head. "It wasn't just for him. I came for you, too."

"You did?"

"Of course, I did."

Her brows lined in confusion. "Even after all this time?"

"A lifetime couldn't erase my feelings for you."

The sound of voices behind us made Lily tense in my arms. "There she is. Lily, honey, why don't you come over here and speak with some of these people?" a woman said. I thought I recognized her as one of Lily's aunts. Maybe her dad's sister.

Lily's anguished eyes met mine. "Take me away from here, Brayden. Please."

Without another word, I wrapped my arm around her shoulder, pulling her tight to me. Then we bypassed the waiting people on the porch and headed down the steps. "Lily? Lily, where are you going?" the woman questioned.

But Lily didn't reply. Instead, she kept her head down as I steered her around the back of the house. When we started for the woods, she glanced up at me. "You're taking me to the treehouse?"

"Is there somewhere else you wanted to go?"

Tears pooled in her eyes. "No," she whispered.

"Look, if it's going to upset you, I'll take you somewhere else."

"Some of the happiest memories I have of you are at the treehouse."

Her words felt like a dagger tearing through my chest. I had just been trying to get her away as fast as I could from well-meaning but irritating family members and mourners. I didn't stop to think that the treehouse probably wasn't a trip down memory lane that we should be taking.

The sounds of bird calls and squirrels scurrying around filled the silence between us as we tromped through the overgrown brush. When I saw the treehouse in the clearing, I exhaled a relieved breath. I had feared it might be gone by now.

"Wait here and let me check it out," I instructed. Lily nodded as I started gingerly up the ladder. The wooden rungs appeared pretty sturdy. When I got to the top, I pushed on the trapdoor. I did a few steps along the floor to test it out. I walked back over to the hole. "It looks fine. Come on up."

Lily came up the ladder, and then I helped pulled her inside. Wrapping her arms around herself, she gazed around the room. "I can't believe how nothing has changed." My gaze fell on the table with the melted candle stubs and lantern. We had them lit each and every time we came here to make love. The air mattress had long since deflated, but blankets still covered it. I spread one out and motioned for her to have a seat.

Once she sat down, her hands ran along the grooves in the floorboard—the grooves I had made with a pocket knife where I etched the date of all the times we had snuck away to have sex. Two teenagers so desperately in love. It seemed like another lifetime.

"What are you thinking about?" she whispered.

"What we used to do here," I answered honestly.

"So was I." With a sad smile, she said, "I'm sure this looks like a real dump to you now."

I shook my head. "I could never think that."

"But you're a millionaire now. You have all the finest things in life. Surely it would be an embarrassment if anyone knew you were hanging out here in some piece of shit treehouse with your inadequate ex-fiancée."

"I sure as hell never said you were inadequate."

"You didn't have to verbalize it. There at the end, I felt it whenever I was with you and from your label's minions." A mirthless laugh came from her lips. "I can only imagine how thrilled they were when we broke up. I bet you're dating some supermodel now, aren't you?"

"I guess I deserve that considering the way I treated you."

"Yeah, you do," she replied bitterly.

"Words are cheap, Lils. You know that better than anybody. I think I could tell you how sorry I am from dusk until dawn, but it wouldn't be enough. You should have actions like me groveling on my knees, begging and pleading for forgiveness, sending you flowers every day. Anything to show you the depth of my regret."

She cocked her brows at me. "You really feel that way?"

"I do."

"When did you come to this epiphany?"

"Not soon enough."

"Exactly when?" she pressed.

"When I heard about Paul."

She sucked in a breath. "So twenty-four hours ago you could have cared less about how you treated me, but then just like that, everything changed?"

"No, it's not like that at all. It wasn't like the day you left I just stopped feeling for you. I was in a fucked up place then. For the first time in my life, I wasn't the responsible one. I was being young and rebellious. Everything was within my reach from money to cars to alcohol. That lifestyle—it fucks with your head. After going through what I did with Tom and Raul, I thought I was stronger than succumbing to temptation of booze."

"I could have helped you be strong, but you pushed me away."

"I know I did. And I'm so fucking sorry I did that." Bringing my hands over my face, I then shook my head. "The truth is that I missed you each and every day we were apart. Most of the time, I would push the thoughts of you away, but sometimes they were harder to do than I thought."

"Every day I kept hoping that you would wake up and realize what you had done. I even had fantasies of you showing up in different places, begging me to come back. But they never came true."

"But I'm here now."

"And what if my father hadn't died? Where would you be?"

"Still lost."

She shook her head. "You wouldn't be here with me."

I growled in frustration. "Dammit, Lily, why does it matter what the reason is? I'm *here*." When she wouldn't look at me, my fingers gripped her chin, forcing her to look in my eyes. "Sometimes it takes a catastrophic event to get you to see the error of your ways. Paul's death did that for me. It showed me at any moment we could be taken out of this world, so you have to live life to the fullest, admit your mistakes, and right your wrongs. That's why I'm here."

Lily stared at me in surprise. "You really mean that?"

"I sure as hell do."

"You hurt me so badly, Brayden," she whispered.

"I know I did. More than anything in the world, I wish I could go back to those months before you left. I would be a different man. I swear that to you." Taking one of her hands, I brought it to my lips. "Just give me a chance, Lily. Please. I beg you. Give me another chance."

"I want to, but I don't think I can. After losing my dad…I don't think I could survive losing you again."

"You won't have to. I swear to God you won't. Please, just give me a chance." Bringing her hand to my heart, I said, "I would crawl through a field of fire and broken glass before I would ever hurt you again."

The agonized expression on Lily's face began to fade. Within her blue eyes, a gleam I hadn't seen in a long, long time burned bright. It took me by so much surprise that I shifted slightly away from her.

"I need you inside me, Brayden."

My eyes bulged at her statement. I shook my head furiously from side to side. "No, no, you don't know what you're saying right now."

"Yes, I do. I'm so dead inside. I want to feel alive again." Her hands came up to cup my cheeks. "Only you have ever made me feel alive."

"I feel the same way about you," I murmured, my resolve slowly fading.

"Then make love to me."

I groaned. "But it's wrong, Lily. You're overwhelmed and grief-stricken. I could never forgive myself for taking advantage of you right now."

With a mirthless laugh, she said, "Oh, now, you become your old honorable self again. How fitting."

"Lily, please. I just swore I would never hurt you again. You know I would do anything to make your pain easier, but I can't do this."

"I'll hate you far more if you deny me, and you will ease my pain by giving me a physical connection." Her hand dropped to my lap, cupping my dick. It didn't need to be reacquainted with Lily. It rose up to greet her like it had missed her. Hell, it probably had. She knew it almost better than I did. As she worked me over my pants, I hissed in a breath. "Give in to me, Brayden."

When she did that special tug that only she knew how to do, I thrust my hips up. That friction was my undoing. I knocked her hand away and tackled her to the floor. I didn't bother getting her out of her dress. Instead, I shoved the hem up her thighs and then jerked down her panties. I fumbled with my belt and zipper. When I finally had my dick free, I didn't bother with any foreplay. I just plowed right ahead.

We both moaned when I thrust deep inside her. She felt so incredibly tight. Almost as tight as when we'd first been together. "Did I hurt you?" I gasped.

"No, you feel so good."

"It's been a long time for you, hasn't it?" I murmured against the shell of her ear.

"Not since you," Lily panted.

I jerked my head up to stare into her eyes with disbelief. Her hands came to cup my cheeks. "There's been no one but you,

Brayden. I don't have sex without love, and you're the only man I could ever love."

Grimacing, I knew I couldn't say the same when it came to being with someone else. I'd whored myself out in the last year trying desperately to forget her. When I stilled my movements, Lily questioned, "Brayden, what's wrong?"

"I'm so fucking sorry that I can no longer say you're the only woman I've ever been with."

"I would have been surprised if you had remained celibate, especially in your profession."

"How can you be so forgiving?"

"Because I know that no matter who you had sex with, you've only slept with me. Right?"

As I stared into her eyes, I wondered how she could possibly guess that with the thirty or forty women I'd fucked over the last year, I'd never actually slept with them. If we ever even made it to a bed, I'd end up leaving or having them leave. Lily was the only woman I'd ever spooned with and woken up to the sunlight streaming across us.

"You're right," I whispered.

"No matter how many women you're with, no one will ever get to have your first but me."

Then I placed a tender kiss on her lips. "No one will ever have my heart but you."

She smiled. "I feel the exact same way. Now make love to me. Please."

"Mmm, I love to hear you beg." I began to flex my hips and slide in and out of her. Being inside her felt like being home again.

Lily's hands slid down my back and grip my buttocks. "Harder, Brayden," she urged.

I gave her what she asked for. Over and over, I pounded into her. I continued right on through the two orgasms she had. Then I finally found relief, spilling myself inside her and crying out, "Lily! Oh God, Lily!"

We lay there tangled together, not speaking and unmoving. When I dared to pick my head up and look at her, I found that she was smiling up at me. "I was afraid you might be having second thoughts after we did the deed," I said.

"No regrets. What about you?"

"None."

"I'm glad to hear that."

Although she looked far more at peace than when I saw her earlier, there was still tension in her eyes. I pushed a strand of hair away from her face. "Lily, I want you to know I'm not going any-where. These next few days I'm going to be by your side every step of the way."

"You really mean that?"

"Yeah, I do."

"I need you so much. I don't know if I can get through the funeral..." Her voice choked off with her sobs.

"I'm here, baby. I'm here."

I don't know how long she cried. My shirt got soaked through with her tears. When she finally finished, her body went limp with exhaustion. I rose up on my knees to tuck my dick back into my pants. I then eased her dress back down her legs. Lily watched me without saying a word. When I finished, I shook out one of the other blankets and then brought it over us. I pulled her to me, wrapping her in my arms.

"Thank you," she whispered. Before I could argue that she didn't need to thank me for a raggedy blanket or taking care of her, she said, "I was thanking God for bringing you back to me."

Her words overwhelmed me. I had such a range of emotions crisscrossing my body. Anger, remorse, grief, fear, happiness-it all threatened to burst out of me. Instead, I closed my eyes and let myself fall asleep with the woman I loved—my other half, my soulmate.

BRAYDEN

THE PAST

After so many years of performing, I rarely ever get nervous anymore. But as I sat in the front pew with Lily and her family, my nerves shifted into overdrive at the thoughts of singing at Paul's funeral. I hadn't anticipated being asked to sing. Anything related to music was the last thing on my mind with Paul's death.

But after Lily and I came back from reconnecting in the treehouse, I went to see her mother. After hugging me so tight I thought she might crack one of my ribs, Marie had asked me if I would sing *Go Rest High on that Mountain.* The Vince Gill song had been a favorite of Paul's. I'd never been much of a country fan, so I wasn't very familiar with the song. Of course, there was no way I could tell a grieving widow no, even if she had asked me to sing while playing the tambourine.

I didn't go back to my parent's house that night. Instead, I stayed at Lily's, and for the first time in our relationship, I got to sleep with her in her teenage bedroom. When she had finally nodded off, I'd gotten my iPod and headphones to listen to the song on repeat. I knew I had to give it all I had for not only Marie and Lily, but for Paul as well.

By the day of the funeral, I had perfected the music and vocals. No one but the immediate family even knew I was going to be singing. We had kept the information close to the vest, so the media wouldn't get word of it and make some kind of spectacle. The local news stations had been covering the story and focusing on Paul's heroism. I could only imagine what he would be thinking if he was alive to see it all.

When it came time to leave the funeral home for the church, the stoicism Lily had shown so far that day faded, and she became distraught. I thanked God I was there for her because I don't know how she would have made it alone. When I started down the aisle of Roswell First Baptist, I had my arm wrapped around Lily's shoulder. She leaned into me, weeping against my chest.

Once the family was seated, the minister began the service. I momentarily zoned out until I heard my name being called. When I didn't immediately rise from seat, Lily nudged me. On wobbly legs, I finally headed for the pulpit where my guitar waited for me. After strapping it on, I stared out into the packed church. There were so many mourners that the doors were opened, and I could see people spilling out onto the yard.

Clearing my throat, I said, "Paul's family asked me to sing one of his favorite songs. It doesn't surprise me that it was a country song. I was just sixteen when I first met Paul, and every time I was at his house, he had the radio on to a country station." I locked my gaze with Lily. "When someone dies, those who knew them often only focus on their good points. But when it comes to Paul, I'm not sure he had any faults. He could have hated me for dating his daughter, but he didn't. We struck up an early friendship that last over the years. While he could have had his doubts about my career path and how I would support his daughter, he never vocalized those to me. Instead, he always encouraged me to chase my dreams as long as I could." I swallowed the growing lump in my throat. "Two years ago, I sat down with Paul to ask for Lily's hand in marriage. He not only gave me his permission, but he gave me such wonderful advice. Unfortunately, I didn't heed that advice, and I let my newfound fame and fortune ruin the best thing in my life." No longer able to fight my tears, I continued on. "I hadn't talked to Paul in over year. I know the greatest regret of my life will be that I didn't get the chance to talk to him one more time to tell him how much his love and support had mean to me. Most of all, I would tell him that I fully intended on doing right by his daughter and to take in all the words of advice he had given me."

Lily's gut-wrenching sob in the front row almost broke me. But I pushed on ahead and began strumming the opening chords of the song. Although tears streaked down my cheeks through most of the words, I didn't mess up or sing off-key. When I finished, I felt like I had given my all. Although it felt oddly out of place, applause accompanied me back to my seat. "That was so beautiful, Brayden," Lily whispered in my ear.

"The song?"

"Everything."

"I meant every word."

She squeezed my hand and then burrowed close to my side. "I know you did," she finally replied.

After the funeral and graveside service, we went back to Lily's house. Once again, it was overrun with family and friends, and once again, we escaped to the treehouse. I let Lily take the lead and decide how we would spend the afternoon. Surprisingly, she began to ease me out of my suit the moment we got up the ladder. When I started to protest, she brought a finger over my lips. "I need to be as close to you as I can right now."

"If you're sure."

She smiled at me before sinking to her knees. When she took me in her hand, I groaned. She worshipped me with her tongue and mouth until I felt I would explode. Thankfully, she eased back and then I dropped down beside her on the blankets. I made quick work of getting her out of her dress.

Instead of diving right in like I wanted to, I took my time palming and kneading her breasts, licking and sucking the nipples into hardened points, and then finally burying my tongue deep between her legs. After she cried out my name and came around my tongue, I gripped her hips and brought her across my lap to straddle me.

She set a slow, sensual pace where we kept our eyes locked with one another. She sought out my hands, which were at my sides, and then she intertwined our fingers together. I realized in that moment what a complete fool I had been. Money, cars, fame—none of it compared to being with Lily. How could this beautiful and amazing woman find it in her heart to forgive me? I didn't deserve it, and I would sure as hell make it my life's work to love her with the respect and adoration she deserved.

We came together, sharing the moment of absolute pleasure. Afterwards, Lily rested her head against my chest, her fingers tracing over the tattoo. "You didn't get it removed," she whispered.

"I thought about it. Even made two appointments to go get it covered it. But I couldn't." I kissed the top of her head. "I think the universe or God was trying to tell me something with that one."

Propping up on her elbow, Lily rested her head on her hand. "And what was that?"

"That you were meant to be written over my heart just the same as you were meant to stay in my heart."

Tears pooled in her eyes before spilling over cheeks. "Fuck, I didn't mean to make you cry."

She shook her head. "They're happy tears really."

"They don't look it to me."

She hiccupped a laugh. "Well, they are." At what must have been my continued skeptical expression, Lily drew in a breath. "I never imagined in the last year that you still actually cared about me. When you never called but that one time or came to see me after I left you in California, I figured you had totally and completely moved on. It never occurred to me that you might be missing me."

"Trust me, I did. Even in my new asshole form, I did."

She grinned. "I'm glad to hear that."

After a few moments of not speaking, Lily's rumbling stomach interrupted the silence. "I think we need to get you something to eat."

"I'm fine."

"No, you're not. You need to eat."

"But I would rather lie here with you." Her bottom lip poked out in her usual pout. "You'll be leaving me tomorrow, won't you?"

A ragged sigh escaped my lips. "I do have to get back."

"God, I'm going to miss you," she moaned.

An idea popped in my head, and I acted on it. "Come back with me."

Lily's brows shot up in surprise. "What?"

"You heard me."

"You want me to come on tour with you?"

"Yeah, why the hell not?"

"Do you really think that's a good idea? I mean, we just got back together. Do we really want to jump right back in the frying pan, so to speak?"

I laughed. "It's something we'll have to face eventually. Why not get it over with now?"

"I guess you're right."

"Can you get away from teaching?"

Lily nodded. "I have the rest of the week off. Of course, my principal told me to take as long as I needed."

"Then there's no reason why you shouldn't come." When she started to protest, I shook my head. "It'll be good for you to get away. It won't do you any good to be sitting around the house right now."

Lily's chin trembled. "You're right."

"So is that a yes?"

She gave me a tentative smile. "Yes, it is."

With a whoop, I rolled us over and began kissing her madly.

LILY

THE PAST

Our plane landed in Vegas around noon. After we got our luggage and headed to the chauffeured driven car, my excitement started to wane. It was replaced by apprehension and fear. Brayden reached over and took my hand in his. "It's going to be all right."

"I hope so."

"What are you worried about? What the guys are going to say?"

"Maybe a little." Deep down, I wasn't worried about AJ or Rhys. They had always been so kind to me, especially when Brayden was treating me horribly. Mainly I was worried about Jake, along with Runaway Train's handlers like Marcus, who had never liked me. Well, there was a time that Jake had been just as sweet and kind to me as the others, but then something had changed when Brayden and I got engaged.

Rolling the window down, I stuck my head out to take in the sights of the Strip. "This is amazing!" I cried, as the slight breeze blew my hair.

"It's a seedy shithole really," Brayden replied.

I turned around to grin at him. "What?" he asked.

"That's exactly the kind of thing the old you would have said."

He laughed. "You're making me sound crazy like I had some multiple personality disorder."

"I think it was more an asshole specific syndrome, but I think you'll make a full recovery," I teased.

"I'm glad to hear that. I hope you'll be my nurse and give me the best care you possibly can."

I reached over to kiss him. "I'll do anything in the world for you."

"And I'll do everything I can to make up for being such a heartless bastard."

"I'm glad to hear that."

The car pulled into the Bellagio. When I walked open-mouthed through the lobby to the elevators, Brayden couldn't help laughing at me. Of course, he also found it funny when I ran in to some people while staring up at the ceiling. "Sorry," I mumbled, my cheeks warming with the extreme mortification I felt.

On the elevator ride up, Brayden took my hand in his and squeezed it. I'm sure he could tell how apprehensive I was about seeing the guys again. When the elevator dinged on our floor, he practically pulled me along behind him. He stuck his key card in the door, and then opened it.

Drawing in a deep breath, I followed Brayden into the suite. "You guys better be decent. I have a guest," Brayden shouted.

"Since when does one of your 'guests' care about seeing a fabulous cock?" AJ asked, with a laugh.

I couldn't help feel a twinge of hurt and pain knowing that Brayden had brought other 'guests' to their hotel rooms. That was the reality, something I would have to learn to accept and forgive. Thankfully, AJ had known Brayden was bringing me back, otherwise his comment would have caused me to want to turn and leave given his acceptance of a 'guest' when he had known Bray had gone to see me after my dad's death

I stepped out from behind Brayden. "Please, keep it covered. I don't want the fantasy of your ten inch wonder dick to be shattered for me."

With a teasing smirk, he winked at me. "You always could see right through me." He came barreling forward to pull me into his arms. He hugged me tight, and I buried my head on his shoulder, inhaling his special scent. It felt good to be held by him.

"I missed you," I murmured.

"Man, have I missed you too! Bad!" When he pulled away, he grinned. "Do you know that no one can make pancakes like you do?

Not to mention none of the girls will clean up after us. You would think after I just rocked a chick's world, she would oblige me in cleaning."

I laughed. "I can't imagine why they would say no."

"Me either." He pushed the hair out of my face, his expression waning serious. "I'm so sorry about your dad."

"Thank you."

"I want you to know that I went to mass and lit a candle for him."

"You did?" I asked, my voice choking with emotion.

"I sure did. Both in Phoenix and here. And let me tell you. Finding a church around here isn't easy."

I smiled. "I wouldn't imagine it would be." I reached up and kissed his cheek. "Thank you, AJ. Thank you for being one of the kindest and most genuine guys I know. You're going to make a lady very happy one day."

He winked. "I already do."

Rolling my eyes, I replied, "I don't mean with sex. I mean, the girl you settle down with."

"Ah, yeah, that one. Give me a few more years before I go that route, okay?"

"I will."

"Hey Lily," Rhys said behind us. I whirled around from AJ to go to his waiting arms. He squeezed me tight, which for Rhys was saying a lot. "So sorry about your dad."

"Thank you." When I pulled away, I smiled at him. "Thank you for the check."

He shifted uncomfortably on his feet. "I don't know what you're talking about."

And that was one of the reasons I loved Rhys so much. He came from his own private wealth before the band, but he never wanted to brag about it. He also gave to people in need not to look good, but because he truly believed they needed it. "It'll really help my mom out a lot. She asked that I thank you, too."

"I'm glad," he murmured softly.

I bestowed a kiss on his cheek too. "You better come over here and give your man a kiss after showing these guys so much love," Brayden said.

I turned away from Rhys just as Jake came out of one of the bedroom doors. He momentarily froze when he saw me.

"Well, well, if it isn't our very own Yoko Ono," he said. Although there was a teasing lilt in his voice, I didn't like being referred to as someone who broke up a band because of her hold on her man.

I strode past Brayden to stand right in front of Jake. His cocky little grin set something off in me. I then did something that I would have never imagined doing before, but my grief, coupled with the last eleven months, was a volatile mixture.

I slapped him.

Hard.

"That's for all the times I sat back and let you treat me like shit! And don't you *ever* demean Brayden's and my relationship again! I'm sorry that you're so self-absorbed that you've never been able to give yourself to somebody else. Maybe one day you'll wake up and see what an egotistical asshole you really are!"

When I finished my tirade, silence echoed around me. I could even hear the sound of the maid vacuuming down the hall. I cut my eyes over to AJ and Rhys, taking in their wide-eyed, open-mouthed expressions. I'd really done it now.

As I braced myself for Jake's retaliation, he merely nodded. "I think you pretty much nailed it, Lils." He turned and walked to the door of the suite. When he got there, he paused. "I really was just teasing you before. You really aren't Yoko Ono. You're way more Paul's Linda. She kept him together, just like you keep Brayden. Hope you guys don't fuck things up again."

And then he was gone. "Well, that was intense," AJ said, breaking the silence.

Covering my face with my hands, I groaned. "I can't believe I did that." When I peeked through my fingers at the guys, they were all still staring at me in surprise. "I'm sorry. That was wrong of me."

Rhys shook his head. "No, Lils. After the way he treated you, he deserved that."

"I agree," AJ replied.

"Really?" I asked.

AJ nodded. "He needed a strong woman to put him in his place. I guarantee you gave him something to think about."

"Well, I could have gone about it differently. I've never hit a man in my life."

With a snort, Brayden said, "That is so not true. You've hit me plenty...especially in bed."

While AJ and Rhys thought his comment was hysterical, I merely proved Brayden's point by smacking his arm. "Easy killer, I have to play with this arm tonight."

Eyeing his expensive looking watch, Rhys said, "Yeah, we better get over to the MGM Grand for rehearsals."

Before I could argue that I would stay here in the hotel and relax, Brayden was dragging me along behind him. Jake appeared to have left without them, so I piled in the limo behind AJ and Rhys.

"So how long are you guys in Vegas?"

"Three nights and three shows."

"Wow, that's intense."

AJ flashed me a wicked grin. "Yeah, well, that's what happens when you become famous rock stars."

I laughed. "I'm glad to see it hasn't changed you."

With a wink, he replied, "Nope, I'm still the same guy I was when we were traveling around on the old clunker bus."

"I hope so." Glancing between him and Rhys, I said, "I don't think I could have bared it if you guys had changed."

Realizing that all the talk of change was a bit of a sensitive subject, Brayden quickly steered the conversation in another direction by rolling the window down and showing me more of the sights along the strip.

When we arrived at the MGM Grand, I was surprised he didn't pawn me off on some of the handlers. Instead, he kept his arm around my waist and led me inside. "While we're rehearsing, you can sit down in the front row."

"Are you sure?"

"Of course I am." He gave me a beaming smile. "I can't wait for you to see the show tonight."

I returned his smile. "Me, too."

A roadie in a headset came up to us then. "Bray, we need you out on stage."

He nodded. "Can you please take Lily down to the first row?"

"Sure."

Brayden leaned over and gave me a kiss before he headed off. I was happily surprised by how attentive he was being to me now that we were back in his world. Once I took my seat, I bounced my leg anxiously as I awaited the guys to take the stage. When Jake came out, his gaze instantly went to mine. Instead of a sneer or smirk, he just merely nodded his head at me. The next thing I knew the guys had taken their places and began to warm up.

I don't think I moved during the next half hour. I was that mesmerized. After all the bars and small venues Runaway Train had performed in, it was really amazing seeing them on a huge stage. I could only imagine what it would be like later tonight with all the lights and then the screaming fans.

When he was done, Brayden immediately came down to find me. "What did you think?"

"Amazing. Seriously amazing. I can't imagine how much better it will be tonight."

A wide grin stretched across his cheeks. "Really?"

"Yeah, really." I gave him a lingering kiss. "You make me very proud."

"Thank you, babe." He pulled me against him and gave me a kiss that had my toes curling. When he finally pulled away, we were both panting.

"Anywhere around here where we can be alone?" I questioned, wagging my eyebrows.

He laughed. "I think I can find someplace."

"Then let's go."

After a storage-closet quickie, Brayden and I emerged to find the band looking for us. When we got into the main dressing room, the guy's eyes widened at the sight of us. My face immediately felt like it was in flames as I tried to smooth down my hair and clothes.

"We were just going to grab some dinner in the restaurant before the show," Jake said.

"Looks like you two have already had dessert," AJ added, with a smirk.

"Shut up," Brayden grunted, while I wished the floor would open up and swallow me whole. It was going to take some time getting used to being around four men again, especially when it came to the free for all of discussing sex.

Trying to change the subject, I said, "Yes, let's eat. I'm starving."

"Guess you worked up quite the appetite," Rhys mused.

At my humiliated squeak, the guys dissolved into laughter. "Damn, it's good having her back," AJ said, as he started out of the dressing room.

When I met Jake's gaze, he smiled, "Yeah, it is good having her back."

LILY

THE PAST

I was half-way in between consciousness and sleep when the hotel curtains were unceremoniously shoved aside and intense desert sunlight streamed into the room.

With a groan, I rolled over onto my stomach, burying my face in the pillow. "It can't be morning already," I muttered.

The bed dipped as Brayden came to sit down. "I forgot how much you weren't a morning person."

"It's not just that." Turning my head on the pillow, I peered up at him. "I only have today left with you before I have to leave."

Brayden's amused expression faded. Scratching the back of his head, he asked, "Can't you take another week off from school?"

"I could, but I probably shouldn't." I reached out to cup his cheek. "I wish I could stay in this hotel room with you for forever."

He brought his hand up to cover mine. "I really don't want you to go, Lily."

"You're not making this any easier."

His expression darkened. "How the hell am I supposed to act? I just got you back. I don't want to lose you again."

Rising up on my elbows, I leaned over to kiss his lips. "You're not going to lose me. Just because I have to go back home, I'll still be right here." I touched the bare skin over his heart.

"That's not good enough," he whispered.

"What do you mean?"

Burning intensity shone in Brayden's eyes. "Marry me."

My heart fluttered at his words, but I tried my best to keep calm. We'd just reconnected after almost a year apart. Everything seemed to be happening at warped speed. "You know, I'm having an odd sense of Déjà vu," I teased, trying to lighten the moment.

Brayden smacked my ass playfully. "I'm serious, Lily."

"How was I to know that? Besides, you're not treating this seriously since you just smacked me."

"Do you want me to get down on my knee again because I will? I'll do anything in the fucking world you want me to if you'll just be my wife."

His words and his earnest tone sent tears springing to my eyes. "Oh Brayden."

"Is that a yes?"

I nodded my head emphatically as I swiped the moisture from my cheeks. "Yes, I want to marry you, too." I leaned over to bestow a soft kiss on his lips. "I really never stopped wanting to be your wife. At least the wife of the person you once were." Leaning my forehead against his, I said, "Thank God, that man is back."

"I promise you he's never, ever going to leave you again."

"I believe you. I really do."

Jerking on my arm, Brayden tried to pull me out of the bed. "Let's go tell the guys the good news."

"Um, have you forgotten you're naked?"

He gave me a sheepish grin. "Okay, let's go shower together, get dressed, and then we'll tell the guys. After that, we'll go ring shopping. I don't want you leaving Vegas without us making it official."

I laughed. "You're really serious about this, aren't you?"

"Yeah, I am. We're getting married, and the sooner the better."

"I like that idea a lot."

"Then let's get going."

"I can't help but point out that I don't think the guys are going to be as excited as you are about us getting married. Well, AJ and Rhys will be happy for us, but I doubt Jake will."

Brayden appeared contemplative. "He might surprise you and come around."

"Really?"

He nodded.

The more I thought about Jake, the more a thought began to roll through my mind. "Let me talk to him first."

Brayden's brows shot far up into his hairline. "Are you insane? You think I'm going to leave you alone in a room with Jake after you slapped him?"

"I can keep my cool." Leaning up, I gave him a reassuring kiss. "Trust me."

He rubbed the stubble on his jaw before he finally nodded his head in agreement. "Okay. But I'll be right outside the door if you need me...or if Jake needs me"

I grinned. "I can handle that."

Brayden then dragged me into the bathroom. After our shower that got way hotter than the scalding water, I slipped into one of the nicer dresses I'd brought with me before sliding into my black knee boots. It wasn't that I was dressing up for my talk with Jake, but more about the fact, I didn't want to look homeless when Brayden took me ring shopping.

When I came out of our bedroom, I found AJ and Rhys lounging around on the couch and loveseat. At the sight of me, AJ gave me a beaming smile. "Oh good, you're up. I'm starving."

I couldn't help laughing at him. "Then I hope you know the number for room service."

He gave me his best puppy dog expression. "But no one cooks pancakes like you, Lils."

"While incredibly flattered, I'm going to have to pass today." Glancing around the room, I then asked, "Where's Jake?"

Rhys snorted. "Toning his masterful physique down in the gym." "Thanks."

When I started to the door of the suite, AJ hopped up. "You're, uh, not going down there to talk to him alone, are you?"

I couldn't help rolling my eyes. "Honestly, first Brayden and now you think I can't be alone with Jake. I appreciate your concern, AJ, but Jake and I need to clear the air."

AJ and Rhys exchanged a glance. I had a sneaky suspicion they might follow me downstairs. "Brayden has some news he wants to tell you."

"He does?" AJ asked.

"Yeah, he'll be out in a minute." With that, I slipped out the door and got on the elevator. On the ride down to the fitness center, I tried to still my nerves. This had to be done. Jake and I couldn't continue to go on like we had, especially not now with Brayden and me getting married.

When I reached the gym, I searched the occupants for him. Just as I was about to leave and go back to the room, I saw the door leading out to the pool and sauna. Jake was gliding under water as he did laps.

Walking around the edge of the pool, I sat down on one of the chairs and took my boots off. Then I eased down on the concrete edge and dipped my feet in the water. As Jake neared me, he jerked his head out of the water. "Hi," I said.

"Hey." As he pushed his wet hair back, he glanced around. "What are you doing down here by yourself?"

"I needed to talk to you."

His brows rose in surprise. "The other day wasn't enough to get your point across?"

I grimaced. "I'm sorry about hitting you."

Jake came to rest his arms on the edge of the pool. "Don't be. I sure as hell deserved it and then some." He gazed up at me. "So what did you want to talk to me about?"

"Brayden and I are getting married."

A range of emotions flickered in his eyes before he finally smiled. "Congratulations. I'm really happy for you guys."

"You really mean that?"

"Yeah, I do." At what must have been my skeptical gaze, Jake sighed. He pulled himself out of the water to sit by my side. "If you had asked me that question a week ago, I would have said no I wasn't. But I was being my usual stupid, selfish asshole self."

Gripping the edge of the pool, I swirled my feet around in the water. "Why do you hate me?" I finally asked.

"I don't."

"Jake, please, I need for you to be honest with me."

Brushing his hand over his face, Jake asked, "Bray didn't tell you about our conversation before he left for Georgia, did he?"

"No. Why?"

"Shit," he muttered. He stared down at his hands for a few seconds before glancing back at me. "I never hated you, Lily. The truth is I hated myself because I cared about you more than I should."

I don't think anything else so shocking could have come out of Jake's mouth. For a moment, I almost wished he had admitted he hated me. I could have worked with that. But learning what he really felt was overwhelming. "How long did you feel that way?"

He shrugged. "A year. Maybe longer."

"Why didn't you ever say anything?"

With a snort, he replied, "Just exactly what was I supposed to say? 'Hey Bray, I like your girl, and I think she should ditch her high school sweetheart and take up with me. Hope this doesn't cause any hard feelings between you and me'."

"I guess you're right."

"It wasn't like I was heartsick and pining away for you, Lils. I just grew to like you more than I should. Then when Brayden started to change, I thought it would be so nice not having you around anymore."

"Ouch," I murmured.

His smile didn't reach his eyes. "I'm an asshole, remember?"

I shook my head. "That's just it, Jake. You can be a really sweet and caring guy. I don't know why you sell yourself short and let the jerk side of you come out so much."

"I don't know either." He reached over and took my hand in his. "I'm so fucking sorry for hurting you, Lily. You never deserved any of the shit I gave you. I don't know why I acted the way I did. I should have just manned up and moved on, appreciated the relationship that we had. But I seem to have a special gift for fucking things up."

"Thank you. Your apology means a lot. I really mean that."

"I promise you that things will be different when you come out on tour with us. You can count on me to do whatever I can to make you feel comfortable."

"I would like that a lot."

He smiled. "This last year without you has been pretty much shit for Brayden."

"It has? I figured he'd been living it up, having the time of his life."

"He did enjoy it all for about a couple of months. But then I think he began to realize it wasn't all he thought it would be. More than that, he started realizing what he had lost. Like me, he's a stubborn jackass who hates to admit when he's wrong. So he just kept going through the motions." Jake shook his head. "He's been so fucked in the head he hasn't been able to write anything since you guys broke up."

I gasped. "Seriously?"

"Why is that so shocking to you? You're his muse, Lily. The person that got him writing songs to begin with. It makes sense that when you were gone, he lost his gift."

"I had no idea. I knew you guys put out a new album a month or so after we broke up."

"All those songs he had already written. Most of what is going on our new album is stuff I wrote."

"I see."

"But he needs you for way more than just songwriting."

"I would hope so," I replied, with a teasing smile.

"You're his soul mate, Lily. He's never going to be any good without you."

My breath hitched at his words. "You really mean that, don't you?"

"I do."

"It works both ways. I'm never any good without him either."

"Then it was high time you two got back together, wouldn't you say?"

"Yeah, I would."

Brayden appeared suddenly behind us. "Everything okay?"

I smiled up at him. "We're fine."

"I'm glad to hear that."

Releasing my hand, Jake then rose to his feet. "I'm very happy for you, Bray. I wish you all the happiness in the world," Jake said, before offering his hand to Brayden.

Brayden grinned before taking Jake's hand. Then he drew Jake to him for a bear hug. "Thanks man, that means so much to me—to both of us."

"You're welcome." Jake glanced between Brayden and me. "You both deserve to be happy."

After echoing our gratitude, Brayden held out his hand to me. "We need to go pick out a ring."

"You know I'd be perfectly happy with the one I had before," I protested.

"I know, but I want us to start fresh."

I rolled my eyes. "You just want an excuse to buy me a big diamond."

Brayden laughed. "Well, that, too."

"So when is the wedding?" Jake asked.

"Tomorrow," I said, as Brayden replied, "Today."

Sweeping my hand to my hip, I said, "I cannot possibly be ready to get married by this afternoon."

"And why not?" Brayden questioned.

"Because I need a dress and time to get ready. Besides, we don't even know which chapel we're going to."

"Yes, we do."

Cocking my head at him, I demanded. "Oh, which one is that?"

He rolled his eyes like he was appalled I didn't automatically know. "The Graceland Chapel."

"You want us to get married at a chapel where an Elvis impersonator officiates the ceremony?"

"Hell, yeah. You know how much I love Elvis. I mean, he's second only because of the Beatles."

"Babe, I'm a huge fan of Elvis, too. I'm just not sure that's exactly what I had in mind when it came to my wedding."

Brayden grinned. "Lily, we're eloping in Las Vegas. Whatever you thought your wedding was going to be like, it's not."

I sighed. "You're right. Okay, the Graceland Wedding Chapel it is."

Pulling me into his arms, Brayden then gave me a long and sweet kiss. "Thank you. Now can we go find your ring?"

"Yes. Then I'll look for a dress for our wedding tomorrow."

"Fine, fine. I've waited this long. I guess I can wait less than twenty-four hours."

With a laugh, I said, "I'm glad to hear it."

LILY

THE PAST

A soft knock came at the dressing room door of the Graceland Chapel. "Go away, Brayden. Even though Elvis is marrying us, I'm still clinging to some traditions, so I'm not going to let you see me right before the wedding!" I shouted.

"It's Susan Slater—Jake's mother," came the muffled reply.

Mortification rocketed through me that I had just been yelling at a perfect stranger. I threw on my robe and hurried to the door. When I threw it open, I gave the tall, graceful woman standing before me my most apologetic smile. "I'm sorry for yelling at you."

She grinned. "It's okay. These boys usually need some yelling to keep them in line."

"That's true," I replied, with a chuckle. Motioning to the room, I asked, "Won't you come in?"

"Thank you." After she stepped across the threshold, I closed and locked the door back. We stood there in an awkward silence for a moment. When I once again realized I was just in my robe, I pulled the lapels tighter against my chest.

"I didn't know you were in Vegas."

Susan smiled. "Jake flew me out here for my birthday tomorrow. He knows with my dancing background how much I've always wanted to see Cirque de Soleil, so we're going to the different shows together."

"That's awfully sweet of him."

"He is always doing the sweetest things for me." Susan then closed the gap between us. Taking my hands in hers, she squeezed them. "Jake asked me to come and see how you were doing."

"He did?"

She nodded. "He was worried you might be having a hard time getting ready on your own—you know, without your mother and sisters."

With sobs rising in my throat, I could merely nod my head in reply. One of Susan's hands came to softly cup my cheek. "Jake is my only child—the long awaited answer to my prayers. I won't have a daughter to help on her wedding day, so it would be my honor to be with you."

Tears stung my eyes at her kindness. "Really?" I whispered.

"Yes, really."

"I-I w-would really love for you to help me get r-ready," I hiccupped through my tears.

Susan laughed. "Oh honey, looks like you've got the pre-wedding jitters."

I shook my head. "I swear I don't have cold feet. There's nothing in the world I want more than to marry Brayden."

"Just because you're overly emotional it doesn't mean you've got cold feet." Her expression softened. "It's only understandable you would be teary considering what you've just been through."

My eyes widened in surprise at the fact she knew about my dad. Score another point for Jake's sensitive side that he had thought enough to tell his mom. "He would've loved the fact I'm eloping."

"Really?" Susan questioned.

With a giggle, I replied, "He always joked that on a chief of police's pay, he would never be able to afford weddings for all of his daughters, so we better start thinking of eloping." As I repeated his words, my father's smiling image appeared in my mind so crystal clear he could have been standing right in front of me. My hand flew to my mouth to try to stop the desperate sobs building in my throat. Without a word, Susan drew me into her arms. Instead of chiding me about how I was going to mess up my makeup or look horrible with blood-shot eyes and a red nose, she just let me cry. Her hand rubbed reassuring circles over my back as my body shook from the emotions ravaging me.

"That's it, sweetheart. Just let it all go," she murmured.

And I did just as she told me to. My heart felt incredibly bruised and broken by the sheer enormity of pain it was holding. It felt as though a large chasm had formed, a gaping, agonizing hole. Having Susan hold me and just let me grieve provided the release I desperately needed—the one I had been denying myself since the funeral. Being held by a member of my own family was not the same as we were trying to comfort each other. Here, Susan simply let me grieve.

Oh, Daddy, I miss you so very much.

Once I finally wrestled a grip on my emotions, I pulled away. Giving Susan a shy smile, I said, "Thank you for letting me do that."

"Don't be afraid to keep doing it either. Our emotions, both good and bad, are what let us know we're alive. You don't ever want to get to the point that you don't feel, especially when it comes to your father." Cupping my chin in her fingers, she smiled. "But at the same time, don't let your grief ruin what is going to be the happiest day of your life. You have your father with you." She placed her hand over my heart. "He's right here, and he always will be."

"Thank you," I repeated again, knowing her words were true, yet still aching for his physical presence just as much.

"You're welcome." Clapping her hands together, she said, "Now, I think it's time we got you ready. Can't have you late for Elvis, now can we?"

I laughed. "No, I don't suppose so."

Taking me by the hand, Susan led me over to one of the plush chairs. She eased me down into it, and then turned back to get my bag. As I twisted my hands nervously in my lap, she did my makeup. Glancing at my reflection in the mirror, I said, "You're awfully good at this."

"It comes from years of being a dancer and then a dance teacher. When I first started out in some traveling ballet companies, we would sometimes do performances in parks where you would have to get ready behind trees. I honed my talent then. It also came to good use later when I opened my own studio. Even the tiniest of ballerinas need some makeup to ensure they look their best under the intense stage lights."

Once she finished, she started brushing my hair in long strokes. When she met my gaze in the mirror, she winked. "I'm even better at up dos."

"I'm so glad you're here and not just for the hair and makeup."

"It's tough being the only girl in the group, isn't it?"

I nodded, which caused a bobby pin to poke me in the head. "Sorry," Susan said.

"It's okay. It's my fault." I smiled. "You know, it's funny because with three sisters, I never imagined I'd ever lament being the only girl somewhere."

"It might sound trite, but I think you're a good role model for the guys."

"I am?"

"Not just for them to be around, but to also make them see how they need a girl just like you."

I snorted. "I'm not sure Jake would ever think something like that, least of all stop being a manwhore for two seconds." When I realized my mistake, I widened my eyes in horror. "I'm sorry."

Susan waved a hand dismissively at me. "You have nothing to apologize for. I know my son and his faults. I just hope and pray that some girl will come along to change him. Then maybe the seeds you've planted along the way will come to fruition."

"I hope so, too."

A loud knock came at the door. "Yo, Lils, you decent?" AJ questioned.

"Well, I—" The door flew open before I could finish. "Guys!" I screeched, jerking on the lapels of the robe.

"Like we haven't already seen you in a robe before," Jake replied.

"I could have been naked, you know," I protested.

Susan laughed as she corralled the boys and pushed them back out the door. "Give me two seconds to get her into her dress, and then you can come in."

Susan unzipped the garment bag. All my life I had envisioned what my wedding dress would look like. I just didn't imagine eloping and having to find a dress last minute. Luckily, I had managed to fall in love with a dress. The satin bottom was form fitted until it flowed out into a small train, and then the beaded bodice came around my neck like a halter top. I'd found it in a designer shop, and thankfully, I had Brayden's credit card on me.

While I felt slightly embarrassed letting Susan see me in my underwear, it was nice having her get me into the dress and zip me up. Standing back from the mirror, tears once again filled my eyes. I truly felt like a bride—a very beautiful bride. "Don't you look absolutely gorgeous!" Susan exclaimed.

"It's because of you."

Susan shook her head. "I just enhanced the overall package, honey. You would be drop-dead gorgeous in a burlap sack!"

I laughed. "Thank you." Jake was so lucky to have this woman in his life. She'd been so wonderful for my heart today.

The door burst open once again, and the guys tumbled in. Their chatter ceased at the sight of me. "Wow," Rhys murmured.

AJ's gaze dipped from my head down to my toes. "Holy shit, Lils! You're fucking stunning!" With a glance at Susan, his cheeks reddened a little. "Sorry, Susan."

"Thank you," I replied, my own cheeks warming because of their compliments and expressions.

Jake took a step toward me, and I couldn't help holding my breath. For some reason, his opinion mattered the most to me. Maybe it had something to do with the rocky road we'd been on since the day he'd first met me. More than anything, I wanted him to acknowledge that what Brayden and I had was the real thing—something he'd never experienced but would one day aspire to.

He cocked his head at me before smiling. "You look beautiful. Absolutely beautiful. You're gonna take Bray's breath away when he sees you."

"Thank you, Jake. It means a lot."

With a wink, he replied, "You're welcome."

"So, are we ready to get this show on the road?" AJ asked, glancing around us. "Cause ol' Bray looked a little shaky when we left him."

"He was?"

AJ nodded. "Pale and pacing the floor."

I swallowed hard. "Like he's having second thoughts?"

A grin spread across AJ's face. "No, it's more like he's scared as hell you're going to jilt him at the altar."

After exhaling the breath I'd been holding, I smacked his arm. "Easy, Bridezilla," he teased.

"You're lucky that Lily doesn't do worse to you," Susan chided.

"She should be used to me by now." Looming over me, he said, "Aggravating people, especially beautiful women, is how I show love."

I laughed. "You're a mess. Always have been and always will be." Standing up on my tip-toes, I bestowed a kiss on his cheek. "But I love you anyway."

"Right back at you."

Groaning, Jake said, "Okay, that's enough of the love-fest. We need to get out there."

"So what do we need to do?" Rhys asked.

Walking over to the table, Jake picked up a basket full of multicolored rose petals. He thrust it Rhys. "You can be the flower girl."

Rhys's dark eyes widened. "Oh, hell no, I won't."

"Look man, you were the last one in the band, so you draw the short end of the stick." Jake shrugged. "That's just the way it is."

Considering how hard Rhys was glaring at Jake, I expected at any moment for Rhys to throw the basket at him. But he didn't. Instead, he gripped the handle of the basket tighter. "This blows."

AJ thumped Rhys on the back. "Aw, but you're such a pretty flower girl."

"Bite me," Rhys snapped.

"So what are you two going to be doing while Rhys is being the flower girl?" I asked.

Clapping his hands together, Jake replied, "Well, I figured AJ would be the ring bearer, and I would give you away."

"Oh, hell no. I'm not carrying some pansy-ass pillow down the aisle!" AJ exclaimed.

Rhys snorted. "It could be worse—you could be carrying this fruity basket."

AJ shook his head. "Besides, I'm the oldest, so I'm the one who should be giving her away."

Jake rolled his baby blues. "Oh please, you're only three months older than me. I hardly think that gives you any rights. Plus, you were an asshole to her for too long."

"I made things right. The only forgiveness I care about is Lily's... well, Brayden's too."

As Jake and AJ stood toe to toe arguing about their roles, I cleared my throat. They both snapped their gazes over to me. "Listen guys, I'm really flattered you both want to give me away, but I was thinking I would just walk alone. You know, as a way to honor my dad."

Jake and AJ mulled over my words for a moment. Then they both shook their heads. "Nope, not happening," AJ said.

"Excuse me?"

AJ closed the distance between us. Placing his hands on my shoulders, he sighed. "If you walk down that aisle alone, all you will be doing is thinking how much you wish your dad could be there and how much you miss him. You won't honor him because you'll be letting his death ruin an amazing moment in your life." One of his hands came to cup my cheek. "He wouldn't want that."

I sucked in a breath at his words. "You're right," I murmured, fighting the tears that filled my eyes.

"Of course, I am," he teased, lightening the moment.

"You really are amazing, you know that?"

"Right back at ya, baby girl."

I leaned up and kissed his cheek. "Thank you, AJ."

"No problem." With a wink, he asked, "So you choose me to give you away, right?"

I couldn't help laughing. "No, I don't." I glanced over at Jake who was watching us intently. "I choose the both of you."

Jake smiled. "That sounds pretty fair."

While AJ nodded, Rhys snorted contemptuously. "Yeah, for you two assholes. I'm the one stuck with the fruity flower basket."

Susan took the basket from him. "I'll be the flower girl."

"But I was hoping you would be my matron of honor," I said.

Her eyes instantly lit up. "Really?"

I nodded. "It would mean a lot to me."

"It would to me, too." She then handed the basket back to Rhys. "Sorry, son. Looks like you're stuck with it."

When Rhys groaned, I stepped over to him as best I could with my gown and train. "Would you really deprive me of walking on rose petals?"

He sighed. "No, I wouldn't."

I leaned in and kissed his cheek. "Thank you, Rhys. I promise I'll make this up to you."

He cocked his dark brows at me. "Does that mean making my favorite meal of fried chicken, fried okra, and homemade cornbread along with a strawberry shortcake from scratch?"

With a laugh, I replied, "Anything for you, flower girl."

"It's a deal then."

Clapping his hands together, Jake once again took the lead. "All right, I think it's time we got this show on the road." As he jerked his head for Rhys to move in front of us, Rhys reluctantly followed his orders. Susan came to stand behind Rhys. Then Jake and AJ offered their arms for me to take.

"Ready?" AJ asked.

I smiled. "I'm more than ready."

Chapter Twenty-Six

BRAYDEN

THE PAST

As I waited for Lily to make her grand appearance, I paced nervously around the altar of the Graceland Chapel. "Easy there, son. Don't want you to wear a hole in the carpet," Elvis said, with a chuckle.

"Sorry."

"It's all right. You're nervous. Happens to most grooms."

"I'm not nervous about marrying Lily. There's nothing in the world I'm more certain of."

"Then what's the problem?"

I grimaced. "Well, I'm afraid I'll never be good enough for her."

Elvis eased his sunglass down his nose to look at me. "Excuse me? I mean, I know who you are."

"You do?"

He nodded. "When you made the reservation, one of the receptionists went crazy. I'm pretty sure when the ceremony is over, she's going to pounce on you for an autograph."

With a shaky laugh, I replied, "Oh, that's fine. I don't mind."

"Like I was saying, you're a rich, famous guy. Why would you worry you wouldn't be good enough?"

I grimaced. "I broke her heart a year ago. Like I was the biggest asshole imaginable even before we broke up. I ignored her, I took her for granted, and I made her feel unworthy." I shuddered. "We've made up, but I'm afraid that she'll never really be able to forget what I did. Like I'll never be able to earn back her full love and trust."

Elvis patted me on the back. "When it comes down to it, most women are far more able to forgive and forget than they should be."

"You think so?"

He nodded. "You just forget what happened in the past. Treat her even better than you did before, and you'll be fine."

"Feels kinda strange getting marital advice from Elvis," I said, with a shake of my head.

He laughed. "You oughta take my advice to heart. Over the years I've been marrying couples, I've seen enough to become a relationship expert."

"I guess that's true."

A woman stepped into the chapel. "They're ready."

"Okay, son, it's time. Take your place."

Adjusting my suit and tie, I then went to stand at the place that had been marked for me. Drawing in a breath, I tried to still my out-of-control nerves. I felt like a complete pansy.

As Jake's mom and Rhys appeared in the doorway, Elvis began to strum his guitar. I'd paid extra to have him serenade Lily as she came down the aisle to *I Can't Help Falling in Love*.

I smiled at Susan as she walked down the aisle. I was so glad she had been here in Vegas so Lily could have a mother figure on her wedding day. If there had been time, I would have flown Marie, along with Lily's sisters, out here for the wedding. But I knew it probably would have been too hard on them after Paul's death.

The appearance of Rhys carrying a lace-covered basket in one hand and then tossing petals with the other caused me to snort with laughter. But one death glare from him silenced me immediately. I don't know how he had gotten roped into being the flower girl.

As Lily appeared in the doorway with Jake and AJ on each side, Elvis began perfectly crooning. "Wise men say only fools rush in. But I can't help falling in love with you."

Jus the sight of her brought tears to my eyes. God, she was so beautiful. She always had been, but something about her in that moment was simply breathtaking. I had to fight the urge to kick myself that this perfect woman was about to be my wife. Even after I had almost ruined things between us, her heart was big enough to forgive me.

I had to swipe my eyes several times before she finally arrived at my side. After Jake and AJ kissed her cheeks, they then went to sit down beside Susan and Rhys. As I took her hand in mine, Elvis sang, "Take my hand. Take my whole life too. For I can't help falling in love with you."

He strummed the final chords of the song. After putting his guitar away, he smiled at us. "Dearly beloved, we're gathered here today to join together Brayden Michael Vanderburg and Lily Marie Gregson."

We went through the vows and then exchanged platinum wedding bands that I had picked up yesterday while Lily went dress shopping. I slid it on over her the diamond engagement ring I'd bought the day before as well. After we'd slipped the rings on our fingers, Elvis smiled, "By the power vested in me by the state of Nevada, I now pronounce you husband and wife. You may kiss the bride."

I didn't have to be told twice. I practically dove at Lily, my hands cupping her face before I brought my lips to hers. I thrust my tongue into her mouth, deepening the kiss. We must have been putting on quite a show because the guys started whistling behind us.

I quickly pulled away to give Lily a sheepish grin. "Sorry about that."

Although her cheeks were red, she laughed. "Don't apologize. That was the best first kiss as a married couple ever."

"I thought it was pretty good, too."

Instead of walking straight on down the aisle, we exchanged hugs with the guys and Susan. Then as Elvis started strumming *Love Me Tender*, we walked out of the chapel as man and wife.

I gave Lily her choice of where we would stay for our Honeymoon night. Instead of the Bellagio, she wanted to stay at the Venetian because as she claimed, "It just seems so much more romantic there."

So after we finished with the necessary paperwork, we all piled into the limo and took off for the Venetian. We had our wedding reception dinner at Zefferino's, one of the restaurants inside the Venetian. I'm sure we would have gotten a few stares considering Lily was still in her wedding dress and veil, but it didn't take too long for fans to spot us. I knew that within a few moments, Lily's and my secret wedding would explode all over social media.

After downing his beer, Jake cocked his head at me. "Any chance you let the label know you were getting hitched?"

"No, I sure as hell didn't. Some of those fuckers cost me my relationship with Lily. I wasn't about to let them try to interfere today." Lily took my hand in hers and squeezed it. I'm sure she was glad I hadn't involved the label handlers either.

He grinned as he shook his head. "Man, I'd love to be a fly on the wall when this shit hits the fan with Marcus and the others."

"You're impossible," I muttered.

After dessert and coffee, we said goodbye to the guys and Susan. Then Lily dragged me over to the canal so we could go on a gondola ride. "You seriously want to do this?"

"Yes, I do. It'll be so romantic."

"At the moment, the most romantic thing I can think of is taking you upstairs and getting you out of that dress," I teased.

She smacked me playfully. "That's not romantic."

With a resigned sigh, I paid for our tickets, and we moved forward in the line. At the sight of us in our wedding finery, people were all too happy to let us go in front of them. We first objected, but after they insisted, we finally inched up. Once we got into our gondola, our driver turned back to the people waiting in line. "Let's give a round of applause for the lovely bride and groom."

A cheer went up through the crowd as people clapped and whistled. "We love you Brayden!" was screamed by two girls at the end of the line.

Ordinarily Lily would have been embarrassed at being called out, but since it was her wedding day, she seemed to be enjoying it. As the gondola glided across the water, Lily laid her head against my chest. "One day will you take me to Venice so I can ride in a real gondola on the canal?"

I smiled down at her. "I think that's a promise I can easily keep. I never knew you wanted to go that much."

She nodded. "I love Italy. I love the idea of traveling anywhere in Europe."

"We have a European tour coming up."

Her brows arched in surprise. "You do?"

"Yep. As my wife, you're more than obligated to come along."

She laughed. "If it works out with my teaching schedule, I'd love to."

At the mention of teaching, I sighed. "What's wrong?" she asked.

"I just hate that you have to go back home in a week. I want you out on the road with me. Can't you quit your teaching job?"

She gasped. "Why would I want to do that?"

"Seriously, Lily, you don't need to work. I make plenty enough money for the two of us."

"But I just started teaching. And I love it."

"Don't you love me more?"

"If you loved me, you wouldn't ask me to choose. You would want me to do the thing that made me happy, just as I supported you all those years."

Deep down I knew she was right. Her dream since we first got together was to be a teacher. I could tell just how passionately she felt about teaching from the way she spoke about it. Leaning down, I kissed her gently. "I'm sorry. You're right. You deserve to do what makes you happy. I can't imagine living a nomadic life on the road with me and the guys would be that thrilling."

"I'll come out to visit you every weekend. I promise."

"And during the summer, you're completely mine. Right?"

She grinned. "Oh yes."

"Good. I'm glad to hear it."

When the gondola ride was over, I happily climbed out and then helped Lily with her dress. I had one thing on my mind, and that was getting the honeymoon started. We would be leaving Vegas in the morning for our next tour stop in Reno, so we had to make use of the time we had.

As I started tugging her toward the elevators, she balked. "What is it?" I demanded.

"I need to do some shopping."

I groaned. "You have got to be kidding me."

Wagging her eyebrows, Lily jerked her head at the store we were in front of. "Oh, okay," I replied, with a smile. She ducked into Victoria's Secret alone. Pacing around outside, I waited for her to make a choice...or several choices. At this point, I didn't need to see her in any sexy lingerie to get me up and running. Right now she could be wearing a burlap sack, and I'd still blow my load. There was something about getting to make love to my wife for the very first time that was so fucking sexy.

After what felt like an eternity, Lily emerged with a bag and a secretive smile. "Now are we ready?"

"Yes, Mr. Impatient, we are."

Taking her by the arm, I once again hurried her to the elevators. Even though I had just been with her last night, I couldn't wait to be inside her again. Of course, this time was monumental because it was the first time we would be making love as husband and wife. It felt a little overwhelming, kind of like the first time we were together.

When we got to the suite, I put the keycard in. After swinging the door open, I grabbed Lily around the waist. "Brayden, what are you doing?" she demanded.

"I'm carrying you over the threshold."

She laughed. "But this is just a hotel room, not our house."

I shrugged. "Doesn't matter. Still wanted to do it." When I set her on her feet, she glanced at me over her shoulder. "Unzip me, so I can go put on your surprise."

"Yes, ma'am," I muttered. I didn't want to just unzip her. I wanted to tear off her dress and start going at it right there on the floor.

Once she was unzipped, Lily slid out of her dress, revealing her strapless bra and underwear. "You're killing me, babe."

"Just wait," she teased before grabbing the bag and running into the bathroom.

I groaned and then started working at getting out of my suit and tie. When I had stripped down to my boxers, I waited patiently on the edge of the bed for Lily to appear. Nothing could have prepared me for when the door opened. It was like an extreme moment of Déjà vu. She was wearing lingerie that looked almost exactly like what she had worn for our first time. "How did you...?"

She smiled. "I was actually going for something in black or red when I saw this." She swept her hands to her thighs. "Real garters this time instead of just the stockings."

"I'm digging them."

With a laugh, Lily crooked her finger at me. "Come here, Mr. Vanderburg, your wife would like to touch you."

"She would?"

"Oh, yes, very much."

I rose off the bed and went over to her. "We really should open a bottle of champagne or something."

"Later," she argued.

"You don't want to take things slow?"

"I want to consummate our marriage."

"Well, I think I can oblige you on that one." I brought my lips to hers in a soft kiss that grew passionate in barely an instant. We tumbled onto the bed in a tangle of arms and legs. Like magnets, my hands went straight for Lily's breasts. I kneaded the sensitive flesh, causing the nipples to harden under my touch. As I began to untie her bodice, Lily ran her fingers through my hair, pushing it out of my face.

When her breasts were free, I dipped my head to suck one of her nipples into my mouth. Lily moaned, scissoring her legs beneath me, searching for friction. While I continued sucking on her nipples, I brought one of my hands between her legs to stroke her over her panties. She arched her hips against me. "Please, Brayden, I want you inside me," Lily begged.

Realizing her need, I slid off her panties and pulled off the bodice. I then rose up sit in the middle of the bed. "What are you—" she began, but I silenced her by lifting her up to straddle me.

"This way I can see you and touch you."

She smiled as she rose up to take me inside her. After I slid all the way down, she began to move on and off of me. As she did, she kept her hands in my hair, her eyes on mine. While I arched my hips to meet her movements, I couldn't keep my hands still. I ran my fingers up and down her spine, I cupped her buttocks to lift her harder on and off of me, and then I stroked her clit until she was screaming my name as she came around my still pumping dick.

It didn't take me long to finish, and I kept my eyes on hers until the very end. When it was over, I collapsed onto my back, bringing her with me. "So what do you think about married sex?"

"Mmm, I think it's pretty amazing." Propping her head up on her arm, she gave me a wicked a look. "I wonder if it's just as good in the Jacuzzi tub or against the wall with the great view of Vegas outside."

I grinned. "I don't know, but you can sure as hell bet we'll try it to see."

BRAYDEN

THE PRESENT

Giovanni shifted the notepad on his lap and reached for a bottle of water. After he took a swig, he motioned to us. "Once again, any time you two need a break, feel free."

I rose off the couch and stretched my arms over my head while Lily took a sip of her Coke. "Yeah, that last bit was a little intense."

At the feel of Lily's hand on my lower back, I turned around. "It's hard reliving it all again. Isn't it?" she asked, softly.

"Only the parts where I was such an asshole." I cringed. "I'm still not sure I deserved a second chance."

"The real you did, and I was happy to give it to him."

"He thanks you from the bottom of his heart." I winked at her as I sat back down. We turned to Giovanni who was watching us intently.

When I cocked my brows at him, he merely smiled. "I'm sorry. It's just in stolen moments like those, I see that you guys really are the real deal, and this isn't just some cleverly spun PR story."

I couldn't help laughing. "No, if I was going to have someone write this, I would sure as hell not have the part where I was a bastard in there."

Lily swatted my arm playfully. "In the end, it's worth it because we see how far we've come, and that what we had was worth fighting for. My dad always said, 'Anything worth having is hard work'."

"That's true. It took some hard work to get us started, but once we did, it was pretty smooth sailing," I replied.

Giovanni nodded. "Let's see. So you guys got married in Vegas, but then I see you had another wedding a month later here in Georgia?"

Lily groaned as she buried her head in her hands. "Yes, that would be correct."

Giovanni glanced from her to me. "Another tough story to relive?"

Peeking at him through her fingers, Lily replied, "Only if you consider that our families were furious with us for eloping and demanded we have a proper church wedding."

"Preferably where Elvis did not officiate," I added.

With a chuckle, Giovanni said, "Oh, I see." His gaze met mine. "Does that mean your parents finally came around about you marrying Lily?"

I nodded. "Yeah, it took them fucking long enough to get with the program. When Paul died, I think they finally realized there was never going to be another girl for me, and that if they wanted to be a part of my life, they would embrace Lily."

"I think it also had to do with the fact they didn't want to miss out on any future grandchildren," Lily said, with a smile.

"That is true. Hell, they've been better grandparents than they ever were parents to me."

"That leads us to another one of my questions. Your son, Jude, was born a little over a year after you got married."

"Fifteen months to be exact," Lily corrected.

Giovanni nodded. "Since you had been together for so many years, did you intend on starting a family right away?"

I chuckled. "Not exactly."

"We always wanted a big family, but no, Jude was a complete and total surprise. One of those birth control failure mysteries." Lily made a face like she didn't like her wording. "I mean, he was very wanted. It's just he was a surprise."

Patting her leg, I said, "At the time, I was only seeing her once or twice a month, so I guess you could say my stored up swimmers were really potent."

Lily squealed, her hands once again covering her face. Giovanni and I both laughed at her reaction. "Hey, it's what happened with the Baby Boomers after WWII. Kinda makes sense it would be the same way for us," I rationalized.

"So you conceived when you weren't actively trying?" Givoanni asked.

"That's right," Lily replied, fanning her reddened face with her hand.

"I like to call it, 'That teeny, tiny .1% of birth control pills non-effectiveness'."

Lily huffed at my side. "Yeah, well, I like to call it an unexpected miracle."

I grinned at her. "Actually, we call him Jude, and even though he's almost twelve and at that know-it-all preteen stage, we still love him."

BRAYDEN

THE PAST

Rolling over in bed, I snuggled closer to Lily's warmth. I lived for the weekends that she got to come along on tour with us. They seemed too few and far between lately. I was going to have to talk to her again about coming out every weekend, rather than every other one. More than anything, I wanted her to quit her teaching job, but she refused. I know it was because she loved what she did so much and had worked hard to earn her degree. But at the end of the day, I was a selfish bastard who wanted her with me twenty-four seven. And it wasn't just my dick that needed her with me all the time either.

Even though we'd been together at least three times last night, I still wanted more of her. The old cliché that absence makes the heart grow fonder was certainly true, especially when it came to my dick. Shifting her long, blonde hair off her shoulder, I then started kissing a wet trail along her neck. My hand slid around her ribcage to cup her breast. When I squeezed it, causing the nipple to harden, she moaned.

Her reaction caused me to buck my morning wood against her backside. Instead of warming up to me, she shifted away. Frowning at her back, I said, "What's wrong?"

"Nothing," she murmured, drowsily.

"Was I too rough last night?"

She shook her head. "I'm just tired that's all."

In our seven years together, she'd never refused me. She was always just as game as I was, especially when I had been gone on the road. Drawing circles on her back with my finger, I said, "Talk to me, Lily."

She glanced over her shoulder. When I saw the tears pooling in her eyes, I sat up straight in the bed. "Oh God, I was too rough last night, wasn't I? If I hurt you, I'm so sorry."

"No, it's not that."

"Then what is it?"

"Please don't hate me."

Her words sent fear crashing from my head down to my toes. "No matter what it is, I could never hate you," I replied honestly.

That statement caused her to burst into tears. Her body shook with the strength of her sobs. Unease prickled over me, and the worst thing I could ever imagine entered my mind. "Is there someone else?" I demanded.

Lily's eyes widened. "NO! No, of course not. How could you think that?"

"You don't want to have sex with me, then you ask me not to hate you, and then you burst out crying. What the fuck am I supposed to think?"

Lily opened her mouth to respond, but then she clamped a hand over it. Throwing back the sheets, she raced from the bed. "You can't go out there naked!" I shouted after her. The last thing I needed on top of everything else was for my bandmates to see my wife naked.

At the slam of the bathroom door, I shot off the bed. When I got to the hallway, a bleary-eyed Jake and Rhys peered out of their roosts at me. Of course, I could still hear AJ snoring. He could sleep through an F-5 tornado. "Dude, what the fuck is going on?" Rhys demanded.

"I wish I knew," I grumbled.

Motioning to the bathroom, Jake gave me a wicked grin. "I haven't heard that much gagging since the last girl who thought she could deep throat me."

I rolled my eyes. "You're a disgusting prick who has delusions of grandeur."

Jake chuckled and then disappeared behind his roost curtain. I rapped my knuckles lightly on the door. "Lils, are you all right?"

Her response came in the form of the toilet flushing. A few seconds passed before the door opened. While her eyes and nose were red from the crying, her face was white as a sheet. She had managed to slip on one of the bathrobes that hung behind the door. Of course, I was still butt naked in the hallway with my junk hanging out. "Babe, are you all right?" I repeated.

"I-I'm pregnant," she stammered.

The world around me came crashing to a halt. Just like the first time I met her and she took me out, I felt the world grow dark around me. No, no, no. Surely, I had heard her wrong. Once I had managed to recover, I demanded, "What?"

"She said she was pregnant," Jake called from behind his curtain.

"I didn't ask you," I growled.

"Then take it to the bedroom." He poked his head out. "And congrats, Hot Mama."

A nervous giggle escaped Lily's lips at his words. "Don't tell me you're happy about me having a baby?" she asked softly.

"Why wouldn't I be? It ain't mine, so I'm thrilled." He stared pointedly at the two of us. "Aren't you happy?"

I threw up my hands in frustration. "This is so fucking wrong! Damn, this bus. There's no fucking privacy!" My voice had raised an octave to where I was practically shrieking. Glancing down at myself, I shook my head. "Fuck, this is surreal. I'm standing here with my balls in the wind for one of the most important announcements in my life!"

"Bray, man, it's—"

"We are so not having this conversation with you!" I shouted at Jake. When Rhys poked his head out of the roost, I jabbed my finger at him. "Or you!" Taking Lily by the hand, I dragged her down the hall to the bedroom. After I slammed the door, I began pacing around the room.

Lily was pregnant. My twenty-two-year-old wife of seven months was pregnant. I was going to be a father. "Jesus," I muttered, raking my hand through my hair.

At a whimper behind me, I turned around. Lily had sat down on the bed and drawn her knees up to her chest. She looked positively grief-stricken. She glanced warily up at me like she expected me at any moment to go utterly batshit on her.

And in that moment, I felt like the biggest asshole imaginable. I mean, what the hell was I doing making my pregnant wife feel like shit? It wasn't like we were back in high school. We had the means to have and take care of this baby. Sure, things with the band were crazy and chaotic, but rock stars had kids all the time. Besides, there was nothing more that Lily and I had ever wanted than to be parents one day. I guess it had come sooner rather than later.

Striding over to the bed, I knelt down in front of Lily. "Baby, I'm so fucking sorry for reacting the way that I did. I was just so surprised."

Her brows shot up. "You're not mad?"

Shaking my head, I replied, "How could I ever be mad about one of my dreams coming true?"

"Oh Brayden," Lily cried, before throwing her arms around my neck. I cradled her trembling body in my arms as she shed what I hoped were tears of happiness. When she pulled away, she smiled at me. "Thank you."

"For being an asshole who made you cry?"

"No. Thank you for loving me no matter what."

I brushed the hair out of her face and then stroked her tear-soaked cheeks. "I'll always fight for you, Lily. I'll always fight for us. Now there's just going to be more of us to fight for."

Lily hiccupped a laugh. "It's still so hard to believe."

"Why didn't you tell me last night?"

"We hadn't been together in so long that I didn't want to ruin it."

"What kind of asshole am I that would make you think a baby would ruin things?"

Her hand came up to cup my cheek. "It's not that. I've been upset myself. We've only been married seven months. You're touring all the time and hardly home. Not to mention, that I just got my first teaching job, and now I'm pregnant. It was like I worked so hard for what?"

"For a college degree that you'll have all your life."

"That's true."

"Besides, you know I hate that you're teaching instead of coming out on tour with me."

"Once again, you have your dream, and I have mine," she countered, softly.

Turning her hands up, I kissed her opened palms. "I know, baby. But there's one dream that we share, and that's each other. Nothing can take the place of that."

"I love you," she murmured.

"I love you, too." I leaned in to place a tender kiss on her lips. When I pulled away, I smiled at her. I reached for the tie of her robe. Her brows lined with confusion when I pushed it open. Bending down, I bestowed a kiss on her abdomen. "And I love you, too," I said to her stomach.

Lily sucked in a breath before her fingers tangled in my hair, and she jerked my head up. "I want you to know you've made me the happiest woman in the world."

"Ditto," I murmured, bringing my lips to hers.

Just as I pushed her back onto the mattress, a loud bang came at our door. "Everything okay in there?" Jake asked.

I groaned. "It was until your nosy ass came knocking!" I shouted.

"I just wanted to make sure Lily was okay."

"Just when I think Jake is a selfish and unfeeling asshole, he goes and redeems himself yet again," Lily said, amusement vibrating in her voice.

"She's fine," I called back.

"Uh, yeah, I'd rather hear her say that herself. You know, so I know there's no coercion."

Lily giggled. "I promise that I'm fine, Jake. Now will you please go away, so Brayden can fuck me?"

As my mouth dropped open in shock at her words, Jake's laughter bellowed outside the door. "You got it," he replied.

Amusement shone in Lily's eyes as she cupped my cheeks in her hands. "I wish you could see your expression right now."

"I'm sorry, but that's the last thing I expected out of your mouth."

"I'd say we're 0-2 on unexpected things said out of my mouth this morning, huh?"

I laughed. "Yeah, I guess so."

"Now come on and make love to your pregnant wife."

"Yes, Mrs. Vanderburg. I'll be happy to oblige you," I said before bringing my lips to hers.

The bus roared down the darkened interstate, taking us from Mississippi into Alabama. Lily lounged on the couch with a pint of chocolate chip ice cream on her lap. Occasionally, Rhys would reach over to dunk his spoon in for a bite. Each time he did, Lily used her spoon like a sword to fight him off. Rhys merely grinned at her antics.

Sitting across from them in one of the captain's chairs, I had a notepad beside me and my guitar on my lap. Jake also had his guitar out.

Lily huffed out a frustrated breath. "You should be ashamed of yourself, Rhys McGowan. Stealing ice cream from a poor, pitiful woman who's forty months pregnant."

"Nice try, Lils. You're only eight-and-a-half months pregnant," he argued, before grabbing another bite.

Lily groaned. "It feels like I've been pregnant forever. I'm so ready for this baby to be born." Glancing down at her belly, she said, "Did you hear that Michael? You can come out now."

"Michael?" AJ questioned, from the kitchen area. "Is that what you guys decided to name him?"

I laughed. "No, that's just the one we're trying this week. Seeing how we like it since it's my middle name."

Cocking her head, Lily said, "Paul Michael Vanderburg sounds very prestigious, don't you think?"

AJ made a face. "Isn't there a hair products dude named Paul Michaels?"

Jake and Rhys snickered as Lily shot Jake a look. "Fine then. Michael Paul. Is that better?"

"A little."

We were on the last leg of a Southern tour that had kicked off in Atlanta and then did a sweep through the Carolinas, Tennessee, Arkansas, Louisiana, and as of last night, Mississippi. After shows in Alabama, we would head home. Because there was no flying involved and she could put her feet up, Lily's doctor had approved her to come along. I didn't like the idea of leaving her behind in her third trimester anyway.

"What do you think about this?" Jake asked, as he strummed a catchy beat.

My brows furrowed. "It sounds familiar."

"How the hell would it sound familiar if it just came out of my head?"

I shrugged. "I don't know. It just does."

"Fine, smart ass. What does it sound like?"

Racking my brain, I then started to strum the melody that was in my mind. Jake snorted. "I so did not just play something that sounded like *Hey Jude*."

"Yeah, you did." The Beatles fan in me kept playing the song not only because I liked it, but because I wanted to aggravate Jake.

When Lily sucked in a harsh breath, I stopped playing. "What's wrong, babe?"

"Nothing is wrong. You wouldn't believe how strong Michael started kicking then."

"Ooh, I wanna feel," AJ said, as he abandoned the arroz con pollo he had been making for us.

She frowned. "He stopped."

"Bummer," AJ muttered.

Absently, I started strumming *Hey Jude* again. Lily started laughing. "He must like the song because he just started kicking again."

My brows shot up. "Seriously?" Wanting to prove the theory, I stopped playing. "Is he still kicking?"

Lily grinned. "No, he stopped again."

With a groan, Jake said, "Jesus, you've already bred another Beatles freak."

AJ motioned to my guitar. "Start it up again, so I can feel him."

Once again, I began playing the opening to *Hey Jude*. This time, I started singing along to. Taking AJ's hand, Lily placed it on her stomach. "Feel him?"

AJ's eyes widened. "That's so fucking cool!" He glanced over his shoulder at me. "Forget a future musician like his pops. I think we have a soccer star on our hands."

"Oh, he knows how to kick. I'll give him that," Lily replied.

Although he tried looking disinterested by it all, Jake asked, "Is he still doing it?"

Lily nodded. "You want to feel?"

Shrugging his shoulders, Jake said, "I guess so." He sat his guitar down and stood up. Leaning over, he put his hand where AJ's had been. A small smile twitched on his lips. "He is strong."

When I stopped playing so I could feel my son kick, Lily dissolved into giggles. "He's stopped again."

Crossing his arms over his chest, Jake smirked at me. "Guess you've got the answer to what to name the kid."

"Jude," Lily and I said in unison.

"Yep, Jude Paul Vanderburg," Jake replied.

And for the remaining two weeks of her pregnancy, whenever we would play *Hey Jude*, our own little Jude would give us a kick or two to let us know he was happy with his name.

Chapter Twenty-Nine

LILY

THE PRESENT

"You were on the road right up until you delivered?" Giovanni asked.

I laughed. "Well, not exactly. We were almost home then. So I had about three weeks before Jude was born."

Giovanni glanced between me and Brayden. "Were you alone for the delivery or was Brayden there?"

With a smile, Brayden said, "Thankfully, we were between tours at the time. Plus, it was right after Christmas, so that's usually a slow season for us."

"And what was it like having your first baby?" Giovanni asked me.

I couldn't fight the smile that lit up my face at the memory of having Jude. "It must be something about his sweet temperament because he was the easiest delivery of the three."

"I think it has something to do with women being difficult," Brayden countered.

"Ha, ha," I replied. Easing back on the couch, a happy sigh escaped my lips. "I remember everything really. How I woke up that morning to find my water had broken."

"I thought she had just peed the bed," Brayden mused.

I smacked his arm. "Anyway, we bundled up and went to Northside Hospital, which coincidentally was the same hospital where Brayden was born. I don't think we were there more than an hour when it was time to push."

Brayden laughed. "Jude was ready to make his appearance that's for sure. With the girls, I think we were there ten or twelve hours before they decided it was time to come out."

"That's true. The girls were a bit more finicky about being born."

"Who all was in the delivery room with you?"

"My mom wanted to be there, so we let her stay in. She was good to stay in the back and let it be about Brayden and me."

"There was probably more than one time that she had to hold my hand to keep me from freaking out," Brayden admitted.

I laughed. "That's true. I'll never forget how pale he was."

Brayden shuddered. "It was seriously scary that first time around. We were both just kids at twenty three. We didn't have a clue really."

"But we made it somehow," I argued.

"Yeah, we did." Brayden shook his head. "I'll never forget how one moment it was just his little blond head there, and then the next he was out and wailing. Seeing him take his first breath, well seeing all my kids take their first breaths, is the most amazing thing to ever happen to me, besides marrying Lily."

Overcome by his words, I couldn't resist bringing my lips to his. Whenever I heard Brayden talk about his children, it made me love him all the more. When I pulled away, I smiled at him. "I love you."

"I love you, too, babe."

When we glanced over at Giovanni, he was smiling at us. "Quite a moment there, eh?"

Swiping the tears from my eyes, I replied, "Talking about our children always does that to me."

"So what was it like when the guys met Jude?" Giovanni asked.

I laughed. "That is a very interesting story."

LILY

THE PAST

After the multitude of Brayden's and my families left the room, I sighed and let my head fall back on the pillow. Exhaustion, like I had never known before in my life, took over my body. It felt like someone had stuck me with a needle and depleted all the energy I had. With a yawn, I glanced over at Brayden. I couldn't help smiling at him as he stood stock-still, watching over a sleeping Jude. "I don't think he's going anywhere," I said, my voice a little hoarse from my previous exertions.

Brayden's hands gently gripped the bassinet. "I know. I just can't stop looking at him." He glanced up at me with tears shining in his eyes. "He's the most perfect thing I've ever seen. To think that I had even a small part in creating him—" a sob choked off in his throat. He shook his head as he swiped the tears from his cheeks. "I'm such a pansy," he muttered.

"No, you're a proud father. And I don't think I've ever loved you more than right at this moment—the one where you wept over your son."

Leaving Jude's side, Brayden came to me. He bent down and bestowed a chaste kiss on my lips. "Thank you for today."

"I could say the same thing to you."

Brayden glanced over his shoulder at Jude. "I was serious about wanting a houseful...or bus full."

"I think it's a good idea *not* to mention another baby to me right after delivering one."

Brayden laughed. "You're right."

When a knock came at the door, I glanced warily over at Brayden. "Just rest, babe. I'll tell whoever it is you're too tired for visitors now."

"But wouldn't that be rude?"

He cocked his brows at me. "Do I look like I give a fuck about what other people think?"

I grinned at him. "No, you look like a man who just won the lottery."

When Brayden opened the door, he didn't get a chance to deliver his spiel and turn the well-wishers away. Instead, Jake, AJ, and Rhys blew past him, their arms laden down with flowers, balloons, and stuffed animals. Without even a hello, Jake demanded, "Well, where is he?"

"Sleeping, jackass," Brayden replied.

"Then wake him up. His uncles are here to see him."

I couldn't help laughing at Jake. Of course, he would have no concept about babies or schedules. All he thought about was himself, so it made perfect sense we should cater to him.

"You're such a dumbass," AJ replied, smacking Jake upside the head. He then came over to me. With a wink, he asked, "Hey Hot Mama, how ya feeling?"

As I pushed myself up in bed, I laughed. "Like I've been run over by an eighteen wheeler."

"Aw, mi amor, you just popped out a kid. I wouldn't expect any less than you feeling like absolute hell. You look a lot better than my sister after my nephew was born." He leaned over and kissed my cheek tenderly.

"Thank you, AJ."

With a wink, he replied, "Anytime."

After Jake sat his balloons and flowers down on the counter, he rubbed his hands together. "Okay, as lead singer, I think it's only fair that I get to hold him first."

"That's total BS," AJ protested, edging in front of Jake.

"Wait your turn," Jake replied.

Brayden glanced at me to survey whether I was onboard with passing our newborn son around. I smiled and nodded. He then went over to the bassinet and ever so gently picked up Jude. As he cradled his son to his chest, a look of pride overcame his face and melted my heart.

He then motioned to Jake. Closing the gap between them, Jake held out his eager arms. He then gazed down at Jude, the corners of his lips quirking up. "Well, he's a handsome little fucker, isn't he?"

I gasped in horror while Brayden only chuckled. I guess a part of me shouldn't have expected anything different from Jake and his notoriously bad foul mouth. Before it hadn't mattered as much, but now I had to resign myself to the fact my son was going to be surrounded by foul- mouthed rockers who weren't always going to be a good influence on him. But at the same time, I knew Jude was lucky to have the three men who were encircling him like adoptive fathers. They would always be there to love and protect him in their own fumbling ways.

"Damn, it's a good thing he looks like you, Lily, and not his pops," Jake mused.

"Dickhead," Brayden mumbled.

Jake glanced from Jude over to me and then winked. "Bet you're surprised I didn't drop him, aren't you?"

A nervous giggle escaped my lips. "Maybe a little."

"You know, I'm not a total dumbass when it comes to babies. I had some practice when Allison was a baby back in the day."

Cocking my head at him, I smiled. "You do look very natural with him."

His eyes widened. "Oh, hell no. Don't even think it."

"One day, Jake Slater. One day you're going to be holding your own baby in your arms."

He shook his head. "Not possible. I always wrap my shit up with my own condoms. Not with one some chick brought that she could have voodoo dolled."

Wrinkling my nose, I countered, "No, not with some random hookup. I meant with a wife."

AJ snorted. "Jake married? Let's wait for hell to freeze over first."

"Believe me, it's going to happen. I don't know when or with who, but it will."

"Whatever," Jake mumbled. Our conversation seemed to dampen Jude's allure because he was suddenly ready to pass him over AJ's eager and waiting arms.

"Such a handsome boy," AJ said, before bestowing a kiss on the crown of Jude's blonde hair.

Jake reached over and lifted up one of Jude's clenched fists. "Looks like Little Man here has some guitar-playing fingers."

Brayden grinned. "I thought as much."

As Jude squirmed awake, AJ cooed and sang to him in Spanish. Surprisingly, it calmed him, and Jude went back to sleep.

When AJ met what must've been my shocked expression, he winked. "Just call me the Baby Whisperer."

I laughed. "I'll know exactly who to come to when he gets fussy."

Pressed up against the wall, Rhys watched AJ and Jude curiously. I jerked my chin at AJ, signaling him to give Rhys a chance. When AJ started toward him, Rhys held up his hands. "Dude, I don't know anything about babies."

"Just give it a whirl. Worst thing you can do is drop him," AJ replied.

Both Rhys and I gasped. "Just teasing," AJ mused, which earned him a glare from Rhys.

Gently, AJ placed Jude in Rhys's arms. I bit down on my lip not to laugh at how still Rhys stood. Like if he even blinked too hard, it might hurt Jude. "He really does look like you, Lily," Rhys said, a smile playing at his lips.

"Thank you."

Rhys's face lit up when Jude's eyes opened, and he stared up at him. "Hey, buddy," he murmured.

While the guys seemed enthralled by Jude now, I couldn't help wondering about the future. "Are you still sure about me bringing him on the bus when I come to visit?"

"Why wouldn't we be?" Rhys asked, as he ran his fingers through Jude's dusting of fine hair.

"Well, babies are a lot of work—"

AJ held up a hand. "Are you insinuating that once you get on the bus, you and Bray are going to expect us to raise the little man while you two have a reconnection fuck fest?"

My face instantly warmed at his words while Brayden only chuckled. "No man, that's not what we had in mind," he replied.

"Then it's fine. Right, guys?"

Rhys and Jake nodded. I hoped, rather than believed, they would still be sincere when Jude started crying in the middle of the night. Of course, they were all so nocturnal that it would be worse during the day when they were trying to catch up on sleep.

Speaking of crying, Jude began to wail, his fists flailing. When I met Rhys's frantic eyes, he said, "I didn't do anything. I swear."

I laughed. "I know you didn't. He's probably just hungry."

All three of the guys froze. "Like for a breast?" AJ questioned, his brows furrowed.

"Yes, he did really well latching on earlier."

Rhys hurried over to the bed and deposited Jude into my arms. "Yeah, uh, I gotta go."

"Me, too," AJ said.

"Same here," Jake echoed.

Cocking my head at them, I grinned. "Who would have thought three notorious manwhores would be afraid of a breast?"

Jake laughed. "Call it what it is, but we're outta here."

"Thanks for coming, guys. It really means a lot," I said over Jude's cries.

"You're welcome, Hot Mama," AJ replied, bestowing a kiss on Jude's forehead and then mine. Jake followed suit while Rhys merely waved at me from the door.

As I pushed down my gown for Jude, I couldn't help laughing at the guys' reaction. Whether they knew it or not, their lives had changed too with Jude's birth. After all, we were one, great big musical family.

BRAYDEN

THE PRESENT

"And after Jude, you waited three years to have another child." Giovanni glanced between us. "Any particular reason? I mean, I do recall Brayden saying he wanted a houseful and for you to be started by twenty five."

Lily and I laughed. "Actually, it was easy to talk about a houseful of kids before we actually had one. Once Jude came along, we realized the work that went into raising a child. Of course, we weren't a conventional family considering Brayden was on the road most of the year, and I was home teaching."

"How did you make it as a single mom?" Giovanni asked Lily.

"Well, I had it a lot easier than most single mothers. Our first home just happened to be Brayden's grandparents' old house, so I was right next door to my mom. My younger sister, Kylie, decided she would go to school at night and be my nanny during the daytime—as long as she got to live rent free at my house."

Giovanni smiled. "That seems reasonable."

"The hardest part was not having Brayden with me, but more the fact that I hated he was missing being with Jude."

"How did you feel about the separation, Brayden?" Giovanni asked.

"It fucking sucked, frankly," I replied.

With a smile, Giovanni questioned, "Can you elaborate on that for me?"

"I felt I was being pulled in two separate directions. My band-mates needed me because we continued to skyrocket in popularity in the business, and then my wife and son needed me to be the father I'd always wanted to be.

Giovanni nodded. "How did you two stay connected?"

"Technology still wasn't at the level of Faceting and Skype, like we had later with Melody. We did do video chats and talk to one another every day. Then I would fly out with Jude to see him two or three times a month," Lily answered.

"That sounds intense," Giovanni remarked.

"It was," Lily replied. Glancing over at me, she said, "I think we waited as long as we did for Melody because we hoped things would calm down some. When I got pregnant with her, I decided I would finally quit my teaching job."

"Finally is right," I said, with a smile.

"And how was it going out on the road with two children?"

Lily and I both groaned. "Very, very hard," Lily answered.

"My greatest regret is we didn't get our own tour bus earlier," I said.

Lily shook her head. "It wouldn't have mattered because I wasn't ready to live on the road full-time yet."

"What changed your mind?"

With a smile, Lily said, "When I saw Mia doing it with Bella, I realized I could do it with two children. I also decided then that I wanted to homeschool the kids while Brayden was out on the road."

I bobbed my head. "Even though I wish we had the bus sooner, I'm still glad that Jude and Melody got to start out their lives with a little more normalcy."

At that moment, a knock came at the hotel door. When I got up to get it, I found it was Melody. "Hey, sweetie, you'll have to go back to AJ and Mia's. We're not finished yet."

She shook her head. "No, it's Lucy."

I didn't even have to call for Lily. She was off the couch in a flash and heading out the door. When I came back to the couch, I gave Giovanni a sad smile. "I guess that makes a good segue into talking about our third child."

"I hope I didn't appear to be treating it as a sensitive subject."

"No, you're fine."

"I know that you and Lily have been very open in the media about her being on the Autism spectrum with Sensory Processing Disorder."

"Yes, we always felt it wasn't something we should hide. Since I was in a position of celebrity, I could raise awareness and funds. With Rhys's help, we've done a lot of fundraising." I shifted in my chair. "Of course, there's a lot of research that argues that SPD isn't a part of the Autism spectrum while other research does. We figured it would be best to combine our efforts with the two."

"I have to be honest that while I was with your children earlier, I didn't notice anything different or out of the ordinary. She only seemed shyer than your other daughter."

"She is naturally shyer and quieter than Melody." I couldn't help laughing. "Considering Melody started talking when she was barely old enough to be walking, it wouldn't take much to be quieter."

Giovanni smiled. "I see."

"But you're right. You wouldn't notice anything right off hand. If you wanted her to give you a hug when you left, she would refuse not just because she doesn't know you, but because she doesn't like to be held or touched. Certain noises that wouldn't bother you or me can send her into a meltdown. To some people, it would seem like little quirks, but it runs a lot deeper than that."

"When did you first discover something was...different about her?" Giovanni questioned.

"Probably when she was nine or ten months old. We thought she was just going through a phase where she hated to be held, which broke Lily's heart. She was used to rocking Jude and Melody to sleep until they were far over a year old, but Lucy began to cry until she was put in her bed. Then she would scream during diaper changes, baths, and anytime we had to change her clothes. Then as soon as we were finished, she would be fine." I sighed as I relived those scary days where we didn't know what was wrong with our sweet little girl, and then the day when we finally found out.

BRAYDEN

THE PAST

I rolled over in bed to find Lily's side empty. Raising up, I squinted my eyes in the darkness. When I didn't see her, I threw back the covers and hopped out of bed. After a glance in the bathroom turned up nothing, I went for the bedroom door. I had three good guesses where she might be, and the strongest led me to Lucy's room.

It had been a hell of a day. Well, if I was honest with myself, it had been a hell of a few months. But today had us sitting in plush leather chairs in the office of Pediatric Neurologist, Dr. Peter Robsten. After our pediatrician had been unable to diagnose what was wrong, we had come to Emory desperate for answers as to what was wrong with our Lucy. She had been through a gamut of testing, which was terribly intense for a fifteen month old.

Then Dr. Robsten gave us the diagnosis we had been expecting to hear: Sensory Perceptive Disorder with Sensory defensiveness, which basically meant she experienced SPD with defensive actions to sound and touch. Although we had a name to go with what our fears and research on the internet had uncovered, it still didn't give us a clear plan ahead on how to raise Lucy.

With the door to Lucy's room already cracked, I slipped inside. Standing beside Lucy's crib, Lily looked like an angel in the moonlight with her white, gauzy gown and flowing blonde hair. I came up behind her, wrapping my arms around her waist. After kissing her neck, I said, "I woke up, and you were gone."

"I couldn't sleep."

"Babe," I murmured.

When she turned back to me, tears glistened in her eyes. "I just kept lying there, searching my mind for what I did differently with her that I didn't with Jude and Melody. Was it because I didn't breast-feed her as long? Was it because she was on the bus so much when she was just an infant? Was it because I gave her those vaccines on time? I mean, we were back and forth on the road with Jude and Melody, so they didn't get theirs until they were a few months older." Her agonized gaze went back to Lucy. "What was it I did wrong?"

A sob tore through Lily's chest. The sound caused Lucy to stir in her cocoon of downy pink blankets. Wrapping my arm around her waist, I drew Lily to me. When she began to cry harder, I led her out of the bedroom. I steered her down the hall and back to our room and onto the bed.

Pushing her long hair out of her face, I stared into her eyes. "I want you to listen to me. There is nothing that you did wrong that caused Lucy to have a sensory disorder. Things like this happen. It isn't a punishment for us or for Lucy. It's just something we have to handle."

"Deep down, I know that. I just want someone or something to blame. She's just a baby. She doesn't deserve to have to go through so much."

I shook my head. "While I agree that it's unfair Lucy is going through this, I'm not going to let you beat yourself up. You're the best mother in the entire world. No one has sacrificed for her children as much as you have."

"Thank you, Brayden," she murmured before she leaned forward to kiss me.

"Do you feel better now?"

She shrugged. "Aren't you scared?"

Taking her hands in mine, I gave her a small smile. "I'm terrified."

"That makes me feel a little better," she admitted.

My brows shot up in surprise. "Really? I thought I was always supposed to be the strong-as-steel man."

"I like it when you're strong, but I also like it when I know that you're struggling just like I am."

"Just don't forget for one minute that we're in this together. You don't have to go through this alone. I'm here for you."

"I think I love you more right now that I have our entire time together," she said, with tears pooling in her eyes.

"I love you, too, baby." I kissed her once again. "Come on, let's get some sleep."

And then I drew her in my arms, and we lay back together. I felt the safest, the securest, and the most loved when I held Lily in my arms. In turn, I hoped she felt the same. I hoped I provided the right loving that helped her feel safe, secure and cherished.

BRAYDEN

THE PRESENT

It wasn't long before Lily rejoined us. "Everything okay?" I asked. She smiled. "Just a minor meltdown due to some of the noises on one of the video games the boys were playing. She's got her headphones on now and is watching a movie. She's fine." Lily turned her attention from me over to Giovanni. "I guess Brayden explained about Lucy in my absence."

"Yes, he did. As a parent of a five year old, I would have to say that you guys are doing amazing with her, as well as your other children."

"Thank you. That means a lot."

"Well, I think that just about wraps it up." Giovanni put his notepad into his briefcase and rose off the couch. "Once again, I cannot thank you two enough for allowing me to sit down with you. I have such a good feeling about this article. I think the entire issue is going to be a hit."

Lily flushed a little at his words while I merely laughed. "Here's hoping our story can sell some copies."

"Oh, I'm sure it will." Giovanni glanced between us. "You two still don't quite understand what an amazing thing you have, do you?"

Taking Lily's hand in mine, I brought it to my lips. "Trust me, I think we get it."

Giovanni smiled. "I'm glad to hear that." As he started over to the door, he said, "Best of luck. I'll see you tomorrow at the wedding."

"Thanks again for coming," Lily said, as she showed him to the door.

When he was gone, I collapsed back onto the sofa. "Oh no, don't get comfortable. We have exactly forty-five minutes before we have to meet the others for the rehearsal."

I groaned. "I'd forgot all about that. I'm dying for a nap."

Lily giggled as she came over to me. "You're showing your age if you're needing a nap, Vanderburg."

"I'd forgo the nap for a quickie," I replied, wagging my eyebrows.

"Thinking about all our past sexcapades has you hot?"

"Mmm, hmm."

Nibbling on her lip, I could tell Lily was giving a quickie some serious thought. "Come on. The kids are being looked after, and we have the whole place to ourselves."

Without taking her eyes off mine, she started backing up to the bedroom. When she crooked her finger, I was off the couch like a shot.

BRAYDEN

THE PRESENT

I stood at the altar of the awe-inspiring Cathedral of St. John the Baptist in Savannah, anxiously awaiting the appearance of the bride. With bated breath, I watched as the precocious Jax and Jules came down the aisle as ring bearer and flower girl. Glancing next to me at Jake, I watched with amusement as he clenched and unclenched his jaw. I'd witnessed firsthand the drama last night when Jax and Jules refused to walk down the aisle. After spending the day at the bridal luncheon, I actually couldn't blame them for wanting to stay back at the hotel to play with the other kids. Of course, I didn't voice my opinion on that one. As Jake kept a watchful eye on them, I'm sure he was just waiting for them to throw another tantrum. But they performed like the absolute angels they looked like.

My attention immediately left the twins and went to the breath-takingly beautiful bridesmaid coming up the aisle in a lavender dress. With her hair swept back on the sides with glittering combs, the rest of Lily's long blonde hair cascaded in waves down her back. It was hard to believe she had just turned thirty four. She looked just as youthful as the day I'd first seen her picking apples. When she met my gaze, she smiled and winked. And after all this time, my heart still did a little shudder and restart.

Just after Lily was Mia and then Abby making their way down the aisle. Because of Allison's eclectic fashion sense, each brides-maid wore a different color of dress. Abby was in pink while Mia was in light blue. When Andrea, Allison's half-sister and matron of honor, came down the aisle, she wore a mint green dress. While she wasn't standing up in the bridal party, Rhys's sister, Ellie, wore a pale yellow dress and held the same bouquet as the other bridesmaids in her lap on the front bench.

Gazing over at Rhys, I surveyed how he was doing. He appeared relatively calm, but I knew on the inside he was probably panicking a little. All grooms did no matter how ready they were to get married. I knew there was no one else in the world for Rhys but Allison. He had just wanted to give her a little time to grow up more before they tied the knot. Now at twenty four, Allison was more than ready to take on the role of being his wife.

The music changed from Pachelbel's *Canon in D over* to *Ave Maria*. The doors at the back of the cathedral opened, and Allison appeared on her father's arm. She certainly was a breathtaking bride. With her dark hair swept back and a glittering tiara on her head, she didn't look like the little girl I'd met so many years ago. She was a grown woman now.

Lily had told me that Allison's dress was reminiscent of Grace Kelly's and Kate Middleton's. Of course as a self-respecting dude, I had no clue what their dresses looked like. All I knew was that Allison looked elegant and beautiful as she glided down the aisle. Her smile was radiant and focused on one person only—her groom.

When she reached him at the altar, tears spilled over his cheeks. I don't think I'd ever seen Rhys cry publicly. But there was something about the love of your life that rendered you so very vulnerable. As the preacher began the ceremony, I couldn't help gazing past the bride and groom over to Lily. I thought about our wedding days—our first in Vegas and then our second at the church back home. In some ways it seemed just like yesterday, but then in others, it seemed like two different people embarking on married life.

We'd had our ups and downs, the good and the bad. We had weathered each and every storm that life threw at us. In the end, it just made us, as well as our love, stronger. Like the old Joni Mitchell song, *Both Sides Now*, that my mother used to love to play, I had been given the chance to see life from both sides—the one with Lily and the one without. It was no contest on how to choose. For me, there was no life without Lily in it.

"By the power vested in me by God and the state of Georgia, I now pronounce you husband and wife. You may kiss the bride."

When Rhys pulled Allison into his arms to lay one on her, applause rang out in the church. They pulled away to smile and laugh at the crowd's antics. Then they started back down the aisle as man and wife. When it was time for me to exit, I met Lily at the middle of the altar. I offered her my arm, and she happily slid hers through it. "You look very beautiful, Mrs. Vanderburg."

She smiled. "And you look awfully handsome, Mr. Vanderburg."

Even though we were supposed to start down the aisle, I stopped to kiss Lily. "I love you," she murmured against my lips.

"I love you more."

And then we walked down the aisle together and out into the sunshine.

LILY

THE PRESENT

Later that night at the reception, I lay with my head snuggled to Brayden's chest under the sparkling lights of the rented tent. Rhys's parents had hosted the reception at their house in the Historic District of Savannah. It was absolutely breathtaking being inside the old home, and the large tent on the back lawn made for an intimate setting. Once the cake had been cut and our children had eaten their way through several slices, along with stops at the chocolate fountain, we sent them back to the hotel with my mother to sugar detox.

As we swayed to the music, I was glad to have some alone time with Brayden. Over my shoulder, I watched as Rhys and Allison danced as close as humanly possible while never letting their eyes stray from each other's. "What are you thinking about?" Brayden asked.

I raised my head. "The happy couple. Us."

"What about us?"

I smiled. "How thankful I am that we're a happy couple after all these years."

"I know what you mean." His brows furrowed a little. "I can't help wondering how the Rolling Stone article will turn out."

"We were honest and told our story. There's nothing to be ashamed of."

"I know. I just dread what might be said about some parts of our past." With a grimace, he said, "It's not that I care about them seeing what an asshole I was. It's more about you being hurt again and again."

"It's okay, Brayden. I promise. Besides, we're the only ones that matter. Don't forget that."

Smiling at me, he said, "I won't."

When the song ended, a screech came over the microphone as Rhys took it from the band leader. "So I just wanted to say on behalf of Allison and myself that we really appreciate your love and support on our very special day. We're so very glad and blessed that you could share it with us. We love you all very much." As applause filled the air, Rhys smiled. "And now, there's something that Allison and I would like to do for a very special couple." Rhys began to search through the crowd. "Brayden, Lily, will you guys come up here please?"

I tensed in Brayden's arms. "What is going on?"

"I don't know." Taking my hand, Brayden led me across the dance floor to the bandstand. When we got there, Rhys winked at me.

"Even though it's mine and Allison's happy day, we wanted to do something for a couple who has meant so much to the both of us. When I first joined Runaway Train, no one was more welcoming or better to me than Lily. And Brayden became the big brother I never had. They've been married for twelve years and a couple for eighteen years. I know I speak for Allison and myself when I say that they have shown me the type of marriage we want aspire to have now and twenty years down the road. They're devoted to each other and to their children."

"Seriously, man, I'm choking up here," Brayden interjected. Both he and I had tears in our eyes from Rhys's speech.

"We ask that you clear the floor and give this very special couple a spotlight dance of their own." Whistles and applause came from around the room. "And while I could have picked any one of the love songs you have written, Brayden, the guys, along with Abby, thought this song best suited the two of you."

"I can't believe they're doing this," I hiccupped through my tears. It was overwhelming being signaled out for a speech that sang your praises, not to mention a private dance.

"Me either."

As the lights dimmed a little, Brayden once again took me by the hand and led me out onto the dance floor. The band leader counted them in, and the music started to play.

Remember when I was young and so were you. And time stood still, and love was all we knew.

As a secret fan of country music, I instantly recognized the song. It was another fellow musician from Georgia, Alan Jackson. And the song was *Remember When*.

You were the first, so was I. We made love, and then you cried. Remember when.

Rhys was right. There probably was no better song that suited all the years that Brayden and I had spent together as well as our beginnings and our battles.

And as the song played on, I kissed my husband under the twinkling lights on the dance floor. I thanked God for all the years we've had and for all the ones that were to come.

When I pulled away, Brayden stared down at me with such loving intensity it made me shiver. "You had your pick of any guy in school. Hell, any guy anywhere. I'll never understand why you picked me."

I smiled at him. "That's easy. You sang to me."

"But you gave me the melody I never knew I had." He took my hand in his and brought it to his chest. "The melody straight from my heart."

The End

About the Author

Katie Ashley is a New York Times, USA Today, and Amazon Best-Selling author. She lives outside of Atlanta, Georgia with her two very spoiled dogs. She has a slight obsession with Pinterest, The Golden Girls, Shakespeare, Supernatural, Harry Potter, Designing Women, and Scooby-Doo.

With a BA in English, a BS in Secondary English Education, and a Masters in Adolescent English Education, she has spent the last eleven years teaching both middle and high school English. As of January 2013, she is a full-time writer.

website: http://katieashleybooks.com
facebook: https://www.facebook.com/katieashleybooks
twitter: https://twitter.com/KatieAshleyLuv
pinterest: http://www.pinterest.com/katieashleyluv/
goodreads: https://www.goodreads.com/author/show/
6546441.Katie_Ashley
instagram: http://instagram.com/katieashleyluv

Made in the USA
Middletown, DE
29 June 2016